Spanish Moon Zephyr

by

Jack Watts

Cover Art: Patty Fitts
Cover Design: Dwayne Bassett
Internal Design: Colin Hawk

Printed in the United States of America

Fiction
Full Moon Frenzy
Snow Moon Queen—not yet published
Crescent Moon Rising—not yet published
Blood Moon Judgment—not yet published
Unholy Seduction—not yet published
The Lords & Ladies of Evangelicalism—not yet published

Non-Fiction
Hi, My Name Is Jack—Simon & Schuster
Recovering from Religious Abuse—Simon & Schuster
We Believe—co-authored by David Dunham, Dunham Books
Prayers for People in Recovery—not yet published
The Search for Reality

TABLE OF CONTENTS

INTRODUCTION

I'm delighted you've come back for my second story about some of the folks I've met in my many years of sobriety. Let me think; it's been more than two decades without a drink . . . and counting. That's the important thing—that it's continuous. Staying sober, which isn't easy in a city like Atlanta, is the way to make your life more meaningful. I certainly used to spend a lot of time getting wasted—with nothing to show for it, I might add.

Marla-Dean Bennington and Sean Kincannon finally figured that out too. As you'll probably remember, my first tale focused on what was required to get Sean sober and keep him that way. Well, I'm happy to report he has been doing just fine. He's been alcohol free and working his program for a while now, and he's definitely a stand-up guy.

He and Marla-Dean have been married more than a year at this point in the narrative. Although the honeymoon has worn off, especially after the baby arrived, they have built a solid relationship, which would have been impossible if either had returned to the sauce. I heard one woman say their little boy, Connor, is "the cutest" child she has ever seen, which certainly pleased his parents.

The woman may be right. The Kincannon's even have a dog. Since Sean has remained sober, the tale you're about to hear goes deeper into the lives of those in recovery. After all, there's more to life than living not to drink. You know that, right?

The following story is about the things that can trip folks up in recovery, and there are a lot of them. Believe me; I know.

I remember when I was a little boy growing up in Boston, my mother used to repeat this rhyme: "*Sticks 'n stones can break my bones, but names can never hurt me.*" When I heard this, young as I was, I believed it. Now that I'm grown, I suspect there isn't a lick of truth to it. A broken bone will heal in a couple of months, but being called a hurtful name can negatively impact you for the rest of your life.

There's another saying I used to hear, but come to think about it, it's something you don't hear often these days: "*Crime Never Pays.*" I've come to wonder if this is true, especially in the times we live? Anyway, that's the aphorism I want you to be thinking about while you're engaged in this story.

I've got an idea—why not make a mental note of what you think right now, and tell me if this story changes your mind? It just might.

At any rate, that's enough of my blabbering. Let's get right to the story, but before I do, let me thank John and Patty Fitts, Anne Alexander, and Dwayne Bassett who helped me with this project.

Maybe we should start with the day Sean and his wife were taking a trip to Lake Oconee. That's as good a place to begin as any.

CHAPTER ONE

"You're My Trophy Husband"

Yes, we can easily afford it, Sean. There's no problem with us buying the house—none whatsoever. I promise," Marla-Dean Kincannon replied to her husband's worrisome inquiry. He was concerned about the two of them incurring an additional financial responsibility. As she was speaking, she smiled coquettishly, which Sean noticed instantly. He was grateful her demeanor was playful and not peevish. Experience had taught him it could just as easily have been the latter.

A moment later, she turned her attention from the road for just a split second to catch his eye. With a mischievous twinkle, she added, "Besides, don't you worry your pretty little head about numbers. You know that causes wrinkles, don't you?" Pausing for a brief moment to magnify the statement's impact, with a wink she added wryly, "Since you're my trophy husband, you have to maintain your good looks. You know that, right?"

With this, she turned her attention to the road, smiling with her eyes, as she continued to drive her Mercedes G-Class SUV toward Lake Oconee—located half way between Atlanta and Augusta, Georgia.

She was eager for Sean to take a look at the waterfront property she intended to buy for their "get-away home."

Growing up in an affluent family, Marla-Dean was committed to using her inheritance to enrich their lives. Sean, whose upbringing included times of scarcity, was always concerned there might not be enough; despite the fact their net worth was well over $10 million—all but a couple thousand coming from what her parents had left her. He realized his concern was emotional rather than substantive, but he needed her reassurance about the purchase, nonetheless.

Being mildly irritated at being equated with a "mimbo"—the male version of a bimbo—Marla-Dean understood full well Sean's reaction would be one of humor, mixed with a small measure of irritation. Knowing him as well as she did, she was spot on accurate. All she needed to do was sit back and wait for him to start laughing, which didn't take long.

Knowing how the scenario was expected to play out, Sean desperately tried to maintain his equilibrium, biting his cheek to keep from revealing how tickled he actually was—but to no avail. His strategy, which had little chance of succeeding, failed miserably. He burst out laughing—just like always—when Marla-Dean reverted to her playful, sarcastic ways. Her irreverence was a regular menu item at the Kincannon household, served up plentifully, each day.

Fearful his laughter might awaken their three-month-old son, she shushed him, but that only made matters worse. Sean, who seemed to laugh at everything Marla-Dean said, did, or even intimated—whether appropriate or not—tried to stifle his laugh, but he couldn't. Tears ran down his cheeks, and his nose started to run as well.

Reaching for one of his wife's tissues, which mothers of infants always seem to have abundantly available, Sean did his best to maintain his composure but, like always, he couldn't. To make matters worse, Marla-Dean scolded him with her eyes for his lack of self-control. This, of course, made him laugh even harder. His exuberance became so contagious; Marla-Dean could no longer restrain herself. She began to laugh as well—not at her well-timed joke—but at Sean's infectious response.

When the moment passed, he just looked at her and smiled, finally returning her wink. Both loved the way they went back and forth. It made their life calm, serene, and easy—at least, most of the time.

Her sarcasm began shortly after they met and never abated—not even a little. In fact, as their love and commitment solidified and deepened, her irreverent responses increased. Knowing he wouldn't walk away, she felt safe, letting it rip whenever the spirit moved her, which was frequently.

Marla-Dean possessed the ability to piss Sean off and make him laugh at the same time, which nobody else had ever done. Occasionally, it was serious and contentious but, more often than not, it was lighthearted and endearing. Episodes like this happened routinely, and she loved her husband because he allowed her to be herself—rarely becoming peevish or offended.

Such was her personality and the playful way they had interacted since meeting two years earlier at the 5:45 p.m. "Attitude Adjustment" meeting of Alcoholics Anonymous at the Buckhead Triangle Club, located in one of the seedier parts of Atlanta. They started seeing one another shortly after Sean picked up his white chip, which signified his desire to stop drinking.

For Sean, making this commitment and sticking to it proved to be the turning point in his life. His dedication to sobriety being genuine, he was getting close to picking up his two-year chip, which was to be given to him by his new sponsor, Jack Watts, the author of *Hi, My Name Is Jack*. His former sponsor, Grant, had relapsed, and Sean hadn't seen or heard from him in quite some time, which saddened and grieved Sean.

Like Marla-Dean, Sean's new sponsor had many years in the program and had been very supportive of Sean's recovery, after the author's latest girlfriend, a vapid, frivolous blond—in a long string of vapid, frivolous blonds—dumped him for a biker. No longer willing to work her program, Jack's former girlfriend chose a new paramour—a hard-drinking ignoramus nicknamed Beam.

Since Sean's sobriety involved a national narcotics-related news story, his early time in recovery had been more adventurous than most. He had been the prosecutor for a drug task force, nearly losing his life, when wounded by a high-powered sniper rifle, in a foiled assassination attempt. Marla-Dean, his girlfriend at the time, was the attending physician at Peachtree Medical, when he was rushed to the emergency room. Close to death, a medical team, headed by Dr. Luke Easton—commonly known as Dr. Big Shot—worked feverishly to save the middle-aged prosecutor's life.

Obviously, the doctors had been successful. Marla-Dean, who lost her first husband to a massive coronary, personally supervised Sean's rehabilitation, and the two married shortly thereafter. With the loss of both of her parents—one shortly before her marriage and the other shortly after—Marla-Dean inherited a substantial portfolio, which she intended to use to improve the quality of their lives. Acting upon this commitment was the reason they were headed to Lake Oconee on a warm Saturday afternoon, shortly after Labor Day, nearly a year-and-a-half into their marriage.

In the back seat was their three-month-old son, Connor—named after a heroic preschooler who was instrumental in uncovering a murder, while only four years old. Now six, the older Connor had moved to James Island, near Folly Beach in Charlestown, South Carolina, where his mother and father were transferred.

Marla-Dean had her child by cesarean section, delivered by Dr. Augustus Porthos, a diminutive obstetrician, who was a descendant of the great French author, Alexander Dumas. Gus Porthos had been a successful physician for many years, but the spending habits of his trophy wife—a tall, beautiful and bosomy red head—had far surpassed his earning potential.

Darden Porthos, who came from the ancestry of William Quantrill, the outlaw general of the Confederate Army in the War Between the

States, had a sweet innocent look that belied her cunning, self-serving heart. Because he was a prominent physician, Darden married Gus, despite the fact he was five inches shorter than she was. When she wore 4" heels, he came up to her breasts, which amused her and titillated him.

At their wedding, she said, "Yes" to status, affluence, luxury and leisure—not to a reversal of fortune. For Gus, she had been wonderful arm candy, enhancing his image of accomplishment and importance, but her incessant demands finally broke him financially, forcing the obstetrician to regroup, downsizing significantly from his opulent, consumptive lifestyle.

Darden was willing to remain married—just as long as Gus was capable of bankrolling her spending requirements. When the going got tough, she bolted, bedding a Polish weapons manufacturer soon thereafter. In essence, she simply changed men without missing a beat or her monthly shopping spree at Neiman Marcus and Versace.

Interestingly, her new paramour, who would eventually become her husband, always wore gray. Because his hair and pallor were also gray, he had a ghostlike appearance, bestowing a cadaverous look upon him. Darden didn't care what color he was, just as long as he had plenty of her favorite color—green.

Destitute, heartbroken, and embarrassed by Darden's abandonment, Gus was left to clean up the mess. Darden didn't even bother to say goodbye—not out of spite; it just never occurred to her that she should have done so. She was finished with him, so why bother? Gus was no longer important so she never looked back—not once. What was the point? Such was her cold, heartless and self-centered nature. Upside down financially and distraught, Gus was left to sell their lovely home on Lake Oconee, among other things.

During Marla-Dean's pregnancy, Gus had mentioned the lake house to her several times, while in consultation, hoping she might be interested. When she finally responded, after months of indifference, he was surprised but as jubilant as a pimpled teenage girl being asked to the prom. He had hoped she would buy it quickly, but with her baby due shortly, she was in no hurry.

Unfortunately for Gus, nobody else showed the slightest interest in the property. It had been vacant for quite some time, and there was virtually no attention being paid to it by realtors. Thus, Gus's financial hemorrhaging continued to diminish his resources month after month, making him desperate to sell.

At the urging of Darden, Gus had originally purchased the property—a five-bedroom, five-bath home, with access to the lake, nestled on two acres of forested land on a dead-end dirt road, which assured complete privacy. He paid $895,000 for the new home several years earlier, when the economy was booming, obtaining a 95 percent loan from the bank because, as a prosperous physician, he appeared to be a good risk.

When the property was initially purchased, Darden was thrilled to have a lakefront home, rewarding Gus the way he liked best—much to his delight. Because the house was completely secluded, however, she became bored quickly, which he had not anticipated. Being secluded is what he desired. He loved the idea of intimate privacy. It would be just the two of them—blissful and carnal. He had hoped they would enjoy many amorous weekends there, but this was not what Darden envisioned—not even close.

She flourished in the limelight and blossomed when others paid fawning attention to her. Spending extended hours in bed with her husband wasn't something she desired, nor would she submit to it. Repulsed by being alone with him for prolonged periods, Darden shuddered at the thought of doing so routinely.

Consequently, the couple traveled to Lake Oconee just a couple of times a year, which made Gus's impulsive decision to buy the property a poor one.

Although in good repair, because of the decline in the housing market, the value of the property had decreased to $495,000, according to the latest appraisal. This meant Gus was seriously upside down. With monthly payments of $5,500, based on the higher value of the home when he purchased it, the continued burden strapped him badly—especially with the alimony he was forced to pay his ex-wife for several years.

Writing her a check every month galled him. He was broke and getting farther in debt while she was gallivanting around the globe, still subsidized by his money, copulating with "The Gray Ghost." Forced to support her, while she was on her back entertaining another man, infuriated Gus. Being a cuckold always does, but he refused to allow himself to dwell on his humiliation.

By the time Sean and Marla-Dean were headed to the lake for the weekend, Gus's only goal was to keep his world from suffering a complete collapse.

When Marla-Dean finally agreed to take a look at the house, Gus had hoped she would make him an immediate offer but, before she would even consider it, she wanted to spend a weekend at the cabin with her family. She needed to get a feel for how the house would fit their needs, which was perfectly understandable from her perspective. She offered to pay Gus for their stay that Labor Day weekend, but he refused magnanimously, telling her it was hers to enjoy. He tried to play it cool, which seemed particularly disingenuous to Marla-Dean. When he handed her the keys to the place, she could see desperation written all over his face. Despite his poor attempts to camouflage his distress, he looked particularly pitiful.

To entice her, Gus had the place cleaned from top to bottom. He went so far as to stock the refrigerator with food, filling the vases with fresh cut flowers. He even purchased a chilled bottle of champagne for the couple to enjoy upon arrival.

の

For Sean and Marla-Dean, the trip to the country was an adventure. They had been very happy living in Marla-Dean's childhood home on

Peachtree Battle Avenue in the old moneyed section of Atlanta, close to the heart of the city. Sean thought it would be sufficient, but Marla-Dean wanted a summer retreat close to home for their son to play and have access to one of the great lakes in the South. Her reasoning made sense to Sean—sort of, but he was still nervous about making such a large financial commitment. He couldn't help it. Fearing scarcity, worrying about money was part of his nature.

As they headed to the lake, rounding out their little family was Asta—the family's wirehaired terrier—named after the dog in the *Thin Man* movie series from the 1930s. The series starred William Powell and Myrna Loy, who were the Sean and Marla-Dean of an earlier generation. Because of the Kincannon's experience as amateur detectives, the "thin man" simile had been a private joke between them since early in their courtship, and it continued to be so.

In the movies, Nick and Nora Charles had a cute, mischievous dog, named Asta who—like his owners—considered himself to be a first-rate detective. In many ways, Asta was the best-loved and most memorable star in the classic series.

In the Kincannon household, Asta was also the star, and she knew it. She was into everything and had as much personality as the home's mistress. To keep Asta from running off, Marla-Dean had an electronic fence installed, confining the dog to their Atlanta yard. Making a mental note to have one installed at their lakefront house, if they bought the property, Marla-Dean told Sean to make certain the doors were always shut tight, knowing Asta would run off, if the opportunity presented itself.

Appraising the house thoroughly, Marla-Dean intended to offer Gus $395,000, having done her homework about property values in the area. But even this "low ball offer" made her husband nervous. When they first married, Sean tried to keep up with the fiscal responsibilities of a major financial player, but it was simply beyond his emotional capacity to deal with so much money, which embarrassed him. Consequently, he pretended to understand the complexities and nuances of Marla-Dean's portfolio. Being a lawyer, bullshit and bravado were part of his repertoire as a good litigator. So, Sean talked the talk, without having a firm grasp of what was significant and what was not. His strategy was simply to hope for the best.

Marla-Dean, realizing such a policy was the recipe for financial disaster, took charge of the money—much to Sean's relief. Instead of chiding him for his lack of financial erudition, however, she learned the intricacies of finance herself. Candidly, Sean was grateful his wife was so multi-talented, and he couldn't believe how lucky he was to have found her.

She felt the same way. Sean was a man of character, with a burning passion to do the right thing, regardless of the consequences. This quality made him particularly attractive, especially since it was a characteristic Marla-Dean had discovered in very few men.

As they were nearing their destination thirty minutes later, the baby awoke, crying for milk. Pulling off the road to allow Sean to drive the remainder of the way, Marla-Dean breastfed little Connor, which was always the most fulfilling part of his mom's day.

As Sean turned into the driveway, he looked at the lakefront property for the first time, falling in love with it instantly. This pleased Marla-Dean even more than she imagined it would.

The house was nestled on a small inlet bay, opening to the lake on the North side. Walking through the front door, Sean headed immediately to the deck, which jettied out over the lake for about thirty feet. The view was magnificent, and the quietness of the bay produced immediate serenity. Surveying the landscape, the only house Sean could see was across the bay about two football fields away.

Gus had told Marla-Dean about the other property, which seemed small across the water. A rich foreign couple owned it. They also owned the woods between the two houses and were unwilling to sell even a small parcel for new construction. As long as the foreign couple owned the house, complete privacy was assured. Unlike Darden Porthos, Marla-Dean definitely liked the idea of tranquility and privacy.

Returning to the living room, Sean took the bottle of champagne out of the ice bucket and put it in a kitchen cabinet, without saying a word. Obviously, Dr. Porthos didn't know his medical colleague as well as he thought he did. Marla-Dean was already seated with Connor in her lap, when Sean turned to look at her. She had been watching every move he made with breathless anticipation. So far, he hadn't said a thing. As it turned out, he didn't need to. He simply smiled—with his broad Irish grin—the one that went from ear to ear. This was all she needed to make her decision. The house would be theirs.

Sean loved it. He thought it was the most peaceful place he had ever seen, and he was certain they would enjoy serenity and solitude while there, routinely rejuvenating their spirits for years to come.

It was a good thought, but that's all it was—a thought. Little did he know it but, as he looked out of the sliding glass doors across the lake on that sunny September afternoon, a new adventure was about to begin—an escapade originating right there at their soon-to-be purchased home on Lake Oconee, in the sleepy little countryside county of Greene, Georgia.

CHAPTER TWO
Spending Time with Jo Ellen

Darden wasn't the only woman who was bored with her husband. If anything, Landria Gordon, now living in Middle Tennessee, wanted to run away from her husband, her daughter, and her confined existence. She found herself shackled, even more than Darden had felt. Landria was trapped, effectively manacled from head to toe. Despite the numerous schemes she concocted in her mind to escape, each was flawed. None would work. Try as she may, she couldn't figure out a successful way to disappear. She knew there had to be one, but she just hadn't discovered it yet.

Sure, she could just get in her car and leave, but that wasn't an acceptable solution—not without taking all of her money with her. Leaving her daughter behind was an option, but not leaving her stash. There was no way that was going to happen. It was hers and she needed it. Being stymied galled and infuriated her, but she would eventually figure a way out of the confining conundrum that plagued her. When she felt trapped, she always found a solution, and she would again. She was determined to discover a way to bolt, and when she was resolute, she never allowed anything to get in her way. She was confident things would work out; they always had before.

Landria just needed to play the game a little longer; that's all, biding her time until an answer and an opportunity presented itself. When this happened, she would vanish and nobody would ever see her again. She would escape, exactly like she had successfully done three times before in her twenty-seven years of life. Just thinking about the looks on the faces of those she had come to hate brought a satisfying, malevolent smirk to her otherwise beautiful features.

Looking in the mirror, she liked what she saw. Everybody did, as well they should. Not quite as tight as she had been before having her child, she still turned heads wherever she went, especially when she was wearing a pair of her low cut jeans—the kind that showcased her snake tattoo coming up out of her vagina. It still had a lascivious effect on men, giving her power over them, which she craved. Men thought with their dicks, and it was easy to fool them—all of them except for Joseph. She had lost her power over him and, try as she may, she couldn't reestablish it. *Damn him*, she thought.

Thinking about him brought back many unpleasant memories. Almost two years earlier, Landria narrowly survived an attempt on her life by her former boyfriend, Pretty Boy Sabarisi. He had tried to murder her by running her down. Later, he was killed, after having shot Sean Kincannon, the state prosecutor for the drug task force. When she saw the details on the news, she couldn't believe her good fortune. God had answered her prayers.

With Sabarisi dead, Landria was no longer forced to hide, fearful of what might happen if she were discovered. For several years, she had been terrified Pretty Boy would find her and exact merciless revenge on her for stealing $978,000, humiliating him in the process.

To her, it seemed like she had been hiding her entire life. Still in her twenties, she had one given name, Lulu, and three aliases—Ginger, Joy, and now Landria. Each had been required in her ongoing effort to hide from her past, but with Pretty Boy out of the way, this was no longer necessary. Surviving his hit-and-run attempt by inches, she was forced to flee Atlanta that same evening. When she arrived in the Nashville area a few days later, she assumed a new identity, setting up a completely different existence, leaving her identity as Joy Fortune behind. To accomplish this, she married the father of her unborn daughter's father. That's right—Landria married her baby's grandfather. At the time, it seemed like a good idea, but it wasn't.

After living with her decision for nearly two years, she realized it was the worst mistake she had ever made. She could have gone anywhere, but she didn't. Instead, she chose to hunt down Joseph's father. Having Googled where he lived, she headed to Brentwood TN, found Dwayne Gordon immediately, seduced him, and married him soon thereafter, telling the older Gordon the child she was carrying was his. He believed her, of course—fool that he was.

She thought it was a brilliant plan, but she had definitely outsmarted herself. Now, she was stuck—trapped like a caged bird. Every time she thought about it, she shook her head in dismay, realizing how foolish her scheme had been.

Now, she was confined to a life she loathed—forced to stay with a man she didn't love—and never would. Even worse, she was required to pretend that she did. Obligated to have sex with him daily, which repulsed her, she found it difficult to fake being satisfied, which she had done routinely with numerous lovers since her early teens.

Fooling egotistical men—all of whom thought they were great lovers—had never been a problem for Landria, but now it was. She had come to dread her evening ritual. Because it granted her a short reprieve, she actually welcomed having her period for the first time in her life.

She didn't hate her husband—far from it; she just detested her loss of independence. In many ways, Dwayne was a decent man. A good provider, he had recently purchased a $1 million life insurance policy for his daughter, putting it into a trust with Landria named as the Executor. Her situation could be far worse and she knew it, but her free spirit wouldn't allow her to be grateful for what she had.

Perhaps it would have been tolerable, if she didn't have the added burden of being a stay-at-home mom. She thought she would enjoy motherhood, but she didn't. Taking care of a toddler required far more effort than she had anticipated, and she didn't like it. Some women were born to be mothers; some weren't. Landria was definitely one of the latter.

Her daughter, who was named Josephine Ellen Gordon, but was called Jo Ellen, was rambunctious, and as cute as she could be. Dark haired, like her mother, she had her father's eyes. A very bright child, Jo Ellen was spontaneous, bringing delight to everybody around her.

Her biological father, Joseph, who was about to begin his junior year at Belmont University, was a stellar student. With substantial God-given talent, coupled with first-rate training, Joseph had a promising future in the music industry, especially since his father was so well connected—both in Christian and country music circles. Joseph's inclination was toward the latter, despite his mother's fervent desire for him to pursue the former.

Landria's husband had no idea Joseph was Jo Ellen's biological father, and nobody was about to tell him either. Dwayne loved the child, whose eyes looked like his. Naturally, he assumed she was his daughter. That she reminded him so much of Joseph when he was a child aided in keeping Dwayne in the dark. He never considered that she wasn't his child; it never even entered his mind. Why would it?

Landria didn't want Dwayne to know the truth; that's for certain. Neither did Joseph. It would have crushed his father. This ensured the secret would remain intact, at least for the time being, regardless of how untenable and volatile the situation actually was.

Joseph's girlfriend, Molly Sullivan, now a senior at Vanderbilt, also knew. Being very protective of Joseph, she would never do anything to harm him. Already accepted into Stanford Law School, Molly planned to move west when she finished her classes, which was just a few months away. Going to school year-round, it seemed like her time at Vandy had flown by.

Palo Alto was a long way from Joseph, but she had plans for her life, as did he. Each accepted being separated as a necessary facet of the journey they were traveling, hopefully together. It was the mature way to look at the future. Living together and being always together, each knew how difficult their parting would be, but neither talked about their separation being permanent. That possibility remained unspoken, but it was a thought in the back of their minds. Because it was too painful for either to articulate, they had a tacit no-talk rule, effectively avoiding the subject.

Each week, Joseph took a break from his studies to visit his "sister," and they played together for several hours. As soon as Jo Ellen saw Joseph's truck pull into the driveway, she ran to greet him, just as fast as her little legs would carry her, calling his name, "Yo-suf," as she did. With arms stretched out wide, he would run to meet her, pick her up, kiss her, and hold her so closely she wouldn't see his eyes misting. He loved Jo Ellen with all his heart, and the toddler knew it.

Watching the two of them together brought a smile to everybody's face, including Landria's. Jo Ellen had been told Joseph was her brother, and Molly was her brother's girlfriend. Because Joseph loved Molly, so did Jo Ellen—but certainly not the way she loved him. For Jo Ellen, Joseph was her favorite person in the world, including her mom and dad.

That Joseph was closer to Jo Ellen than her mother certainly was unique. Perhaps the mother-daughter bonding problem stemmed from Landria's bitterness about being shackled to Dwayne, an imposition she resented and never came to accept. Nevertheless, in her own way, Landria loved her daughter, but there was a hesitancy about it the child sensed. It made Jo Ellen feel unsafe, even as a small child. There was no hesitancy with Joseph though, not in the least. When she was with her brother, she knew she was completely safe, and nothing else in the world mattered.

When he left, she always cried, begging him to stay longer, which infuriated Landria. As he drove away, Landria was vexed and refused to comfort her daughter, choosing instead to look at her sobbing child with contempt, disdain, and even a little anger.

This pattern replicated itself weekly, including summers, varying little from one week to the next. Once Joseph began his college studies in Nashville, shortly after Jo Ellen's birth, he never took a break or returned to his mother's home in Atlanta for more than a day or two at a time. This is how important spending time with Jo Ellen had become.

Although her father, Joseph transformed his paternal inclinations into that of a brother, knowing it was in Jo Ellen's best interest—his father's too. At first, it was difficult but, like so many complicated situations in life, over time, what he considered abnormal became tolerable, then acceptable, and finally natural. Obviously, this was a strange family situation, but it was also Tennessee, where incest wasn't uncommon—not like in other parts of the country.

When Molly accompanied Joseph to visit Jo Ellen, which was about half of the time, she always maintained a watchful eye on Landria. Molly was like a cheetah stalking a gazelle—just daring Landria to make a false move with Joseph. Both women understood this dynamic. Each loathed the other without coming right out and saying so. Because it was the South, and the conflict was between southern women, this little dance of rivalry went unnoticed by everybody other than the two of them. Since both had been intimate with Joseph, it was normal behavior between jealous felines.

Joseph understood what was happening, but only after Molly pointed it out to him. Every once in a while, he got an earful when they were driving back to campus. Had she not told him about Landria's intentions, he never would have recognized what was happening. It would have simply passed by him—just like it would have most guys. Infuriated that he could miss something this obvious, Molly just shook her head, thinking he was oblivious, never realizing that most men are equally obtuse. Women hate this characteristic about men, but it's a trait that generally serves men well, keeping them blissfully ignorant about much of what occurs in their lives.

༣

Meanwhile, as the months passed, eventually becoming close to two years, Landria's marital discontent never diminished—not even a little. Miserable with her lot in life; she wanted to run, but she couldn't—not without the funds she had stolen from her former lover. Her stash was now nearly $850,000—a little more than what she possessed when forced to flee Atlanta—thanks to compound interest and never having to tap into the account.

Her husband, Dwayne, didn't even know the funds existed, but Joseph did. Unfortunately, Landria couldn't do a thing with the money—thanks to her "son-in-law." As part of the demands he extracted from her to keep quiet about Jo Ellen's parentage, Landria had reluctantly given Joseph the username and password to her Wells Fargo account. Initially surprised she had so much money; he knew she might use it to disappear. Therefore, using an iPhone application, Joseph maintained constant vigilance on her account, rendering her stash of funds useless for any potential escape plans. Fearful of never seeing Jo Ellen again, he insisted on keeping close tabs on the child's mother.

Joseph had Landria exactly where he wanted her, and that's precisely where he intended to keep her. Having been her sexual partner for several months, Joseph understood Landria's nature intimately. Having been badly fooled by her once, he would never allow himself to be fooled by her again.

Molly helped him with this. Particularly disdainful of Landria's sluttish snake tattoo, which had enamored Joseph, as well as his father, she reminded Joseph repeatedly that Landria was no better than a whore—just in case he might have forgotten. Always wary of Landria, Molly jogged his memory about "that woman" several times a week, whether he needed the reminder or not. As nearly every guy knows, women can be petulant about potential rivals and former girlfriends.

Since Landria had skipped town three times before, leaving others holding the bag each time, Joseph didn't need to be reminded about what kind of woman she was. He wasn't about to lower his guard and allow Landria to disappear again, especially now that Jo Ellen had become such an important part of his life. To ensure she couldn't just pick up and leave, he also had her movements monitored by a detective agency. They kept close tabs on her.

When informed he had found Landria in Nashville and that she had married his father, Joseph's good friend, Sean Kincannon, was flabbergasted and shook his head incredulously at this unexpected and bizarre turn of events. Understanding the situation well, Sean knew Joseph's instincts to have Landria monitored were justified. This is why the affluent lawyer offered to pay for the detective service, which Joseph accepted appreciatively.

Although Landria had not been told she was under routine surveillance, she knew. Being sneaky by nature, she always knew when she was being watched. This infuriated her, of course, but she couldn't come right out and confront Joseph about it. Besides, being straightforward was never Landria's way of dealing with a situation anyway. Having passive aggressive tendencies, she chose another way to get even.

When Joseph came to visit Jo Ellen, Landria always wore her low cut jeans, revealing her snake tattoo, knowing he remembered where the serpent originated. It was a subtle reminder that sex with her was always an available option for him. Pretending she didn't do this on purpose, she hoped it would tantalize the college student—just like it had several years earlier, when she seduced him, while still an underage high school student. Such was her spiteful, sensuous, and seductive nature.

Landria knew that even if the tattoo didn't entice Joseph, it would certainly infuriate "his bitch girlfriend." From Landria's perspective, this was even better than tempting Joseph. When Molly saw it, Landria was certain her rival would make Joseph's life a living hell, which was precisely what happened.

Although Molly and Joseph didn't fight much, Landria's snake tattoo was a constant source of friction between them. When Landria flaunted it, Joseph's heart sank, knowing there would be hell to pay driving home. He also knew he would be celibate for several days thereafter.

Like his son, Joseph's dad also loved the tattoo. It aroused him regularly and played a prominent role in their sex life. Before his daughter was born, Dwayne couldn't believe his quality of intimacy with Landria. It delighted him to no end, just like it would any guy in his forties who was married to a beautiful woman in her twenties.

In the beginning, she had really been into him but, since the birth of their daughter, Landria had become hesitant and passive. At first, this confused Dwayne but ultimately it became very bothersome. Try as he may, he couldn't understand why there had been such an abrupt change in her level of sexual interest. Saddened, he felt powerless to rectify the situation.

Like most men, he convinced himself it had to do with his technique, so he read a book about Tantric sex, hoping this would help, but it didn't. When he whined, asking what was wrong, she denied there was a problem. She told him he was being silly, but Dwayne knew better. Clueless about what was really the issue, he tried everything he could think of, finally doubling down on his efforts to enhance his performance by increasing his dosage of Viagra. He was certain that if he remained aroused longer, that would work. Consequently, his expenditures on male enhancement medication became substantial.

On the afternoon the Kincannons arrived at Lake Oconee, as Sean was unloading the car, which was filled with groceries and the necessities to care for their infant son, when he opened the front door, he took his eyes off of Asta for a split second. Spotting an opening, Asta bolted and was gone in a flash. As quick as lightning, she disappeared into the woods before Sean could grab her. Infuriated with the dog and with his own stupidity, he could do nothing but swear, which he did profusely. For the dog, the lure of the woods was too great, and Sean was not dressed to chase after her, nor did he intend to scour the thick woods searching for her fruitlessly.

Returning to the kitchen where Marla-Dean was unpacking, he hissed, "That damn dog got out, and I have no idea where she went." Somehow making it her fault, he added, "I told you we should have left her in Atlanta."

Irritated that he had let Asta get away, coupled with his avoidance of responsibility for allowing it to happen, Marla-Dean replied in her don't-mess-with-me tone, "I told you to keep the door shut, Sean."

"I know you did," he replied contritely, after a long moment to determine whether or not he wanted to fight about it, which might spoil their entire weekend. Ultimately, he decided he was in a poor position to defend himself, which would have been a losing battle with Marla-Dean.

Sighing, she concluded, "It will be all right. Asta will come back when she's hungry."

"But she's not familiar with the area. She may never come back," he lamented.

"Yes, she will, Sean. She can smell us. That dog has part bloodhound in her. I'm sure of it."

Sighing, Sean simply shook his head, as he returned to the SUV to finish unpacking.

Sure enough, after dinner, Asta returned hungry. Feigning contriteness with her eyes and lowered head, the dog was fearful she might be in trouble. Because Asta looked so cute, Marla-Dean just smiled. Being relieved to see Asta, no reprimand was given.

When Marla-Dean looked closely at Asta, however, she noticed the dog was quivering and whiny. There was something different about her that worried Marla-Dean. Going outside to take a look around, she didn't spot anything unusual. Nevertheless, she wondered what had troubled Asta so much the dog couldn't stop shaking.

CHAPTER THREE
This Is Sadomasochistic

Thursday, after the long Labor Day weekend at the lake, Marla-Dean was scheduled to work the evening shift at Peachtree Medical, along with her colleague, Dr. Luke Easton, the man who had become well known as a medical expert on the television program, *On the Record,* hosted by Greta Van Susteren and *The Kelly File,* hosted by Megyn Kelly. Nicknamed "Dr. Big Shot," for reasons he refused to divulge on TV, Dr. Easton had actually become accustomed to the name—something he thought he would never do.

Returning to the emergency room in a part-time capacity, Marla-Dean had agreed to work six twelve-hour shifts a month. She returned—not out of necessity—but out of her love for medicine. It was her first calling. Being a skilled physician, she didn't want to abandon her practice completely. Besides, Connor was in good hands with his new nanny, Winky Weller, who was now living in the Kincannon's guesthouse, over the garage at their Peachtree Battle home.

Before Marla-Dean went on duty at 7 p.m., she agreed to meet with her gynecologist, Dr. Porthos, to discuss making an offer for his lakefront property. In an effort to recover as much of his investment as possible, Gus wanted to sell the house without using a realtor, which was acceptable to Marla-Dean. They had agreed to work out the sale privately, pleasing both.

She was willing to make an initial offer that was $100,000 less than his asking price, knowing she would come up a little, but not much. Sitting at the same table where she and Melissa Gordon—the charge nurse and Luke's girlfriend—had enjoyed many meals, she waited patiently for Gus Porthos to arrive.

Five minutes later, wearing a tailored lab coat and a broad smile, Dr. Porthos walked up, held out his hand warmly, and sat down, ready to seal the deal. Anxious to get right to business, Gus asked, "Well, what did you and your husband think of the place, Marla-Dean?"

"Gus, we just love it. It's beautiful. It's even more peaceful and serene than I thought it would be."

"Wonderful. I was certain you would like it," he said, barely able to contain his glee.

"Gus, we want to buy it, if it's still for sale, that is?"

Surprised she would even ask; he dismissed her apprehension instantly. "Of course it is, Marla-Dean. It's a real steal at only $495,000. You know I originally paid a lot more for it, don't you?"

"I do remember that, Gus. My husband and I are prepared to offer you $395,00 for it. We're basing our offer on what similar properties are selling for in the area," she added quickly, although somewhat defensively. Trying to be professional and detached, she hoped he wouldn't realize she was just as anxious to buy, as he was to sell.

When Gus heard how much less her offer was than his asking price, he winced noticeably. Trying hard to remain cheerful, while not spoiling his only opportunity to unload his albatross, he countered sheepishly, "But Marla-Dean, it is worth much more than that. I paid $895,000 for it, and I'm only asking $495,000. It's worth every penny of it, and you certainly can afford it."

"Gus, my husband and I do like the house," she countered. "You've done a marvelous job with it, but our offer is about what the house is worth in today's market—not about what we are capable of paying. This is all my husband has authorized me to offer," she added calmly, wisely making Sean the villain in the conversation.

She was fully aware she had the upper hand, of course. Knowing the true value of the house, she wasn't about to pay more than it was worth. Although Gus didn't know it, this was why she was negotiating the deal rather than her husband.

Using the tactics of pleading, imploring and whining, Porthos went back and forth with Marla-Dean for a while. But she was a shrewd businesswoman, and Gus's negotiating skills were substantially inferior. Plus, his situation necessitated him to make the deal.

Finally, looking at her coldly, resigned to his fate, with flared nostrils, Gus said, "Well, it doesn't seem like I have much choice, do I? All right, have it your way; it's yours for $425,000." Contemptuously, he asked, "Will you at least pay for the closing costs?"

"Certainly," Marla-Dean replied, accommodatingly.

"Oh, and one other thing," he snipped. "I think it would be best if you found yourself another gynecologist." With that, he walked off, nearly in tears, blaming bitches like Marla-Dean and his ex-wife for his financial ruin, never taking one iota of responsibility for creating his own mess, ensuring he would replicate his error with another woman in the future.

As Dr. Porthos rounded the corner, muttering curses under his breath, Marla-Dean flipped open her cell phone and called home. Answering immediately, without even saying hello, Sean asked, "What happened?"

"Mr. Kincannon, we are now the owners of a beautiful home on Lake Oconee."

"And?"

"And, it only cost us $425,000, which makes it a good investment, as well."

"What a woman. I probably would have . . ." he started to say, when she interrupted him.

"I know, Dear. You would have paid far too much for it, bailing out Gus in the process but, with me around, you don't have to worry your pretty little face about numbers. You remember that it causes wrinkles, don't you?" She added playfully.

"I do remember, darling," he replied, choosing gratitude over irritation, which might have led to a pointless quarrel. As each sat quietly holding the phone, neither said anything for a long moment. Both were pleased, obviously. Nothing else needed to be said.

In the ER, the triage nurse, Tanisha Brown—an excellent gatekeeper for the unit—had things moving smoothly. As Marla-Dean checked the board to see what was upcoming, nothing major was imminent, which made her smile. It meant the night might be uneventful. As Melissa Gordon, the charge nurse, approached her with a smile, Marla-Dean asked where Melissa wanted her to start.

While Melissa was bringing her up to speed, both women were startled by Dr. Easton's raised voice. He could be heard all the way from Room 3 to the front desk, yelling, "Holy shit; I don't believe this. Your ass isn't an amusement park, you know? What kind of fool are you?" A moment later, he added, " You haven't changed one bit; you know that?"

Surprised, but curious, the women looked at each other with startled amusement. Smiling, they tried to cover their mouths to squelch and conceal their laughter, but couldn't. Both giggled like teenagers. Without saying a word to one another, knowing something interesting was occurring, both turned and walked quickly to Room 3.

As they opened the door, they saw a man lying face down on a gurney with his exposed rear raised high in the air.

In the ER, doctors, nurses, and orderlies witness many things. Nevertheless, being mooned like this definitely surprised both Melissa and Marla-Dean, requiring both women to bite their lips to keep from laughing out loud. On the verge of losing control, neither looked at the other, knowing a single furtive glance might initiate unintended pandemonium. Although an understandable human reaction, laughing definitely would not have been a professional response to the situation.

Dr. Easton was busy rummaging through his surgical instruments, trying to find a pair of long, narrow forceps. Barely noticing that Melissa and Marla-Dean were there, Dr. Big Shot continued to berate his patient's foolishness.

"What in the world were you thinking? This could precipitate some serious medical consequences. Did you know that?" Not waiting for a response, he added, "Of course not!"

"Turning his head, the patient whined, "I know, Dr. Easton. I'm sorry; I'm so embarrassed to be back here."

"You should be," Easton scolded—devoid of compassion.

Curious about why Luke wouldn't relent, Marla-Dean walked to the patient's side and realized it was Ring Man, the patient who gave Dr. Easton his nickname—Dr. Big Shot—several years earlier, by ejaculating in his face. This time, instead of having three metal rings choking his erected penis to enhance his sexual pleasure, Ring Man had something inserted in his rectum for a similar purpose.

Marla-Dean wanted to remain a while longer to enjoy what was happening, but she couldn't. Over the intercom, Tanisha had just called, telling her to report to Room 5, where her first patient was waiting. Melissa, however, stayed to watch, as well as to help, if necessary. Still somewhat tickled, she made certain to avoid catching Marla-Dean's eye as she left, fearful of initiating pandemonium from laughter.

Dr. Easton finally located the instrument he had been hunting. After coating it with K-Y gel, he walked between Ring Man's exposed buttocks, took a deep breath, and inserted the forceps into the man's rectum unceremoniously. The man's entire body lurched and grimaced from obvious discomfort, but Dr. Big Shot could not have cared less. In less than fifteen seconds, the physician clasped the foreign object and pulled it out quickly—somewhat mindful of his patient's distress.

Ring Man groaned as the doctor retracted the object, becoming nauseous during the procedure. In fact, the patient had to make a concerted effort not to vomit, knowing that if he did, it would have made his situation worse. When the doctor was finished, Ring Man lowered his derriere and curled up in a fetal position, trying to comfort himself physically, as well as emotionally.

As Dr. Easton held the object he removed from Ring Man's rectum up to the light, Melissa had expected to see a gerbil, but that's not what it was. Instead, she saw a shoe polish applicator—the type with a brush on the tip of it. She knew what it was instantly, having used one to polish her son's shoes every week before church for years.

Evidently, Ring Man's partner had inserted it a little too deeply and was unable to retrieve it, necessitating a trip to the ER, inflicting further humiliation upon Ring Man, who had become legendary at Peachtree Medical.

As Luke was finishing with his patient, Melissa excused herself. Walking back to the Triage Desk, she poked her head into Room 5 to see if Marla-Dean needed anything, but Dr. Kincannon indicated she didn't.

Twenty minutes later, as Ring Man was being discharged, intent on assuaging his wounded ego, he walked up to Tanisha at the triage desk. Having regained his composure, he was incensed at being the subject of ridicule and humiliation. In an effort to regain his dignity, he turned to Tanisha, and said, "I'll have you know my name is not Ring Man. It's Lance Rector, and I never want to be referred to as Ring Man again. Do you understand me?"

Not intimidated one iota by this nitwit's theatrics, Tanisha turned and looked at him. With obvious contempt, she replied, "Your real name is even worse."

With that, she turned her head away from him indifferently, as

Lance and his new partner left Peachtree Medical, fuming at her contemptuous dismissal.

❧

As Marla-Dean began her examination of her fifty-year-old female patient, she realized something wasn't right about the situation immediately. The woman had come to the ER complaining of back pain. Lying on the gurney, wearing a surgical gown and a sad, embarrassed look on her face, the woman's countenance seemed odd to the doctor.

As Marla-Dean was about to begin her examination, she instructed the woman to raise her gown. When the woman did as she had been instructed, the first thing the doctor noticed was significant bruising around the vagina and inner thighs of both legs. Instantly, Marla-Dean stopped. As she stepped away, she also noticed bruising on the woman's neck, which the patient had attempted to camouflage with a generous supply of foundation. Taking a long, appraising look, Marla-Dean simply turned to the woman with questioning eyes.

The patient didn't say a word but, by the look on her face, she understood a response was required. Knowing this was certain to happen—but unprepared for the embarrassment that would accompany it—the patient turned her head, indicating an unwillingness to respond. When Marla-Dean saw this, she simply stood back and waited, refusing to continue her examination without receiving an explanation.

A long tense moment ensued, making both women feel uncomfortable. Finally, the patient blinked. Addressing the doctor, Anne Morrow-Steiger simply said, "It was consensual."

With obvious concern, Dr. Kincannon began to reply, but her patient interrupted, cutting Marla-Dean off before she could say a thing. Imploringly, with her hand held up, palm open—like a stop sign—Anne turned to the doctor. With tears in her eyes, she pled with Marla-Dean in a quivering voice, "I told you it was consensual,

Doctor, and it was. I promise it was. Can you please just forget about the bruises and help me with my back? That's all I need. Will you help me with that, please?"

Although hesitant, out of compassion for the woman and gratitude that her husband, Sean, was gentle, Marla-Dean simply nodded that she would.

Proceeding, she gave her patient a complete examination, including X-rays and ultra sound. When the examination was complete and Anne finished dressing, regaining a measure of her dignity in the process, the two women sat to discuss Anne's medical situation. As Marla-Dean was writing Anne a prescription for pain medication, she looked at her patient with concern. Realizing this, Anne blushed, knowing what was coming next.

Being unapologetically straightforward, Dr. Kincannon asked point blank, "Did your husband do this to you?"

"No, it wasn't him. Besides, I'm divorced," Anne responded immediately. After a long pause, while Marla-Dean waited patiently for her to continue, the woman hung her head, shamefully. "It was my boyfriend. But it really was consensual, Doctor." Being a little defensive, Anne added, "There's nothing wrong with it. He just gets a little rough with me, that's all."

Shaking her head in disagreement, Marla-Dean replied, "That isn't true, Mrs. Steiger. Your bruising is not normal, but I'm neither your therapist nor your minister. I'm just your emergency-room physician." Waiting for Anne to give her full attention, which she did after taking a deep breath, Marla-Dean continued. "Your bruising is more than your boyfriend getting a little rough with you. By allowing him to do this, you are putting your safety at risk."

"No, I'm not," Anne responded dismissively, desperately trying to avoid being confronted by the truth she adamantly refused to acknowledge or even consider.

"You most certainly are, Mrs. Steiger." Marla-Dean countered, knowing her patient's denial could lead to catastrophic consequences.

She added, "I don't know who has done this to you, but your injuries are not normal. Your partner's behavior is sadomasochistic, and it's dangerous. In addition to the medication I'm prescribing for pain, I'm also making a psychiatric referral. You need help. If you don't get it, you could end up dead."

Anne just sat on the examining table stoically, as Marla-Dean's words pierced through her.

"Do you understand what I have just said?" Marla-Dean inquired.

"Yes."

After forcing her patient to confront the harsh reality of her situation, Marla-Dean looked at Mrs. Steiger for a long, awkward moment.

Finally, with tears streaming down her cheeks, Anne Steiger broke, telling Marla-Dean she would take her advice and obtain the professional help she needed. With this, the woman stood, picked up her purse, and left, grateful her ordeal in the ER was over.

Anne promised to get help. It was a promise she intended to keep, but she never did. The reason she didn't was simple. The lure of her sexual addiction was greater than her need for safety. Although middle-aged and the mother of two, the spell Amiglio Sabata had cast upon her was powerful and enticing. Despite the pain he enjoyed inflicting upon her, she knew she wanted more. It was a compulsion that required sating. Just the thought of it made her tingle. Amiglio was this alluring; she couldn't help herself. Addicts never can.

CHAPTER FOUR
She Had to Have More

As Anne drove out of the parking lot at Peachtree Medical, she wanted to get as far away from there as she could, and as quickly as possible. Speeding down the road, she merged onto I-85 headed north, passing everybody in front of her. Mortified by her experience, she could hardly breathe.

Before checking into the emergency room, she had been concerned about what her medical examination might entail. That's why she had been so hesitant to go, but she had no idea Marla-Dean would be so confrontational. *Thank God my doctor was a woman*, she thought. *What if it had been a man?* She would never have been able to live down her embarrassment.

Driving helped settle her nerves somewhat. It allowed her to reflect upon the direction her life had taken since her divorce. Just thinking about it, she had to shake her head. Despite her predicament, this brought a wry grin to her face. If one of her girlfriends had told her ten years earlier she would be consumed by a sexually obsessive relationship with a brutal Mexican, she would have laughed, telling her friend she had lost her mind, but this is exactly what had happened.

As Anne continued ruminating, she couldn't believe the turn of events her life had taken. It made her think about her two daughters. At least both of them were at Auburn—her alma mater—shielded from what was happening in their mother's life. Anne was grateful they weren't around to witness their mom's self-destructive midlife crisis. And that's exactly what it was—a phase—nothing more. She was fairly certain of this, but the traumatic event she had just endured was beginning to make her wonder—just a little. Maybe there was more to it than she had been willing to admit.

Although she had begun to question her behavior, she hated being judged by her doctor. Just thinking about it, galled and infuriated Anne. That bitch knew nothing about her life and all she had endured over the years. If she had, she would have shown more compassion, instead of being so confrontational and condemning. Dr. Kincannon definitely needed to develop better communication skills. Going over the events repeatedly in her mind, Anne finally realized the doctor couldn't have understood what was really happening. *How could she?* Anne thought, as her anger over her humiliation abated—just a little—further calming her nerves.

Unlike so many of her high school friends, Anne had waited quite a while to marry, knowing those who wed early were more likely to divorce. Having a mother who had been married three times and divorced just as many, Anne wanted to avoid producing a broken home at all costs. Hating the way her mother behaved around potential suitors, when she was young, Anne never wanted to be like her mother—a flirtatious divorcee.

Anne believed she had made a wise and prudent decision by waiting until her late-twenties to marry William Steiger, nearly a quarter century earlier.

It wasn't as if she had multiple options. Although striking, she was by no means beautiful. Petite, with a trim figure, she had a great smile and was very funny, but at Auburn University, where there were thousands of beautiful young women, Anne was easy to overlook. Consequently, she had few dates and even fewer boyfriends.

When William Steiger met her at a fraternity party one night, he was smitten. Showing genuine and sustained interest, she responded, and they became an item, getting married a year later. Having two daughters, after being married several years, she was content and looked forward to the future.

Her husband, Bill Steiger, was a confident young man who was ready to take on the world. He intended to make a name for himself. A big talker, with swagger to match, Anne believed he would be successful and a good provider for their little family, but this wasn't the case.

Bill's grandiose ambitions never materialized into anything sustainable, regardless of the effort he put forth. Disappointed by one botched opportunity after the other, he began to drink heavily, self-medicating the disillusionment he felt over his failed career. In the process, he became an alcoholic. Living in denial about this for many years, like others addicted to booze, he steadfastly refused to seek the help he needed. Embittered, he blamed everybody other than himself for his lot in life.

Bill's alcoholic behavior put a terrible strain on his marriage.

Despite her determined efforts to hold everything together—for the sake of their children—after twenty years of frustration and enabling, Anne finally had had enough. Being the sole breadwinner by this time, she threw him out of the house and finished raising their two daughters as a single mom.

For Anne, life was much easier without him. Once he was gone, she only had two children to rear instead of three.

For Bill, it was different. Without Anne to regulate his life and temper his alcoholism, his drinking escalated, while his ability to cope with life diminished proportionately. Drinking more than ever, he became delusional frequently. As his life continued to deteriorate, he ended up living in squalor, completely dependent on his government check for long-term disability. His humiliation complete, he came to despise the hand that fed him, wholeheartedly embracing a conspiracy theory that villainized the President and his evil cohorts—the Illuminati.

Once single, Anne's life also changed dramatically. As often happens with women who endure a great deal and have never been fulfilled in life, she blossomed in her husband's absence. Being free, amorous, and desirable, she became as flirtatious as her mother had been a generation earlier. To complete her transformation, Anne's sexual appetite, which had long been dormant, resurfaced, and it required substantial sating.

Her husband was a diminutive man. Although his ears were large, as were his toes, fingers, and nose, there was one appendage that was quite small. Anne thought she had come to terms with her husband's shortcomings, but she hadn't.

During their entire marriage, she never refused her husband's sexual demands—not once—but she had never been completely satisfied by him either. Not terribly bothered by this, she simply accepted it as her lot in life, realizing that men were more concerned about sex than women anyway. None of her girlfriends seemed to enjoy sex, so she didn't believe she was missing much anyway.

Soon after her divorce, however, Anne became intimate with a massive hulk—a gargantuan that was the antithesis of her former husband. Bill Steiger was bright, while her new boyfriend was nearly a dullard. Her former husband was verbal, while Anne's new guy was stoical and taciturn. Despite being crude and ignorant, which Bill wasn't, her new guy had one thing Bill didn't, and Anne soon realized just how important that one thing was.

No longer a chore to endure before closing her eyes at the end of the day, Anne loved having sex with her new boyfriend, starting the first time they became intimate. She especially loved the feeling of being overpowered and dominated by the Cretan—something her husband was incapable of doing.

Anne's new guy drove a Harley and drank Jim Beam to excess

regularly, which didn't seem to bother her. She had become used to drunkards. Still as quick-witted as ever, Anne began referring to her new guy as Beam. Completing the comparison, she spitefully nicknamed her former husband, Pencil, which added to Steiger's humiliation immeasurably. She hoped the new sobriquet would piss him off, which it did.

Now free and thrilled to be experiencing regular orgasms, Anne loved the feeling of being with a real man, but this was Beam's only redeeming quality. Plenty good enough for a while, she eventually required more to remain interested in the relationship. Besides, her daughters loathed Beam and made fun of his ignorance and lack of erudition regularly. Weary of defending him, Anne finally lost interest and sent him on his way, taking up with Amiglio Sabata soon thereafter, believing he would be a more suitable alternative.

Although she knew very little about Amiglio, Anne became intimate with him on their first date. As an aging fifty-year-old woman, with her sexual clock ticking, she saw no reason to abstain. Besides, Amiglio was not the kind of man who was about to take no for an answer. After the first time, they had sex three or four times a week for about a month before things changed. By that time, she was hooked, which was precisely what Amiglio intended. This was when he introduced his sadomasochistic behavior into the relationship.

The first time he hurt her, while they were making love, Anne was surprised. It was completely unexpected. At first shocked, she balked and tried to push him from her. Refusing to comply, he became increasingly forceful, subjugating her in the process. That's when things changed. In an instant, in the twinkling of an eye, she abandoned her resistance. To her astonishment, she liked his brutish forcefulness. Being overpowered by him helped her achieve a sense of pleasure she had never anticipated. She didn't even know such an experience was possible.

Once having achieved it, however, her life changed. She could never return to the confines of what she had experienced before. Just the thought of it was unacceptable.

From then on, she couldn't get enough of the cruel, detached Mexican, who became increasingly rough with her. He was never attentive or tender, but this didn't seem to bother Anne—not any longer. Whatever he wanted, regardless of what it was, she provided. Slavishly compliant, she became totally obsessed with her lover in the process.

Their relationship was intense, filled with raw passion and little else. Amiglio, who had had numerous similar relationships over the years, soon grew weary of Anne and started looking for a new paramour to bed and beat. Although married for many years and the father of two sons—both nearly grown—Amiglio did what he pleased, when he pleased, with whomever he desired. This was the lifestyle he demanded, and nothing short of death was going to prevent him from pursuing it.

His wife, Gabriela, had come to terms with his brutish sadomasochism years earlier. As the mother of his children, he never brutalized her, but they no longer had sex either, which was fine with her. Their relationship had been asexual for more than a decade.

Gabriela was a good mother. Having plenty of money and all the freedom she desired, she provided Amiglio with a modicum of respectability, but little else. She didn't love him and hadn't for a long time, but she knew better than to leave him—that was for sure. Nobody left Amiglio; he left them.

Although Amiglio might have been bored with Anne, she certainly wasn't bored with him. Not close to being ready to end their relationship, if it could be called that, Anne's obsession intensified as Amiglio's cooled. As a result, she became clingy, needy, and whiny, which repulsed the Mexican gangster, driving him further away from her.

By now, Anne was starting to become a problem. Despite this, at one level, the Mexican enjoyed being hounded by her and continued to have sex with her often. Loathing her, while also desiring her, he became increasingly brutal as time passed.

As her cravings intensified, Anne's possessiveness finally became a nuisance. Having had his fill, Amiglio told her to get lost, which was tantamount to a death threat.

A wise woman would have received this clear message and understood it, counted her losses and moved on, but not Anne. Consumed by her carnal obsession, she couldn't. Choosing to believe he really didn't mean what he said, she unwisely continued her pursuit. The further he withdrew, the greater her obsessive compulsion became.

Possessive and insanely jealous, she began to stalk him, never fully understanding the type of man he was. Thinking he was an importer, she had no idea cocaine and marijuana were the products he imported. The target of numerous investigations—all aimed at putting him behind bars for the rest of his life—Amiglio was known to authorities nationwide as an underworld kingpin. Even Sean Kincannon had tried to convict him twice, failing both times.

Had Anne fully comprehended the situation, perhaps she could have walked away, but probably not. Her need was simply too strong. It trumped her ability to think rationally—just as completely as Amiglio's forcefulness had trumped her ability to tell him no, when he began hurting her.

Two days before she went to the emergency room, Amiglio had discovered Anne snooping around his house in Gwinnett County. Realizing she had been discovered, she felt embarrassed. Abandoning her hiding place, she walked to her car, intent on leaving as quickly and quietly as she had come. Instead of sending her on her way with a firm reprimand, however, Amiglio chose an alternative means to rebuff her.

Confronting her at her car, he grabbed her, raising her skirt, as he did. Ripping off her panties, in the front seat of her SUV, he forced himself into her. This time, he was more brutal than he had ever been before, severely injuring her in the process.

At first, she was terrified he might kill her, but his brutality ended up exhilarating her—just like it always did. By the time he was finished, which didn't take long, she had achieved the greatest pleasure she had ever known, intensifying her toxic addiction to her gangster in the process.

Sneering when he was finished, Amiglio wiped himself off contemptuously with her disheveled skirt, ruining it with stains. Looking at him, she could see that he was clearly repulsed by her. Sneering as he zipped up, he simply walked off, never uttering a word. He never even kissed her—not once—during the entire encounter. As she thought about it later, she couldn't remember if he had ever looked at her.

Humiliated, exhausted, and physically hurt, Anne drove home and bathed. She tried to function normally that evening but couldn't. The following morning she could barely get out of bed, and the only reason she did was to retrieve some much-needed ibuprofen. As her pain intensified rather than diminished, she became genuinely alarmed her injuries might be severe. She also noticed the bruising on her neck, where he had choked her during orgasm. The marks had darkened appreciably, becoming quite noticeable.

Unable to cope with her injuries, she reluctantly went to the emergency room, where Dr. Kincannon had given her a heavy-duty narcotic for pain, along with some sobering advice about the possible negative consequences of her behavior.

Being sexually fulfilled at the time, Anne accepted the wisdom of her doctor's advice. In one sense, it scared her straight, so Anne made a vow to never go near her violent paramour again.

It was a vow she intended to keep and did maintain for a while— but not for long. She couldn't. When her depraved yearnings returned, she didn't have the resolve or the intestinal fortitude to stay away from Amiglio. Consumed with wanton desire, she had to have more, and she knew where to get it. Regardless of what the consequences might be, she intended to have sex with Amiglio again.

CHAPTER FIVE

"La Vas a Matter!"

When Anne's ex-husband Bill, nicknamed Pencil, saved Sean's life by intervening in an assassination attempt, Pencil was certain he would be championed by one and by all. He deserved special recognition. He was America's Hero, after all, relentlessly fighting the President and the Illuminati in their attempt to impose a dictatorial rule on the land of the free and the home of the brave.

Foiling their evil machinations was Pencil's purpose in life; and a righteous calling it was. Bearing this heavy mantel was his lot, bequeathed to him by his late-friend, Terrance Bruce—a noble patriot—murdered because he had become a nuisance to the forces of Evil. Having come too close to proving the President and the Illuminati were destroying the foundations of the American way of life, Terrance had been murdered, but nobody knew how much he had already confided in Pencil before being eliminated.

After successfully completing his first assignment, when he shot the assassin on the roof, preventing the murder of the district attorney, Pencil was eager for his next task. He assumed it would come quickly, especially since he had proven his worth by taking out Pretty Boy Sabarisi and not getting caught.

Although Pencil didn't know the assassin's name when he shot him twice—first in the abdomen and then right between the eyes—Pencil discovered who he was from watching TV. He learned everything he needed to know, gaining most of his knowledge from the best news reporter in Atlanta, Jaye Watson.

Watson got to the bottom of things, which a man of action like Pencil always appreciated. Watson reported about Sabarisi's drug connections in New Orleans, conjecturing that the drug lord wanted District Attorney Kincannon out of the way because of his high conviction rate. The reporter also explained how prevalent drugs had become in the Southeast. Having foiled their plans made Pencil's chest swell with pride. His intervention had been in the nick of time, saving thousands of kids from becoming hooked, perhaps even his own two precious daughters. Although Kincannon had been critically wounded, he survived the attack, which he would not have done without Pencil's heroic efforts to save the day.

Hero or not, Pencil was concerned the Atlanta Police Department might break into his apartment and apprehend him for shooting the sniper. Always vigilant, Pencil's senses were more acute than ever for several months after the incident.

Because the police never came, Pencil's pride in his accomplishment appeared justified. He had outsmarted them all—the police, the President, and the Illuminati. With the help of Megyn Kelly and Greta Van Susteren, he had done it. A master sleuth, he was ready for his next assignment, which he was certain would be given to him by Megyn, as she broadcasted her program, *The Kelly File.*

To understand her secret messages, which were specifically meant for him and no one else, he was forced to wear the dreaded University of Georgia football helmet, which contained a secret antenna. To tip him off that a cryptic message was forthcoming, Greta Van Susteren touched her hair during the last segment of her show, *On the Record.*

When she did this, Pencil understood he was to put on the helmet and pay close attention to every word Megyn Kelly spoke, knowing she had something important to communicate to him.

Eager for a new adventure, Pencil paid rapt attention for weeks, but nothing of interest happened. Weeks turned into months, but Megyn didn't provide him with a new escapade. After waiting for more than half a year, Pencil's euphoria turned to despair. Consuming more vodka than ever, he passed out before 9 p.m. frequently, missing Megyn's show as often as he watched it.

Isolating, his alcoholism became life threatening, and his two daughters were the only people in the world who seemed to care whether he lived or died. But they were off at college, leading their own lives, so he rarely saw them. Worst of all, his whore ex-wife had sent them to Auburn rather than to his alma mater, LSU. This embittered LSU's most loyal fan even further.

Pencil hated Auburn—just like he hated Georgia and Alabama. The only reason he tolerated Auburn was that's where he met Anne at a fraternity party, during his senior year at LSU. Traveling back and forth regularly to see her on weekends, he actually had some very pleasant experiences at Auburn, but that all changed when she divorced him and started screwing that Neanderthal, Beam.

Now divorced for several years, he still couldn't believe she had done this to him. After dumping Beam, he was certain she was ready to admit her mistake, but she hadn't made any overtures toward reconciliation—not yet, anyway. He was certain she would apologize after he was proclaimed a national hero, but that hadn't happened either, much to his chagrin. For whatever reason, Megyn was still keeping his heroics under wraps.

Now, The Whore was screwing someone else. He was certain of it, but he still hadn't figured out who it was. In time, he would. It would be nearly impossible to hide lascivious behavior from a world-class detective like him, and he knew it. Being so accomplished made him grin.

In the meantime, until Anne came to her senses and took him back, he was free to enjoy the good life, including drinking a quart of vodka a day and passing out regularly. Still believing he was just a social drinker, he lived in denial, as his alcoholism continued to take its toll on his mind and body, ravaging both.

The purchase of the property on Lake Oconee went smoothly. Marla-Dean had her attorney draw up the papers and, since the Kincannons paid for the house with a cashier's check, there were no banks involved with a vested interest. After the house passed inspection, it became theirs in a matter of weeks.

At the closing, Gus Porthos continued to display an attitude of brusque contemptuousness toward Marla-Dean, which made their meeting quite uncomfortable for everybody other than him. Still unwilling to take responsibility for his situation, Porthos scolded Marla-Dean non-verbally, making her the proxy for the venomous hatred he continued to maintain toward his ex-wife, Darden.

Long gone, his former "trophy bride" rarely thought of him. She was busy enjoying a two-week cruise on the Danube River with her new paramour, the Gray Ghost.

By the time the property was Sean and Marla-Dean's, it was already the first week in October. So, the Kincannons decided to spend the following weekend at their new lake house. Anxious to settle in, Marla-Dean wanted to take a couple of outings before it started to get cold, knowing weekends in the winter would not be as enjoyable.

This trip, they included Connor's nanny, Winky. Excited to get away from the city, Winky had everything packed and ready to go by noon on Friday. Anxious to beat the traffic out of town, the family left soon thereafter. Being a big football weekend, they were concerned the traffic might be horrendous, and it was.

Since the Dawgs were playing Auburn, Sean had a 60" flat screen

TV installed the day after the closing, making certain the cable worked properly. He was all for going to the lake, but he wasn't about to miss the Georgia game—that's for sure. Bulldog fans are like that—Auburn fans too.

Like many women, Marla-Dean could not have cared less about football, which bored her. In a moment of candor, she once asked her husband, "Why do you like football so much, Sean? They only do two things—run and pass. It's always the same. I just don't get it!"

Looking at her as if she had a screw loose in her head, he just stared at her for a long moment. Then, he raised an eyebrow, shook his head, and changed the subject—never answering her question, which he considered ridiculous. Properly rebuffed and somewhat embarrassed, she never asked again, realizing football was "his thing" and not hers. Allowing him to enjoy it in peace was a wise strategy—one few women were smart enough to embrace. Many tolerate it but exact painful reparations for their martyrdom at a later time.

As they drove to the lake, Winky was so excited she could hardly sit still. She loved her job. Having a highly developed maternal nature, caring for Connor and Asta was not a difficult chore. Plus, it provided her with a reprieve to deal with her broken heart.

Named Burma Weller by her mother, because the woman supported missionaries working in Southeast Asia, Marlene Weller's favorite movie growing up was *Paper Moon*. She particularly liked the character Trixie Delight, played by Madeleine Kahn. Having a small bladder, Trixie needed to make frequent bathroom stops to go "winky-tinkie."

When Marlene married and had Burma, making a restroom stop was referred to as going "winky-tinky." Picking up the phrase quickly, the toddler shortened it to going winky, which was really cute and pleased her parents. Hence, Burma was nicknamed Winky soon thereafter, and the name stuck. As you can imagine, Winky rarely discussed the origin of her nickname. Nevertheless, it befit her personality, which was cute, engaging, somewhat frivolous, and funny.

At the insistence of her father, Winky attended nursing school at Mercer. Hating the sight of blood, pus, and every other human discharge, being a nurse was a poor profession for Winky to have chosen. While training on the floor one day during her junior year, she was told to cut the toenails of an older patient. Looking at the woman's feet, Winky saw that the nails were thick, brownish-yellow, and smelled. To her, they resembled claws rather than toenails.

Disgusted, when she bent down to perform the task, her stomach lurched and she nearly vomited. Knowing she just couldn't do it, Winky quit the program on the spot. Leaving the woman with uncut toenails, Winky simply walked out of the hospital and changed her major that afternoon, finishing her degree in a program more suitable to her inclinations—fashion merchandising.

Winky loved clothes almost as much as she loved jewelry. Things that sparkled fascinated her. In her garage apartment at the Kincannons, her closets were bulging with clothes. She also had half a dozen hanger boxes filled to overflowing, which required a corner in the garage for storage. In fact, Winky spent most of her paycheck on clothes and jewelry. Not having to pay rent, food, or utilities, she had substantial discretionary income. What she didn't spend on outfits and costume jewelry, she spent on her hair, nails, and anything else that might attract "the right man." No expense was spared to accomplish her goal.

Looking good is important to nearly every woman, but Winky took it to the nth degree, going so far as to have laser surgery to correct as many issues as she could think of, despite the fact none of them were necessary. Such was her obsession to look "perfect," when the right man came along, which never seemed to happen.

Raised Southern Baptist, in Cuthbert Georgia, she was fanatical about tithing, giving away large sums of her paycheck each month to TV evangelists. If a poufy-haired preacher whined about a special need, she gave. Some women are addicted to soap operas; Winky was addicted to the religious channel, funding just about anybody who asked—anybody other than Ernest Angley. She didn't like him. She believed a faith healer who needed a toupee was a fraud.

Having been crushed in a romantic relationship by a narcissistic glutton ten years her senior—a miscreant involved in numerous shady real estate deals—she went to the emergency room one evening to obtain a prescription for an anti-depressant. When Marla-Dean examined her, she took pity on the twenty-six-year-old and offered to help.

Several days later, they met at Starbucks. After checking out Winky's background, Marla-Dean offered her the job of being Connor's nanny. Being eight months pregnant at the time, Marla-Dean needed the slot filled, and she liked Winky from the moment she saw her. Because Winky was funny and vivacious, Marla-Dean thought she would fit into their family well, and the doctor was correct.

Although a little scatter-brained and as vain as a B-List Hollywood actress, Winky could make a five-letter word sound like it had four syllables, which Marla-Dean thought was charming. Winky was genuinely cute and witty. Although not traditionally pretty, because her teeth were far too big for her mouth, when she smiled, she radiated, making the overall effect delightful. She also had a trim figure, which made Marla-Dean certain the "right man" would come along sooner or later. Until then, she intended to allow Winky to heal from her broken heart, while helping raise Connor in the process.

Ready to make a new start in life, Winky jumped at the opportunity. Having been with the Kincannons from shortly before Connor's birth, she became an integral part of their family within a few weeks.

As they pulled into the driveway of their new lake home late Friday afternoon, everybody was excited, especially Winky, who had her own room adjacent to Connor's. After unpacking, the family had a wonderful dinner, enjoying the calm, relaxing evening breeze.

The following day was equally pleasant, especially since the Dawgs beat Auburn in a very competitive game. By the time it was over, Sean was exhausted from the emotional ordeal, which seemed silly to Marla-Dean. His obsession with football continued to mystify her.

Since Auburn was favored, Sean was on pins and needles from the start of the game to the finish. This wasn't the only college football upset of the day. In Nashville, the Commodores of Vanderbilt beat mighty Alabama, which surprised Sean. The only SEC rivals Vandy ever beat were Kentucky and Tennessee, so this sent shock waves across the nation.

After watching football for most of the afternoon and early evening, Sean was ready to retire early. Being a cool evening, he left the sliding glass doors open, allowing the gentle breeze from the lake to fill the master bedroom.

A little before midnight, Sean was awakened by voices that appeared to be coming from the deck. It seemed like people were right outside the bedroom—just a few feet away.

Petrified, his senses became acute. Instantly vigilant, he sat straight up in bed, listening intently. The first voice he heard was a woman's. High pitched, it had a frightened aspect to it that was unmistakable and unnerving. The woman seemed terrified. Her voice was followed immediately by a man's voice. His was angry, harsh, and authoritative.

Startled but cautious, Sean got out of bed as quietly as he could. Then, he tiptoed on the carpet until he reached the deck. Fearful someone might be right outside; Sean didn't make a sound. Muffling his breathing, the only sound he heard was his heartbeat, which sounded as loud as a base drum. Full of apprehension, he finally stepped out on the deck. As he looked around, he couldn't see anything that shouldn't be there.

The moon being full, he had a clear view of everything, including the house across the bay, which still had its lights on. The night was as calm and still as it could be, with nothing but a gentle breeze coming from across the lake to cool his face. With his senses alert, he continued to look and listen, but he neither saw nor heard another thing.

Perplexed, he was certain he had heard a woman's voice, followed by a man's. It wasn't a dream, nor was it a figment of his imagination. With nothing left to do, he returned to bed, sleeping restlessly the remainder of the night, knowing something was amiss.

Having breastfed Connor an hour earlier, Marla-Dean was exhausted and slept through the entire episode, never hearing a thing.

Because Winky's room was on the other side of the house, she wouldn't have heard the voices anyway. Besides, she was watching a sermon being preached by Charles Stanley—one of her favorites. This required her complete and undivided attention.

Sean wasn't imagining things, and he knew it. He had definitely heard something, but he couldn't make out what it was—not because the words weren't clear and discernible, but because they weren't spoken in English.

Had the Porthos' still owned the home, the events of the evening might have turned out differently, but they didn't. It now belonged to Sean and Marla-Dean Kincannon. Had Gus' ex-wife, Darden, been there, she would have understood immediately what had been said and would have known where the voices came from. You see, Darden spoke fluent Spanish, having studied the language at the University of Seville for two years. She would have been so alarmed by what she heard, she would have told her husband to call the police immediately, but that didn't happen. No longer married to Gus, she was a continent away, traveling in Europe with her new lover.

What came across the lake from the house on the other side, carried by a gentle zephyr, made the voices seem much closer than they actually were. It was the woman's voice that said, "*Parate Amiglio! La vas a matar!*" Within a second, the man responded, "*Cayate mujer si intiendes lo que es bueno para ti.*"

None of the words made sense to Sean but, had Darden heard them, she would have understood exactly what they meant. Terrified, she would have turned to her husband and said, "Someone is being murdered."

If asked what made her think this was true, Darden would have answered, "The woman said, 'Stop it, Amiglio. You'll kill her.'" Continuing, Darden would have added, "The man replied, 'Shut the f--k up, woman, if you know what's good for you.'"

But Darden didn't hear what was said; Sean did. Having no idea what the words meant, he simply went back to bed—troubled but clueless.

CHAPTER SIX
This Was Her Chance to Escape

Earlier that day in Nashville, Dwayne Gordon went to the Alabama vs. Vanderbilt football game, accompanied by his son, Joseph, and his son's girlfriend, Molly. The Crimson Tide was expected to win handily. Whether in Nashville or in Tuscaloosa, the Tide routinely throttled the Commodores. If Vandy remained competitive for a half, it was considered to be a moral victory. Because this year's game was expected to be a blowout, there were more Alabama fans attending than Vanderbilt's, the latter choosing to stay at home rather than witness a slaughter.

As the game progressed, however, Vandy hung in much tougher than anyone had predicted and actually led at halftime 15 to 14, thanks to five field goals. Surprised to be attending such a competitive contest, Dwayne and his guests were witnessing a far more competitive game than they anticipated.

At halftime, when Molly excused herself to go to the ladies' room and to buy each of them a Coke, Dwayne and Joseph had a few minutes to themselves, which the father used as an opportunity to speak candidly. Somewhat reluctant to initiate a serious conversation, Dwayne finally began by saying, "Son, I really appreciate the time and effort you have put into your sister, Jo Ellen, I really do. You can't imagine how much this pleases me."

As he said this, his eyes misted. Blinking back a tear, he added, "The Lord has given me a second chance, providing me with a beautiful wife and a lovely daughter, restoring my relationship with you too. I am a blessed man, and I know it."

Joseph just looked at his dad but said nothing. In spite of becoming a regular part of his father's life, his dad had never been this transparent with him before. Such candor surprised Joseph. Like all young men, Joseph desired validation from his father but, now that it was actually happening, it made him feel uncomfortable, especially since their entire relationship was based on a lie. By being affirmed like this, Joseph actually felt a deep sense of shame for participating in Landria's duplicity. He nearly confessed the entire thing, right then and there, but for some reason, he held off.

Unaware of what his son had been thinking and feeling, Dwayne continued with his affirmation. "I love the time we spend together, especially time at the house, seeing the way you and your sister react to each other." Smiling, he nudged his son playfully, adding, "Sometimes, I think she loves you more than me—her own father."

In response, Joseph smiled and blushed, as a tear welled up in his eye. Changing the subject, Dwayne became more serious. His smile faded, being replaced by a furrowed brow. Joseph knew this was his dad's way of showing concern. Finally speaking, Dwayne said, "I'm okay. You don't have to worry about me." Taking a deep breath, he added, "but something isn't quite right between Landria and me. I can't put my finger on what it is, but something is wrong. I can just feel it."

Discarding his reticence and feelings of ambivalence, Joseph focused intently on what his dad had to say, keenly aware of the problem's origin. Again, Joseph was on the verge of confessing everything, but he decided to hold his tongue until his dad finished. As he was listening, Joseph was working up the courage to be scrupulously honest.

Unaware of what his son was thinking, Dwayne came right to the point, knowing their time of privacy might be short. Molly was certain to return any minute. Proceeding straight to the bottom line, he announced; "A while ago, I took out a $1 million life insurance policy, setting up a trust, primarily for your sister but some of it is for you. I allocated more for her because she's so much younger. You understand that, right?"

"Of course, Dad. I don't want anything. I just want to be with you guys."

Choking up when he heard this, which he realized was one of the proudest moments of his life; Dwayne was forced to pause for a moment before continuing. Taking a deep breath to regain his composure, finally exhaling, he replied, "Thank you, son. You have no idea how much that means to me. But let me tell you why I'm bringing this up. I'm not sure what's going to happen between Landria and me. Until I do, I've changed my will to make you the Executor of my estate. Landria doesn't know what I've done, and I don't intend to tell her. It would just make matters worse, but I would feel more comfortable with you being in charge of things."

Just then, they looked up and saw Molly making her way across the aisle to their seats, taking one cautious step at a time while holding three Cokes. Knowing he only had a second, Dwayne clasped his son's forearm. Looking straight into his son's eyes, Dwayne asked, "If something happens to me, can I count on you to make sure that all of your sister's needs are met?"

Nodding his head affirmatively as he answered, Joseph replied, "Yes Dad, absolutely."

This was precisely what his dad needed to hear. Satisfied, Dwayne refocused on the football game, as Molly arrived with their drinks and halftime ended. Handing each of them a large Coke, Molly sat down and the three watched the Commodores outplay the Tide in the second half, finally winning 29 to 21. It was a great day for Vanderbilt and for the Gordon family.

Realizing he had missed his opportunity, Joseph became ambivalent once again, not knowing whether he should tell his dad about Landria or not. It was a real dilemma.

Later that evening, long after Dwayne Gordon had said goodbye to Joseph and Molly, he continued to fret about what was happening in his marriage. He and Landria never fought; neither did they bicker. There just wasn't any depth to their relationship. It was devoid of passion, and he couldn't understand why. With the exception of co-parenting Jo Ellen, their marriage seemed lifeless, especially their sexual life, which was crushing.

Since he was so much older than Landria, her lack of enthusiasm, which had nothing to do with her willingness to participate, made him feel inadequate. This is the downside, when there is a significant age differential between the man and the woman. Guys are just like this. When they think their virility has been judged and found wanting, it adversely affects their self-esteem—not just occasionally, but constantly. Women don't get this about men, but guys don't understand women either. For a woman, sex is far more emotional than physical, while it's the exact opposite for a man.

It's only physical for women in the movies, probably because directors are men who want women to behave in the wanton ways they depict on film. This creates unrealistic and unfulfilled expectations for everybody, but it's the American way.

Encouraged by the "carpe diem" attitude of the Commodores, who refused to quit or accept defeat against the Crimson Tide, Dwayne Gordon decided to put some life back in his marriage by seizing the moment. To help, he popped three 100mg. Viagra tablets, which would certainly bolster his performance, but it was six times what was recommended, a dangerously high dosage.

By 10 p.m., Jo Ellen was already settled for the evening. Landria was ready for bed as well, dreading her nightly ritual. As she slid between the sheets, she was surprised to discover her husband was already hard as a rock, but it pleased her. It meant he would be brief, and she would be able to get to sleep sooner, rather than later.

Intent on being as pleasing as possible, Dwayne did everything he had done in the past to arouse her, but none of it was successful. Finally mounting her, he felt particularly virile but also a little lightheaded. In fact, as he moved rhythmically, the colors of objects began to change. This concerned him a little but certainly not enough to stop what he was doing.

As his passion intensified and he neared ejaculation, Dwayne felt a sharp, piercing pain in his chest that arrested his movement. Stiffening, he rolled off of his wife, crashed to the floor, and began thrashing about, writhing in pain. Gasping, unable to take a deep breath, he knocked over the bedside table, which made a terrible noise.

Shocked by everything that had happened in just a few seconds, Landria jumped out of bed and reached for her cell phone to call an ambulance. She was certain her husband was having a heart attack. As she was about to dial 911, Jo Ellen, hearing the commotion coming from her parent's bedroom, became frightened and began to cry for her mother.

Panicked, Dwayne fought the piercing pain as well as his inability to breathe. With his eyes beseeching his wife for help, she just stood above him frozen, either unable or unwilling to assist him.

Although Landria intended to dial 911, she hesitated—just for a moment. While frightened by what was happening, she suddenly had a moment of clarity. She realized this was her chance to escape. In His mercy, God was answering her prayers, and she knew better than to intervene. Fighting the urge to vomit, she said to her husband, "I need to go check on Jo Ellen. Once I get her calmed down, I'll call an ambulance for you."

With that, she walked out, shutting the door behind her. Putting on her bathrobe as she headed down the hall to her daughter's room, she was shaking like a leaf. Entering Jo Ellen's room, she picked up her daughter. The child was nearly frantic. Soothing her, as only a mother can, Landria held her tightly, grateful for the noise of her toddler's crying. It was loud enough to drown out much of the noise coming from her husband, who was fighting for his life.

Several times, Landria started to put Jo Ellen down and run to her husband's aid, but she checked each of her impulses, refusing to act the part of a Good Samaritan. To allow Dwayne to die alone—just because it would free her—was cold, even for Landria. She didn't love him, never had, but to permit him to die like this, without raising a finger to help, was difficult for her to do.

Nevertheless, it was necessary. She had made her decision and acted accordingly. She did exactly what she needed to do—nothing. The thought of the extra $1 million from the life insurance policy entered her mind, but she refused to allow herself to be driven by monetary gain. The sliver of conscience she still possessed wouldn't allow her to be this cynical and mercenary.

As she thought about her situation, she was also afraid that Dwayne wouldn't die. Maybe it wasn't a heart attack after all, and he might live. What would she do then? How could she explain herself? She didn't know, but she would think of something. She always did. At bare minimum, she could pretend to enjoy making love again. That would fool Dwayne—buffoon that he was.

Sitting on the chair beside Jo Ellen's bed, she rocked and sang to her daughter, calming the child as she did. In the other room, Dwayne's thrashing finally stopped, just as suddenly as it started. When Jo Ellen went back to sleep five minutes later, Landria put her down and tiptoed back to the master bedroom, terrified he was still alive.

Still shaking, she opened the door just a crack and saw Dwayne's lifeless body on the floor, exactly where she had left him. Opening the door further, she looked at his face, which was reddish blue, looking waxy. His eyes were open and bulging. His pupils were fixed and dilated—without even a spark of life remaining.

Sighing with relief, she was certain he was dead, but she waited another five minutes just to be sure. Then, she opened her cell phone and dialed emergency services.

Answering, the dispatcher said, "Nine-one-one; is this an emergency?"

"Yes," Landria answered, still shaking and on the verge of becoming hysterical.

"What's the nature of your emergency?"

"My husband is having a heart attack in our bedroom. I just stepped out to call you. He is in terrible pain, and I don't know how to help." She added, "Can you send paramedics and an ambulance right away?"

"Yes ma'am. What is your address?"

After providing the information to the dispatcher between sobs, Landria implored the dispatcher to hurry.

Assuring the distressed woman that help was already on the way, the operator asked, "Is your husband's airway clear? Is he able to breathe?"

"No, he has been choking badly. Please hurry!"

After being assured the ambulance had already been dispatched; Landria disconnected. Sitting on the bed where she had been making love to her husband thirty minutes earlier, she cried. She was free, but she had paid a terrible price to achieve it. Dwayne probably would have died anyway, but she would never know that—not for sure. What she did know was he didn't deserve to die the way he did, without hope, without help, or without the comfort of his wife.

By choosing a path of depraved indifference, she had ripped a gaping hole in her soul, and she knew it. But with him out of the way, she had also attained her freedom, which she deserved to have. With him dead, she was also much richer. She would have Dwayne's million dollars, plus access to her own funds. Joseph could no longer threaten her with exposure. His power over her had ceased the moment

Dwayne took his last breath.

She was free, which was exactly what she wanted. At the same time, she wondered if she would be able to live with herself, knowing what she had done. She thought she could; what other choice did she have?

With sirens blazing, the ambulance raced up the street, arriving at the Gordon residence soon after being summoned. Meeting the paramedics at the door, Landria cried and beseeched them to hurry, while there was still a chance her husband might be saved.

Bounding up the stairs, the two men entered the room. Just as soon as they saw Dwayne, however, they stopped their hurrying. There was no reason to rush. Having been in similar situations many times before, they knew a dead body when they saw one. Going through the motions, they lifted Dwayne Gordon's corpse from the floor, strapped him to a gurney, and wheeled him out of his home, trying to console his grieving young wife as they did.

The ruckus awakened Jo Ellen again, as well as numerous neighbors, forcing Landria to give an encore performance to her role as a grief stricken widow. It was another half hour before she was able to close her front door and be alone with her daughter.

Once by herself, she had to perform her most difficult part, playing the same convincing role for Joseph. Putting Jo Ellen down for the third time of the night, she picked up her cell phone, took a deep breath, and called him.

Joseph's phone rang several times, finally going to voicemail. Knowing she couldn't leave such an important message on his voicemail, she hung up. Waiting a couple of minutes, she called again with the same result.

With no alternative, shaking from head to toe and fearful of Joseph's reaction, Landria called Molly's cell. Answering immediately, with a sleepy voice, Molly said, "Hello."

"Molly, This is Landria. I need to speak with Joseph right away. This is an emergency."

Now completely awake, Molly replied, "Just a minute, Landria. He's right here. I'll put him on."

Realizing Molly was covering the phone, Landria heard muffled voices speaking briefly before Joseph picked up the phone a few seconds later. He said, "Landria?"

"Joseph. I'm sorry I have to disturb you like this. I tried your cell, but you didn't answer," she said, beginning to cry.

"What's wrong?" Joseph asked, jumping out of bed, anxious to hear what was so urgent that Landria needed to call him in the middle of the night.

Taking another deep breath, she said, "It's your father. He's had a heart attack."

"What? Is he all right? Where is he?"

"No, he's not alright," Landria lamented. "He's dead, Joseph. Your father is dead," she repeated, bursting into tears again. These tears were real, partly from sorrow but mostly from being is such a stressful situation.

When he heard the news, a myriad of emotions flooded Joseph's mind, along with many questions, but they would have to be answered later—not now. Although he had substantial responsibilities in life, in many ways, he was still a little boy whose dad had just died. Without saying another word, he simply disconnected. Looking at Molly, he told her what had happened.

Then, he began to cry. Loving him more than ever, Molly put her arms around and let him sob for a very long time.

CHAPTER SEVEN
"The Woman Is Dead"

Early the following morning, at 6:15 a.m., Pencil was startled awake by two Atlanta policemen who had just thrown him roughly from his chair to the floor. One put his knee into Pencil's back, forcing all the air from the diminutive man's lungs. The huge cop twisted Pencil's hands behind his back, handcuffing him immediately. Chambering a round, which was an unmistakable sound, the second officer held a gun to Pencil's head, pressing the muzzle roughly into the temple of America's Hero. This ensured Pencil's total compliance.

Apparently blindfolded, Pencil had no idea what was happening. Nevertheless, he offered no resistance, which he knew would be futile. He was as frightened as he had ever been. Having been sound asleep just a few seconds earlier, he was clueless about what was happening and powerless to prevent it.

Shaking from head to toe, Pencil's fear got the best of him. He wet his pants, which he had not done in a long time. As this was happening, he didn't even know he was doing it. That's how frightened he was.

Witnessing Pencil's incontinence, the horrified cop hopped off of the suspect's back immediately. Not wanting to have the man's urine all over him, the officer was determined to stay out of the line of fire. Furious at this turn of events, the cop hissed, "You idiot. I can't believe you pissed all over yourself. What kind of man are you?"

To show his displeasure, the infuriated cop pressed his baton down hard on Pencil's back, while simultaneously raising Pencil's manacled hands, wrenching the suspect's shoulders in the process. The pressure produced excruciating pain, and Pencil howled in agony. Next, the officer placed his knee on Pencil's back a second time, forcing the air out of his lungs again, twisting Pencil's neck as he did until the helpless man feared it would snap. Finally relenting, the officer tightened the handcuffs on Pencil's hands until they hurt. It was difficult for the shackled suspect to maintain circulation in his hands.

All of this was done to punish the hapless arrestee for urinating all over himself, making a foul-smelling mess in the process. The officer's behavior was definitely punitive, but none of it would leave a mark, nor would it cause bruising. This would render any protestation made by Pencil as nothing more than an unsubstantiated allegation.

Still blindfolded, Pencil continued to cry in agony, sobbing like a rebuffed teenage girl, wetting himself further in the process.

After what seemed like an eternity, the cop relented, easing up on the pressure, allowing Pencil to breathe normally. Although such treatment might seem excessive and unusual, it isn't. It's how law enforcement has come to operate throughout America, especially since the 9/11 terrorist attack on the Twin Towers.

Informed by the other cop—in no uncertain terms—not to move, Pencil did precisely as he had been instructed, being as still as he knew how to be. With his eyes covered, he had no idea what was happening, other than his pants were wet and uncomfortable. Not being able to see definitely added to his confusion.

As he lay there, however, his mind raced, trying to figure out why the cops had come. His assumption was they had somehow discovered he was the person who had shot the sniper nearly two years earlier, but that didn't make sense. If this was the reason, why were they being so rough? He had actually done them a service by shooting Pretty Boy Sabarisi, which they must have realized. After all, it wasn't like Pencil had shot Mother Teresa.

Nevertheless, he was nervous they might find his gun, but he doubted they would. He had hidden it masterfully. Thinking about how clever he had been, he smiled—just a little. He might be in handcuffs, but he was definitely smarter than the two dragoons who had just arrested him.

Most of all, he wondered why he had been blindfolded? He had never seen this occur on TV or in any of the movies—not even in the Jason Bourne flicks. He considered asking about what was going on, but he thought better of it, remaining still instead. He definitely didn't want his shoulders wrenched or his neck twisted another time.

For whatever reason, there seemed to be a scurry of activity in the room, but he couldn't figure out what it was. A minute later, the cop who pointed the gun at him made a call, which was answered immediately.

The arresting officer said, "The anonymous tip was legit, sir. We have the perp in custody. We need the CSI unit dispatched right away. The woman is dead, and it appears she has been here for a while. He strangled her."

After listening for a long moment, the cop added, "We're going to take a picture of him. When we apprehended him, he was wearing her panties over his face, covering his eyes and nose." As the cop waited for his superior to stop laughing, which Pencil distinctly heard in the background, the cop added, "I shit you not, sir. He's still wearing them. I'll text you a photo," which the cop did, laughing derisively as he did.

Now completely bewildered, Pencil couldn't imagine what was happening, but he didn't like the sound of it one bit. *A dead woman,* he thought? *What dead woman? There was no woman in his apartment? What were the cops talking about?*

For the first time, he wondered if he was being set up—just like

Terrance Bruce had been a couple of years earlier. Most of all, Pencil wondered what the cop meant by, "The woman is dead." Mystified, Pencil had no clue, but he listened intently, trying to figure it out. More than anything, he wished he wasn't blindfolded.

Pencil's thoughts were interrupted, when the officers grabbed his arms and hoisted him to his feet. As they did, his soggy jeans slid to the floor, infuriating both of the cops. One asked where he kept his pants? Pencil responded by saying he had another pair of jeans hanging on his closet door.

Returning a few seconds later, one of the cops helped him out of his wet jeans into the dry ones, cursing under his breath that he had to do so.

Pushing Pencil down on the sofa, one of the cops commanded, "Don't move while I take these panties off of your face. Do you understand me, you little pervert?"

"Panties, what are you talking about?" Pencil asked. "I don't have any panties on my face. You've blindfolded me." By saying this, Pencil was standing up for himself for the first time, although he remained seated compliantly, as instructed.

Laughing contemptuously, the cop bent down one inch from Pencil's ear and said, "Listen to me, you little shit. If you move even one inch, you'll regret it. Do you understand me, you little prick?"

Smelling Skoal on the cop's foul breath, which made Pencil's empty stomach lurch, he replied, "Yes sir." He knew he was close to being roughed up again.

Unable to see, Pencil, master sleuth that he was, focused keenly on each sound, trying to figure things out. He heard one of the cops put on surgical gloves. He was sure because there was a snapping sound that accompanied its completion. To make sure he was right, Pencil tried to smell the unmistakable odor of latex, but he couldn't. For some reason, the only thing he could smell reminded him of The Whore, his ex-wife, Anne, which further perplexed him.

Then, the officer opened something that might have been a Ziploc bag, which Pencil suspected would be used for gathering evidence. This frightened him even more, and he nearly wet his dry jeans. Gathering all the willpower he possessed, however, he controlled himself. It was a small victory for America's hero, but it was something.

Walking quickly to the suspect, the gloved officer carefully removed something that was draped over Pencil's eyes and nose—but not his mouth. Pencil assumed he had been blindfold, but this wasn't the case. It wasn't a blindfold at all; it was a pair of women's black panties, which the cop put into the marked evidence bag. Then, he zipped it shut and placed it into a larger bag.

Pencil had never seen the panties before. As he squinted his eyes, trying to focus, while adjusting to the light, he scrutinized the two policemen. By the look on Pencil's face, he was clearly perplexed, which surprised both of them. He had never seen either cop in his life, but they were standing in his living room, dwarfing him by their size. This was no delusional nightmare.

Pencil had been certain there were just two cops, and he was right—one was white and the other black. Looking at the white cop quizzically, Pencil asked, "What's this all about?"

Telling Pencil to shut up, the cop wouldn't allow Pencil to talk, commanding him to keep his mouth shut until they had read him his rights. When Pencil heard this, he knew he was in big trouble. The President and the Illuminati had finally gotten to him—just like they had Terrance two years earlier. Worst of all, Pencil had passed out and hadn't seen *The Kelly File* on Friday night. Since the program wasn't aired on Saturday nights, Megyn had no way of warning him about what was going to happen. He cursed himself for having been so lackadaisical; knowing the consequences of taking his eye off the ball might prove to be a fatal mistake.

Just then, the black cop took a small step sideways. Having had his view blocked, Pencil noticed a woman's bare leg protruding from behind the cop, which had been hidden from his sight at the other end of the living room. Shocked but curious, Pencil moved his head forward slightly, without taking a step, which he had been commanded not to do. When he did, he saw the lower half of the woman's body. Nearly naked, with her skirt raised above her waist, she wasn't moving. Alarmed, Pencil took a step forward to see who the woman was. When he did, he was thunderstruck, as a searing pain pierced his heart. It was Anne—his ex-wife.

Disheveled, with her mouth open and her eyes bulging, she was disfigured, having obviously been brutally attacked. She had bruises on her neck, arms, and vaginal area. Clearly dead, she was gray and looked more like a waxed mannequin than a human being.

Instantly horrified, Pencil yelled, "Anne!" Then, he ran to her— just like any loving husband would run to his wife—oblivious to the commands of the policemen who screamed for him to stop.

Suddenly, he didn't care what they said or what they did to him. He was no longer afraid. His wife needed him. To Pencil, she was no longer The Whore. She was his wife, and she needed her husband's help. As he got closer, a hand grabbed his handcuffs from behind, impeding his progress. As he pulled, in his single-minded effort to reach her, the much larger cop was unable to halt Pencil's advance. With superhuman effort, America's hero—filled with resolve—pushed forward, despite the cop's determined efforts to thwart his progress.

Knowing he had to get to her was the last thought that went through Pencil's mind, as the nightstick came crashing down on his head, stopping him dead in his tracks. When the blow struck him, he collapsed to the carpet, not quite able to reach her, which seemed like a perfect metaphor for their failed relationship.

CHAPTER EIGHT

He Felt It in His Bones

For a full moon Saturday night, the ER had been relatively uneventful. Tanisha kept things moving at a good clip and, best of all, so far nobody had died. That evening, Dr. Luke Easton was the senior attending physician. Without either Melissa or Marla-Dean to keep him company, he put his nose to the grindstone and worked with one patient after the other, moving them through the process at a brisk clip, tending to all expeditiously. He was always methodical, but he was also being very efficient, which was unusual, especially for him.

Most of the cases had been routine, requiring little thought or effort. There had only been one notable exception. A man in his late twenties or early thirties had been brought in after being involved in a serious, high-speed accident on I-285, near Spaghetti Junction in Atlanta.

Unconscious, the injured man had been strapped on the gurney by the paramedics who moved him very carefully; fearful he might have sustained a spinal injury. Just as soon as Dr. Big Shot saw him, he ordered an immediate X-ray. The unconscious man remained immobilized, strapped to the gurney.

Rushed to radiology, where an X-ray was taken, Luke accompanied the unconscious patient; concerned something more serious might be discovered. When Dr. Easton looked at the X-ray, however, he noticed something unusual—a .38 caliber pistol. Reading the X-ray, it looked like the weapon had been surgically implanted in the unconscious man's lower back, which would have been impossible.

Relieved there was no trauma to the spinal cord, Dr. Easton called the paramedics into the room, while the man was still unconscious. Then, Luke carefully reached beneath the man, while the paramedics watched inquisitively. Being as dramatic as a magician with a mesmerized audience, Dr. Big Shot removed the weapon the man had hidden beneath his belt.

When the paramedics saw what the doctor had in his hand, they looked at each other and then back at Dr. Easton. In stunned horror, they realized the seriousness of their mistake. Their surprise quickly turned to concern, knowing their procedural error could have lead to serious negative consequences. When Luke saw their troubled looks, he couldn't help himself; he started to laugh. This broke the tension, and the paramedics followed suit.

As it turned out, there was nothing seriously wrong with the man who awakened shortly thereafter. Because he had been carrying a concealed weapon, however, the paramedics informed the police who placed the man in custody. They kept him handcuffed to the gurney until Dr. Easton released him. At that point, they intended to transport him to the hospital wing of the Garnett Street Pre-Trial Detention Center in downtown Atlanta.

Carrying sketchy ID, the man, whose name was Ernesto Rodriquez, appeared to be an illegal alien residing in New Orleans. The other passenger, who had been in the car with Rodriquez, left when his friend was placed in the ambulance, probably because he was also an illegal alien.

Rodriquez, who had been brought in a little before 6 a.m., had been

Big Shot's last patient of his shift. Because of the potential seriousness of Rodriquez's injuries, Luke had spent considerable time with him, as a precautionary measure.

Dr. Luke Easton was notorious for spending too much time with patients, which slowed down everything in the ER, at least according to Melissa Gordon—the charge nurse. She could be hell on wheels when she needed to be, and it was rare for Luke to cross her.

Melissa was also Dr. Easton's girlfriend and had been for quite some time. In this role, she had steadfastly supported him through the process of his bitter and acrimonious divorce from his socialite wife, Patricia.

Although Patricia had initiated the split, she wasn't at all pleased to see the last of her husband—not out of her love for him—but with him gone, her affluent way of life came crashing to the ground. She may not have missed his insatiable sexual demands, but she definitely missed the pampered, luxurious lifestyle he provided her.

Sultry and beautiful, coupled with a figure to die for, men had always found Patricia desirable. Since being sensuous was available to her whenever it had been required in the past, she thought it would still be there. She assumed that losing Luke would be nothing more than a minor bump in the road, and she would return to her life of affluence on the arm of a different man in record time. That, however, had not proven to be the case. In fact, her experience was the exact opposite.

As gorgeous as she was, she was also in her mid-forties. Most of the men she would consider acceptable—meaning filthy rich— didn't give her a second look. They chose women ten-to-fifteen years her junior, which she had not foreseen when she divorced her husband. Ironically, numerous guys in their mid-twenties did pay attention to her, but all they were interested in was having sex with a MILF—a distasteful acronym Patricia had been unfamiliar with while married. Now, being an attractive single mom, she had come to loathe it.

Still a barista at Starbucks, Patricia's fortunes remained stagnant, while the clock ticked, diminishing her marital potential as each day passed. Nevertheless, she was determined to be optimistic. After two years of making cappuccino for her former tennis girlfriends, as well as for her enemies—people like that loathsome Sean Kincannon— she feared her best years had passed. Forced to consider this painful possibility, she wondered if she was destined to live the rest of her life in drudgery, envious of others, and never regaining the opulence she missed so badly.

Melissa Gordon's fortunes, on the other hand, had also changed, but she was more optimistic about her future. Now that Luke was around and they had become a solid couple, she had most of what she wanted in life, but she still wasn't happy—not really.

Having been emotionally estranged from her son for nearly two years, there was a void in her life she was certain would never be filled—not as long as the chasm between them existed. Her heart was broken, and she feared it would never mend.

Now away at college in Nashville, she disapproved of Joseph living with his girlfriend, Molly. But what could she say about it? Not a damn thing! Not since Luke Easton practically lived with her. To even broach the subject with Joseph would make her look like a hypocrite, and for good reason, it would have been hypocritical.

Compounding her feelings of guilt, Luke wanted to move in, but this was something she simply could not allow. Melissa had been firm about maintaining separate residences. Although he spent the night with her more often than not, she wouldn't make their de facto living arrangement into a de jure one. Something about it just didn't feel right. Regardless of how she tried to justify the situation in her mind, she couldn't. Her deeply ingrained value system wouldn't allow it.

The two were definitely lovers, but Melissa's Christian convictions always gnawed at her about their living arrangement, which a hedonist like Luke couldn't even conceptualize. He seemed peaceful and settled with their situation, but she wouldn't allow herself to become complacent. She just couldn't, so she continued to live a conflicted life, with equal parts of joy and misery, hope and despair, sexual ecstasy followed by nearly debilitating guilt and remorse.

Having been celibate for a decade after her divorce, Melissa had focused her attention exclusively on raising her son, making a determined effort to provide him with a Christian home, despite being a single parent. After Joseph's disastrous dalliance with "that tramp"—the one flaunting a snake tattoo coming out of her vagina—the subsequent confrontation, initiated by Melissa, produced a permanent breach in her relationship with her son. She desperately wanted to bridge the growing chasm between them, but she feared it might never happen.

By becoming intimate with Luke, she had acquiesced to her carnal needs. In her mind, this made her behavior no better than what she had condemned in her son. Obviously, her lover was a more suitable paramour than Joy, but that didn't excuse Melissa's behavior. In her mind, she just couldn't make it right. By living a lie, she knew she was being a religious charlatan. Although deeply enmeshed with Luke and happy much of the time, she knew she could never embrace her new lifestyle—not and be okay with herself. Although her soul was tormented, at least she was no longer lonely.

When Joseph came home for a weekend, Melissa felt particularly fraudulent about her relationship with Luke. Although her son's trips to Atlanta were rare, whenever he came, she insisted Luke pack up everything and put it in his trunk until Joseph returned to college.

Luke obediently complied with her demands, but he didn't like it. Each time, it put a strain on their relationship, making their future together seem somewhat tenuous. Once the crisis abated though, things eventually normalized between Luke and Melissa. This had been their pattern since Joseph left for Belmont University two years earlier.

⟡

As his Saturday evening shift was ending at Peachtree Medical and the full moon was giving way to early morning sunlight, Luke pondered about how dramatically his life had changed in the past two years. Melissa loved him; Patricia never did. Thinking about this, he began to gather his things and head for his locker. He was certain he had seen his last patient, but he was mistaken.

At 6:52 a.m., an ambulance rushed a man into the ER. The man's head was bleeding profusely from being struck by a nightstick. Luke immediately noticed the man was handcuffed to his gurney. Normally, an arrestee would be taken directly to Grady—the city hospital—but this prisoner had been brought to Peachtree Medical. The man had already lost quite a bit of blood, and Peachtree Medical was much closer. Although Dr. Big Shot had never seen him before, the man on the gurney was America's Hero, Bill Steiger—a.k.a., Pencil.

While trying to stop Pencil from reaching Anne and compromising the crime scene, the white officer had been forced to use his nightstick to subdue the suspect. Not being able to aim well, the blow struck Pencil firmly, but it was also somewhat glancing, ripping a large piece of Pencil's skin off in the process, similar to being scalped. Falling to the floor instantly, Pencil was out cold. Being a very vascular area, the blow to Pencil's head bled profusely.

Calling for an ambulance, while trying to keep pressure on the wound, Pencil was rushed to Peachtree Medical, where Dr. Easton had been winding up his evening shift. Due to resurfacing on I-75, Luke's replacement was stuck in a Sunday morning traffic jam—the one day of the week when traffic was normally light. With no alternative, Luke tended to Pencil.

After being X-rayed, where no fractures were discovered, all that was required was for Dr. Easton to sew the arrestee's scalp back together, which he did. Although not a difficult procedure, it required nearly an hour to complete. Fortunately for Pencil, only one transfusion was required.

By the time Dr. Easton finished, Pencil, whose scalp had been numbed, was awake, and he had been read his rights. Incoherent—with a splitting headache from the blow—as well as from a hangover, Pencil was deeply disturbed. His ramblings, which were disjointed, focused on the President and the Illuminati. Somehow, the enemies of America had finally won by killing his ex-wife.

To Dr. Easton, who smelled the alcohol on his patient's breath, the man appeared to be quite delusional, so he paid little attention to what Pencil was saying, concentrating on being a good seamstress instead.

Handcuffed to his gurney the entire time, Pencil may have seemed crazy to others, but not to himself. Unable to move and deeply sorrowful, Pencil couldn't get the image of Anne's gruesome face out of his mind. It was not only the look of death but also of terror. As he was lying there, his senses returned, which meant he was beginning to sober up—a little anyway.

Pencil's mind began to wonder what had happened and how Anne had come to be in his living room? Being completely inebriated, he had no idea what had occurred, other than he had not killed her. Drunk or sober, he was certain he would never do anything like that.

Strapped down, he was completely helpless, as a nurse scraped his fingernails and swabbed his penis for evidence of rape. Stripped, he was photographed, and the nurse searched his entire body for scratches, which his victim might have inflicted defensively. This was standard procedure for a man suspected of raping and murdering a woman.

Knowing that protestations of his innocence would be futile, Pencil's demeanor was passive and compliant. America's Hero had finally succumbed to his adversaries, acknowledging he had been defeated.

Pencil wasn't the only one who wondered what had happened in that apartment. The Atlanta Police Department wondered as well. They sent a Crime Scene Investigation unit to William Steiger's residence to gather evidence, which was necessary to develop a theory about how Anne Morrow-Steiger was murdered. The case seemed pretty straightforward but, with so many guilty suspects being acquitted in recent years, police departments nationwide were required to redouble their efforts to gather every scrap of evidence available, knowing there could never be too much.

As the detectives knocked on the doors of Pencil's neighbors to discover if anybody had heard or seen anything else out of the ordinary, the crime scene techs were busy putting things together in the suspect's apartment.

The anonymous tip had been received at 5:32 a.m., saying that a woman had been screaming for her life at a nearby apartment, which was rented by Bill Steiger. The cell phone used to make the call was a throwaway, which was the first odd thing about the case. The second oddity was none of the suspect's neighbors had either seen or heard a thing. If a woman had been screaming, surely it would have awakened someone, the lead Crime Scene Tech, who was also an excellent investigation, speculated.

This wasn't the only thing that bothered the CSI team leader, Lance Rector—Ring Man. The victim hadn't put up a struggle, which was puzzling. It seemed logical the victim wouldn't allow her ex-husband to rape her willingly. Also, clearly brutalized, Lance wondered how such a small man could have caused so such trauma, without using a weapon of some sort. What bothered Lance the most, however, was the time of death. The victim seemed to have been dead several hours before the time of the call. Rector knew dead women don't scream, so who had the anonymous tipster heard, certainly not the woman in Steiger's apartment.

Knowing he would need answers to these questions and many more, Lance was interested in what the autopsy would reveal. Being curious by nature, as his previous sexual escapades would indicate, Lance decided to take a much more thorough look at the apartment than he might have under different circumstances.

Going through Pencil's drawers, he discovered several female panties that were soiled, which disgusted him. As his stomach lurched, he placed them in an evidence bag, sealing the bag quickly, while muttering that the suspect was "one sick freak."

As Lance continued his investigation, he realized Pencil's apartment contained no reading material other than a solitary copy of *Shooting Times Magazine*, which was sitting on the back of the commode, opened to a page featuring a pistol with a silencer. The magazine was well worn, but there was no gun, which made Lance wonder why the suspect had such a fascination with this type of weapon?

Something wasn't right. He felt it in his bones, which is what made Lance excellent at his job. Looking around for nearly an hour without much luck, Lance finally noticed a screw in the floor vent in Pencil's bathroom that had been painted over. The paint was chipped, which meant the vent had been opened since being painted, while others in the apartment hadn't been.

Unscrewing the bathroom vent and removing the facing, Lance carefully looked down the hole with a flashlight but saw nothing. A little over a foot down, the air vent bent at a right angle. Reaching down, hoping not to find a dead rat, Lance felt around and discovered a pistol that had been taped to the upper side of the vent just past the bend. Being cautious about how he retrieved it, Lance pulled out a loaded .22 caliber pistol.

Looking at it, Lance realized there was much more to this story than a guy raping and murdering his ex-wife. What he didn't know was his discovery would change Pencil's life forever, as well as the lives of many others.

CHAPTER NINE
"There Are Some Things You Don't Know"

By 9 a.m. on Sunday morning, Luke had returned to his condo from the ER, showered, brushed his teeth, and done everything necessary to prepare for bed. With the shades drawn tight and his cell phone on vibrate; he finally closed his eyes after spending a long night working in the ER.

Melissa didn't expect to hear from him until mid-afternoon, when they would finalize their dinner plans with another couple. After a long week for both, they were looking forward to a glass of wine and a casual dinner at Canoe, an elegant restaurant, located on the Chattahoochee River near Vinings. It was the other couple's favorite spot.

While Melissa was putting on her make-up, getting ready to meet her good friend Barbara Baird at church, the phone rang. Not expecting a call, she was startled when she heard the quavering, emotion-filled voice of her son say, "Mom."

Instantly, her senses were on high alert, "What's wrong, Joseph?" she asked as her mouth suddenly became dry and her legs weak.

"It's Dad," Joseph replied. After a long moment of tense silence, thick with anxiety, he added, "He's dead, Mom. Dad's dead."

"What?" she asked—both surprised and horrified.

"He's gone. He had a heart attack last night."

"Oh no; I can't believe it. He never had any heart problems."

"Molly and I were just with him at the football game," Joseph added. "He seemed perfectly fine, but he wasn't." Beginning to whimper, Joseph repeated, "He's dead, Mom, and I'll never see him again."

"I'm so sorry, son. I just can't believe it. I never expected anything like this to happen," Melissa replied, trying to process what she had been told. Like her son, she was in shock that her former husband had died so abruptly, without the slightest indication that anything was wrong.

"I still can't believe it, Mom."

"I know. He was in the prime of life." Shaking her head sorrowfully, she added absently, "His poor wife and daughter. My heart aches for them."

"I know, Mom. I'm so worried about Jo Ellen," Joseph added.

As Melissa was trying to assimilate the news and process how she felt about it, Joseph began to sob gently. In the background, she heard Molly comforting him, which stung Melissa. She was his mother; that was her job, not Molly's. Nevertheless, Melissa was grateful Joseph wasn't alone—not during such a difficult time—especially being so far away from home.

Rising to the occasion, which meant attempting to take control, Melissa said, "Joseph, what can I do to help?"

"Nothing Mom. I just wanted to let you know."

"But, there must be something I can do?" she pressed.

"No, Mom. Thanks, but there isn't."

Changing direction, she said, "Joseph, I'm glad you called me." Working out an alternative scenario, still intent on becoming involved, she continued, "I want to come to Nashville for the funeral. Will you let me know when and where the funeral will be?"

"No. You can't come, Mom. I'm sorry, but it just wouldn't be appropriate."

"Of course it would be appropriate, Joseph," she replied, with moderate indignation. "I was his wife. I have a right to come, and I want to be there."

"I know you do, Mom, but it wouldn't work. You can't come. It's as simple as that," he said firmly. "I mean it."

"Are you sure?" she beseeched.

"I'm sure," he replied, establishing a firm boundary, which Melissa acknowledged and grudgingly accepted.

For what seemed like a very long time, both just held the phones to their ears, without saying a thing. Melissa wanted to comfort her son, but she didn't know what to say or do. Fearful of saying the wrong thing or of sounding hypocritical, since she had divorced his father, she remained silent.

Joseph was silent for a different reason. His mind was racing, pregnant with thought. Finally making a decision, which necessitated forming a plan, he said, "The funeral will be some time in the middle of the week—probably Tuesday or Wednesday. When it's over, I'll call and let you know, okay?"

"Of course."

"Then, if it's all right with you, I'm going to come home next weekend. Can I, Mom?" he asked.

"Certainly, son. It's always all right. You know that."

"Thanks." After another long pause, Joseph added, "There are some things you don't know—things you need to know. When I get home, I'll tell you all about them," he added, taking charge.

Surprised, but pleased, she replied, "Whenever you're ready, son."

A moment later, he said goodbye, and hung up the phone. When he did, Joseph began to reflect. The day he met Landria, when she introduced herself as Joy, all he wanted to do was get laid—that's all, nothing more. His friends were doing it, but none of them created the mess he had. Just thinking about it increased his sense of guilt and remorse. And now the final blow; his father was dead because of what he had done.

He felt guiltier than Landria, although his feelings were neither rational nor accurate. He still remained a kid in many ways, being just twenty. When something tragic like this happens, kids always believe it's their fault. Feeling as low as he ever had, brokenheartedly, he began to cry. Holding him very close, Molly gently stroked his hair and rubbed his shoulders, comforting him, just like she had done the evening before, when he first heard the news.

When Melissa disconnected, she was not only surprised to hear about Dwayne's passing but also about her son's intention to have a long talk with her. Delighted, it was what she had desired and prayed for constantly. She also wondered if Dwayne's death might help facilitate healing between Joseph and her. In her heart, she was certain this would be the case, which meant Dwayne's passing, as tragic as it had been, would also have a higher purpose. Reflecting on her conversation with Joseph and all that it might entail, for the first time in years, she entertained fond memories of her ex-husband.

After settling herself, she took a deep breath and finished getting ready for church. While putting on her dress, Melissa made a commitment to pray for Dwayne's wife and child, whom she had yet to meet. Now that Dwayne had passed, she fully intended to rectify that. Being magnanimous, she even considered befriending Dwayne's young widow.

Melissa also intended to ask Barbara Baird to pray for them. *Barbara is such a godly woman*, Melissa thought. At such a time as this, she was grateful to have such a supportive friend.

That same morning at Lake Oconee the Kincannon household was in full swing. Everybody was at the kitchen table. Having already been breastfed, Connor was as happy and content as he could be, smiling and cooing for his mom, dad, and Winky. After finishing a breakfast of orange juice, scrambled eggs, English muffins, grits, and coffee, Sean told Marla-Dean and Winky about his experience shortly before midnight.

Mesmerized, each woman offered various explanations, but none seemed plausible. With no enlightenment forthcoming, the women finally changed the subject to discuss the activities they had planned for the day.

Having cooked breakfast, Sean left the clean-up duty for the ladies. Putting a leash on Asta, he went outside to scout around, hoping to discover the source of the voices. As he continued to think about what he had heard the previous evening, there was something about the tone of the ghostly voices that he found disturbing. He wasn't certain what it was, especially since their words weren't spoken in English, but he was bothered nonetheless.

Sean was hopeful Asta might smell something and earn her keep as a bloodhound, but she didn't. Still baffled but without answers, he was forced to put the matter in the back of his mind as he rejoined the women in the house.

The night before, when he had been scared about the safety of his family, he became acutely aware of exactly how remote they were—in the negative sense. Knowing how vulnerable being that isolated actually could be, he made a mental note to purchase a shotgun when he returned to Atlanta.

If Marla-Dean objected, he didn't care. Because their safety was involved, he would insist. He never wanted to be as unprotected as he felt the evening before—that's for sure.

After lunch, they repacked the car and headed home. Sean thought that, with any luck, they would make it back in time for the second half of the Falcon's game, which was being played in San Francisco. He liked pro football—not as much as he liked the Dawgs—but he did enjoy watching a good pro game.

While Joseph was informing his mom about Dwayne Gordon's sudden demise, at Peachtree Medical the ambulance used to transport injured prisoners arrived. Manacled, Ernesto Rodriquez was loaded on the truck to be transported to the hospital wing of the Garnett Street jail. While lying there, his mind was racing, wondering what was going to happen to him? Being in custody, his options were minimal. He was worried about the police, but he was far more concerned about the inevitable problems he would have with his accomplices.

While speculating about his future, the rear doors of the paddy wagon opened, and another prisoner was placed beside him, secured to the right side of the truck—parallel to him. After checking the other man's manacles to make sure they were secure, the guards stepped out of the vehicle, shutting the doors behind them. In dead silence, both men laid in the dark, nursing their injuries.

When the guard started the truck a minute later, the interior lights came on. After adjusting his eyes to the light, Ernesto turned his head to the side, meeting Pencil's stare immediately. Although heavily bandaged, Pencil's look bore a hole right through Ernesto. Unnerved, the Mexican recoiled reflexively, rattling his manacles in the process. Closing his eyes and shaking his head, he prayed, "Madre de Dia, perdoname. Jesu Christi, perdoname."

In Brentwood, after the paramedics removed Dwayne's body, Landria had difficulty sleeping. By the time she finally nodded off, Jo Ellen woke up for the day at her normal time, hungry and playful. With no choice in the matter, her mother got up as well, made a cup of coffee, and fed her daughter some cereal.

Having escaped being confined twice before in her life, leaving each of her tormentors unconscious in a puddle of blood, she was accustomed to having her circumstances change rapidly. In those situations, however, she had carefully orchestrated the change. This was different. Although welcomed, it was a shock and totally unexpected. Heart attacks always are.

Now that it was over, she needed to formulate her plans rapidly, and she couldn't make any mistakes. To get what she wanted, she needed to be at the top of her game.

The first thing she did was change the bedding, including the mattress pad. As she was thinking about everything else that was required, the front doorbell rang. Wondering who would just drop by on a Sunday morning, she was greeted by a neighbor who handed her a tray of cold cuts, sliced cheese, and crackers.

Thanking the woman, Landria talked to her for at least five minutes—five minutes she couldn't spare. When the woman left, Landria realized she would never be able to plan her escape, if she had to speak to Dwayne's friends who "just wanted to stop by" and pay their respects.

If the situation had been different, she might have welcomed their comfort, but not this time. She couldn't. By eleven, Jo Ellen was ready for her morning nap. Just as soon as Landria put her daughter to bed, she pulled down the shades, turned off all the lights, and sat down at the kitchen table to make a list. She titled it, "My Next Life."

Smiling snidely, she thought, *This time, I'll have nearly $2 million, and nobody will ever find me. Jo Ellen and I will be gone for good.*

Arriving in Atlanta from the lake house at 6 p.m., Sean turned on the TV to watch the remainder of the Falcons' game, which they lost in the final minutes—a frequent occurrence for the Falcons, who had been perennial losers for most of Sean's life.

If her husband had not turned on the game, Marla-Dean might have been able watch the local news. If she had, she would have seen a photo of Anne Morrow-Steiger, as well as Anne's ex-husband, William

Steiger, who was being held in connection with the woman's brutal murder. The story, which ran again on the evening news—long after Marla-Dean had retired for the evening—wasn't significant enough to warrant a featured story by Atlanta's best reporter, Jaye Watson or even Morse Diggs. By Monday, Anne's murder was old news, so Marla-Dean was unaware that she actually held a significant piece of the puzzle.

Having had no break over the weekend, when they arrived back home, Marla-Dean told Winky she could have Sunday evening off, which delighted the young lady. With nothing planned, Winky went to Barnes & Noble to check out the latest releases in the religious section. More than anything, she loved biblical prophecy, especially about Israel's role in the future, but her interests also included anything to do with prosperity theology. This is the false promise propagated by some TV evangelists where you give the TV personality $200, and they promise that God will give you $2,000 in return.

Marla-Dean had tried to explain to Winky the difference between this twisted perspective and what the New Testament actually taught, which was not quid pro quo materialism, but her explanations were to no avail. Winky listened, nodding her head in agreement, but being easily mesmerized by the manipulation of TV evangelists, she returned to her old pattern of sending a check—just in case Marla-Dean might be wrong.

Having heard a stirring TV message by Joyce Meyer while at Lake Oconee—about giving away possessions you cherish for the love of God—Winky was intent on being obedient to this mandate. Ordering a tall skinny latte at the Starbucks in the bookstore, Winky saw a very sad Central American woman sitting by herself, looking forlorn and downcast.

After paying for her drink, Winky removed her pearl and diamond cluster ring, which was her favorite piece of costume jewelry, took a long look at it, and made her decision. Acting upon it, Winky approached the woman and said, "Here, this is for you. The Lord told me to give it to you."

With that, and nothing more, Winky handed the ring to the woman, squeezed her hand gently, and walked off, headed for the religious section of the bookstore. In the entire exchange, the Spanish woman didn't say a word. As Winky was leaving, however, she turned her head and saw a smile on the woman's face. Feeling good about herself, Winky knew she had been obedient and done the right thing.

Purchasing two of Joel Osteen's books a few minutes later, Winky headed for her garage apartment to begin reading. As she was driving home, however, she began to think about her ring. She loved that ring. It was her favorite piece of jewelry. Although she felt guilty for having second thoughts, she wished she hadn't given it away. The woman obviously didn't speak English, so she probably didn't even understand the sacrifice Winky had made.

By the time Winky reached Peachtree Battle Avenue, she regretted her decision. Turning around, she headed back to Barnes & Noble to ask the woman for her ring back. If she needed to, Winky intended to buy it from her. Realizing she had made a terrible mistake, she was intent upon rectifying her error immediately.

Parking quickly, she went straight to the table where the woman had been sitting, but she was gone. Disheartened but determined, Winky walked through Barnes & Noble several times looking for the woman, but she was no place to be found. The woman had vanished, and so had the ring.

Berating herself for being such a fool, she drove home, determined to keep her foolish adventure to herself. If she told Marla-Dean, Winky knew she would get a look that would make her feel even more ridiculous than she already did. If Sean heard about it, he might laugh. He laughed at everything, which she liked most of the time, but certainly not about something like this.

CHAPTER TEN
"That's the Wild Card, Isn't It?"

On Tuesday morning, at 9 a.m., Crime Scene Inspector Lance Rector walked into the office of Detective Michael Renfro to discuss the pending case against William Steiger. Renfro had taken the position once held by Detective Chuck Gerulitis, who had retired and moved to Palm Harbor, Florida to live out his years in ignominy.

Detective Renfro, a graduate of Georgia Southern University, was a handsome young man in his early thirties. At one time married to a woman with a borderline personality disorder, his ex-wife had made his life a living hell for three years. Having had his fill of consanguinity, Michael vowed to never marry again. Instead, he spent most of his time focused on his career, which had been developing nicely.

Having worked with Rector before, Michael knew Lance was gay, but he also knew the man was skilled, insightful, and methodical. Lance, on the other hand, liked and respected Michael. Although handsome, Lance had never considered making a pass at him—not once. Working well together, they had become friends of a sort, which pleased both. In fact, having a gay friend made Michael feel enlightened.

Entering with a pumpkin spice latte in his hand, Lance sat down in the detective's office to discuss Steiger's case. Opening the conversation by holding his drink high, with an apologetic look, Lance said, "Sorry, Michael, I should have brought you one of these. They're yummy." Getting to business, Lance added, "Have they made a decision about whether or not to charge William Steiger?"

"Almost, but not quite," Michael replied. "On the surface, it seems like a slam-dunk case, doesn't it?"

Having no idea what "slam-dunk" referred to, Lance ignored Michael's response and pressed forward. "On the surface, I suppose it does, but I'm not sure. There are several things that just don't add up."

"I know."

"Want to review them with me?" Lance inquired.

"Sure."

"Well, there was obviously animosity between the victim and her ex-husband, which did provide him a strong motive, especially since he owed her a small fortune in past due child support. Plus, she was found dead in his apartment with him asleep, sitting right there in front of her—with her underwear over his face—the pervert. It's hard to fathom how this could have happened unless Steiger is the murderer?" Lance stated rhetorically.

"That does seem like the obvious conclusion, doesn't it, Lance?"

"Yes, it does," he replied—not showing his hand, like a good poker player. "There was also vaginal fluid located on Steiger's penis. That's pretty condemning; don't you think?"

"I do," Michael replied cautiously. "The suspect had motive, means, and opportunity."

"Correct," Lance acknowledged.

"Then, why are both of us so troubled about this, Lance?" Michael asked, candidly.

"Because of the inconsistencies, damn it," Lance asserted, laying his cards on the table. "First, the anonymous call came at 5:52 a.m., but—based on her liver temperature—we've determined the woman must have died between 11:00 p.m. and 1:00 a.m.—hours before the anonymous phone call. And the call was made from a throwaway phone, for goodness sakes. Who does that? And why would they?"

Michael just shrugged his shoulders, nonplussed.

Taking a sip of his latte, Lance added, "And the guy who tipped us off has never come forward. Putting all of this together, the whole scenario seems odd to me. How about you?"

"Definitely! We've got some problems—big ones. Now, let's hear the rest of what you've got, Lance," Michael requested.

"There's a lot more," Lance replied. "Okay, here goes." Putting down his latte, he started. "If her ex had rough sex with her, which would have been rape, why weren't any of his pubic hairs on her corpse? And why weren't any of her vaginal hairs on him? I've never seen a rape where there wasn't, have you?"

"No," Michael admitted.

Continuing, Lance said, "Worse than that, we did find pubic hair from another man—a non-Caucasian."

"That doesn't necessarily mean anything, Lance. She could have had sex with someone else earlier in the evening, right?" he asked.

"That's true, but the seminal fluid we found inside her, which somebody tried to swab away, definitely was not from her ex-husband." Pausing for a minute, he gazed at Michael with a quizzical look. "There's more. The bruising on the victim's neck, where she was strangled, came from hands that were much larger than those of her ex-husband. Have you seen how small and petite Steiger is?"

"Yes, I have," Detective Renfro admitted.

Now on a roll, Lance continued, "If her ex did this to her, I want to know why there weren't any scratches on him? By the way, her toxicology labs came back completely clean—no drugs, no alcohol, no nothing. She was conscious and alert when this happened. There is no way she would have just let him screw her and then strangle her to death—not without putting up some kind of resistance. And why didn't any of his neighbors hear a struggle? It just doesn't make sense, Michael. I don't believe all of these inconsistencies are possible—not for one minute—do you?"

"No, the whole case is troubling," Renfro admitted.

"One more thing," Lance added. "There was nothing under his fingernails or hers that would link him to her death. Without wearing gloves, which weren't discovered at the crime scene, how could this have happened?" he asked.

Detective Renfro just raised an eyebrow in response.

"All of these things bother me, but nothing bothers me as much as this," Lance remarked, looking at Renfro for dramatic effect—his specialty—taking a sip from his latte to heighten the anticipation.

"What?" Michael asked curiously, mesmerized by Lance's drama.

"The victim was sprawled on her back, but her blood lividity shows she had been on her side for hours after her death, which means the way we found her isn't the position in which she died."

"Really?" Michael replied, as he watched his "slam-dunk" case dissolve before his eyes, knowing that most defense attorneys, based on these facts, would obtain an acquittal.

Lance continued, "It looks like she was on her side for a long time and then placed on her back with her legs spread open." Looking straight into Renfro's eyes, Lance concluded, "I don't think her ex did it, Michael. I think someone else killed her and staged it to look like Steiger murdered her. That's what I think."

Mulling over what Lance had said, Renfro offered a rebuttal, "But Steiger wouldn't just sit there and let all of this happen—not without putting up a fight of his own. That doesn't make sense to me."

"It *does* makes sense, if you take into consideration his blood alcohol was 3.1% when he was taken into custody. The guy had passed out and would have slept through a tornado. Being that drunk, I don't think he could have gotten it up to screw her anyway," Lance added with a knowing smile.

As serious as the discussion was, Michael couldn't help himself;

he laughed as well. With a wry grin, he added, "Having had a little experience with this myself, I get your point—no pun intended." When he said this, both grinned at each other's humor. Michael added, "And I'm nearly twenty years Steiger's junior."

As the conversation was culminating, Lance said, "I'm curious about what ballistics will reveal about the gun I found. That's the wild card in this, isn't it?"

"It certainly is," Michael agreed, as the meeting came to an end.

While Lance was walking out, he added, "I've got to be in court in Forsyth this afternoon—wherever the hell that is. I'm having the ballistics report sent directly to you. When you get it, text me what it concludes, okay?"

Renfro nodded affirmatively that he would, as Lance shut the door behind him.

Taking a deep breath, after his conversation with the crime scene tech, Michael realized he had more questions than answers. *This case is anything but a slam-dunk,* he thought.

In Nashville, Dwayne Gordon's funeral was held at the First Baptist Church of Brentwood on Tuesday afternoon. It was a beautiful warm day, sunny and mild. The celebration of Dwayne's life was well attended. Several major artists from both the Christian and country music communities were in attendance, which pleased Landria.

Joseph, who was accompanied by Molly, sat beside Jo Ellen, next to the widow. Definitely not comprehending what was happening, Jo Ellen wanted to sit on Joseph's lap, which he welcomed. Looking up at him, she smiled, which he returned. She was so young, innocent, and vulnerable. Giving her a big hug, he remembered the promise he had made to his father—a promise he intended to honor, regardless of what it required to do so.

Even though he gave the eulogy, Joseph was numb throughout

the service, which seemed surreal. When the funeral was complete and Dwayne was interred, as the mourners were headed out of the cemetery, Landria touched Joseph's arm and asked if she could speak with him privately. Hearing this, Molly took Jo Ellen's hand and walked ahead of Joseph and Landria.

Slowing her pace to provide additional distance and increased privacy, Landria said, "Joseph, I'm so sorry about your father. I could see how close the two of you were becoming. I want you to know I fully supported that."

In response, Joseph just nodded his head.

Landria continued, "I want you to know I did everything I could to save his life, but it wasn't enough. I wish I had been trained in CPR, but I wasn't. I felt so helpless, unable to do more than I did." As a tear came to her eye, she added, "I know you might not think so, but I truly loved your father. He was so kind and gentle, and he was a wonderful father. I'm going to miss him badly. I know you will too."

She waited for a response, but Joseph just looked at her, nonplussed.

Being on a mission, the widow added, "I hope you know how difficult this is going to be for me. It will be very hard for Jo Ellen too. She's so young. She doesn't understand anything about what's happening, does she?"

"No, she doesn't," Joseph replied, finally speaking.

"She keeps asking where her daddy is," Landria added.

When he heard this, Joseph winced but didn't say a word.

Continuing, Landria began to make her point. "This is why I want to finalize all of this as quickly as possible. You understand, don't you, Joseph?"

"Of course, I do, Landria," he affirmed.

"Thank you, Joseph. I want to have Dwayne's Will read as soon as possible."

Joseph nodded that he understood, implying he thought it was a good idea as well.

Landria continued, "I've scheduled a lawyer for tomorrow afternoon at 4 p.m. I know that's sooner than you might have expected, but I do want to get things settled—for Jo Ellen's sake."

"I understand. Where do I need to be?" he asked.

Providing him with the address, he promised to attend. With this, she gave him a brief maternal hug, turned, and caught up with Molly and Jo Ellen who had already reached the funeral limousine.

At 6 p.m. that evening, as he was driving back to Atlanta from Forsyth, Georgia, Lance received a text from Detective Renfro. It said, "Meet me at Joni P's at 6:30. Urgent." Having no idea what was happening, he replied, "K" and stepped on the gas.

Arriving at a quarter to seven, Lance started to rant about the deplorable traffic situation in Atlanta, but Michael held up his hand firmly, telling him to stop, which Lance did immediately.

Simply saying, "Watch this." Michael pointed to the large television at the end of the bar. After ordering himself a piña colada, both men stood at the bar to watch. The local news resumed soon thereafter. As the lead story, the District Attorney, Wilbur Kenyatta, was holding a live press conference. With aspirations to become the first African-American governor in the Deep South since Reconstruction, he intended to show how tough on crime he intended to be.

Stepping to the podium, which had been strategically placed in front of the state capitol, he came straight to the point. With a dozen microphones in front of him, he announced, "I want to thank the press for coming here this evening on such short notice." Looking at his audience—the voters of Georgia—he asserted, "Today, I am announcing my intent to file charges against William Steiger for the murder of his ex-wife, Anne Morrow-Steiger, and also for the murder of the gangster commonly known as Pretty Boy Sabarisi. Ballistic tests have revealed the pistol found at Mr. Steiger's residence was definitely the weapon used to execute Mr. Sabarisi nearly two years ago."

Although the news conference continued for another ten minutes, this statement was all the two men at Joni P's needed to hear. Lance looked at Michael with his mouth wide open, knowing this simple case was about to become a national story. Returning his look, Michael said, "Kenyatta wants to be governor, and he thinks convicting Steiger will be his ticket to win the election."

CHAPTER ELEVEN

"A Burned-Out Alcoholic Murderer"

O n Wednesday afternoon at 4 p.m., Joseph Gordon walked into the law office of Mengele, Specht, Hassan and Bundy to partici-pate in the execution of Dwayne Edward Gordon's "Last Will and Tes-tament." Landria Gordon, wife of the deceased, was already present, seated, and waiting. When Joseph walked in, she rose and greeted him with the kind of embrace one would expect from the grieving widow of a close family member—warm but appropriate.

The lawyer, Richard Morton, having had no knowledge of the family dynamics, behaved in a charming and ingratiating manner, clearly enamored with the beautiful young widow. Going through a painful divorce himself, he thought Landria Gordon might prove to be the answer to his financial downturn, if he played his cards right. Consequently, he had been particularly warm and engaging when she arrived several minutes before the deceased man's son, which provided the lawyer and the widow with an opportunity to chat and become better acquainted.

Landria, who loved the libidinous attraction of men, recognized

Morton's yearnings instantly. Using this to her advantage—as usual—
she welcomed the man's attention, as she played the role of a helpless
woman in need of a strong, confident, and self-assured male leader.
Being her favorite role, she played it magnificently.

Believing he was in charge, Morton had actually become a willing
pawn in Landria's impending drama. The lawyer was a short, paunchy
man in his late forties. His hair was sparse, but what little he had,
was slicked back and hung over his collar. Dressed magnificently, his
sartorial splendor was a display of his affluence and success. He always
sported the right cufflinks—precisely the right ones—to augment his
monogrammed and stiffly starched shirts.

Morton thought he was God's gift to women, and Landria's
behavior was a validation of this conviction. It was to be expected.
Women always loved him.

In his duty as an officer of the court, Morton intended to use his
pettifogging skills to protect and enhance the standing of the virtuous
beauty sitting before him. He particularly liked the way she crossed
her legs in a revealing and slightly lascivious way.

When Joseph arrived, Morton was instantly distrustful of the
handsome young man, considering him to be a potential rival for
Landria's affections. Why he felt this way he didn't know, but he did.
Obviously a woman of Mrs. Gordon's sophistication would be more
interested in a man of the world like him than in a schoolboy like her
stepson. Nevertheless, the lawyer didn't like the young man. Being a
lawyer though, he camouflaged his disdain for Joseph quite well.

Having no idea what the Will contained, since another partner
had executed the document, Morton intended to be an advocate
for Landria's position, if a conflict arose. After chatting for a few
minutes, Morton opened a portfolio containing the sealed document,
which Landria had helped her late-husband create several months
earlier. Knowing what it contained, she had already made her plans
accordingly. She couldn't wait to see the look on Joseph's face when
Dwayne Gordon's "Last Will and Testament" was read, knowing she

would control everything—including the small allowance bequeathed to him. Having been under his thumb for nearly two years, she longed for the upper hand. She even considered making him beg for sex before giving him his monthly stipend. She probably wouldn't screw him, but she did like the idea of screwing with his mind.

As Morton opened the envelope, he caught a gleam in Landria's eyes for an instant and recognized the malevolence in their beautiful sparkle. Taken aback, he blinked and looked again. The second time, it was gone, which confused him, but Morton knew what he had seen. If lawyers are good at anything, it's discerning the evil intent of a client. Being more self-protective than horny, he backed away from his original inclination to support her. He did this without saying a word or revealing his change of position in any way.

Looking at the document for a long moment, while Landria and Joseph sat waiting—both confident they knew what it contained—the lawyer began to read its content.

By the time he finished, Landria sat frozen, stupefied by what she had just heard. On the outside, her look was as calm as it could be, but on the inside, she was bitterly resentful of her late husband. She had never loved Dwayne, but now she loathed him. That duplicitous prick had made Joseph the Executor of everything—the $1 million in life insurance, the company life insurance policy worth $250,000, the house, the artwork, and all of the home's furnishings. Landria—Jo Ellen's mother—would only receive a stipend of $2,500 a month, dispersed by Joseph, and she would only receive that for as long as she remained single. That was it—nothing more.

Indignant, Landria instantly regretted spreading her legs for that buffoon for as long as she had. After his betrayal, she no longer felt guilty for letting him die. He deserved to die like that for what he had done to her. She hoped he was rotting in Hell, where horny bastards like him belonged.

Although close to incensed, Landria recovered quickly. Her internal rage was unnoticeable—a trait seductive women like her learn to master. Perplexed, she informed Morton that she had helped her husband draft the Will, and it made her the Executor of the estate. She asserted, "I was here, in this very boardroom, when he signed it six months ago. I was made the Executor—not Joseph."

Looking down at the Will, Morton said, "Mrs. Gordon, the original Will was amended recently, and its terms are quite specific. Joseph Gordon is the Executor of Dwayne Edward Gordon's estate—not you."

His pronouncement, which was delivered sharply, cut her like a knife. Wounded, she lost her composure—just for an instant. Nearly hissing, she said, "But my husband never said a word to me about this—not one word." By the way she said it, it appeared as if Morton had double-crossed her as well as her husband.

No longer enamored, Morton replied, "Mrs. Gordon, the Will is crystal clear. Joseph is in charge—not you. To protect our client's interests, our firm will defend Dwayne Gordon's choice in court if need be. Now, my advice to you is to try and work with the Executor, your stepson, to provide for you and the needs of your daughter—as he sees fit."

Censured and rebuffed, Landria didn't utter another word. She simply stood, revealing more leg than necessary, sneered at the fat, pompous lawyer, letting him know he would never have another chance with her, and left. She didn't even look at Joseph when she walked out.

Once the door was shut behind her, Joseph and the lawyer exhaled audibly, grateful their ordeal with Landria Gordon was over.

When Joseph left a few minutes later, he thought he would give Landria a few days to calm down before he spoke to her about his plans for taking care of Jo Ellen. This would give his stepmom time to reflect on the situation and hopefully become more reasonable.

Because he intended to drive to Atlanta for the weekend, he thought he would call Landria when he returned to Nashville on Sunday afternoon. Although it was just Wednesday, it seemed like a month since he had last seen his father at the Alabama-Vandy football game the Saturday before, but it had just been four days. He was emotionally exhausted, but he knew that talking to his mother about everything would be equally draining. He dreaded the trip but had to go. He had no choice. It was the right thing to do.

In Atlanta, the District Attorney's news conference had generated more media hype than Kenyatta's political consultant, Arthur "Swag" Wheeler, had anticipated. Delighted Kenyatta's name recognition would increase substantially from the avalanche of free publicity certain to accompany the Steiger case; Swag anticipated no downside to what was about to transpire.

The defendant was "a nobody"—a man who had been in-and-out of rehab and mental facilities for years. Being a deadbeat dad, never supporting his two daughters, was an added bonus. By coming down on him with both feet, Kenyatta's appeal to women voters would increase dramatically.

Women were the key to Kenyatta's electability. Everybody knew this. If you intended to be the governor of Georgia, you had to win the female vote, and this would help him do so.

Additionally, because Steiger was nearly a street person, he had no funds to hire adequate counsel. He would be forced to rely on a public defender—some hapless attorney Kenyatta's chief prosecutor would decimate in court. Ecstatic at the prospects for their candidate's future, Kenyatta's gubernatorial election team encouraged the media frenzy, which didn't require much.

When the story broke, it was a major news item in Atlanta and throughout the state, but it also received national attention, especially by Nancy Grace—a native Atlantan—and by Megyn Kelly. Having covered the story in depth nearly two years earlier, it was a natural story for Megyn's show, *The Kelly File.*

When Kelly's producer saw the particulars of Steiger's arrest, her eyes lit up, knowing this was a story that had legs. It was something her program could follow, off-and-on, for the next year, maybe longer. Stories like this helped keep Kelly's ratings high. Jumping on it immediately, before Nancy Grace's producer could, Ceci Drawdy called the two guests she had used in the past—Dr. Big Shot and Captain Barbara Baird of the Etowah Police Department. Both responded favorably and agreed to be expert witnesses throughout the duration of the trial.

Next, Ceci called Sean Kincannon, but he was unavailable. He was in Valdosta Georgia, taking depositions for a murder trial. He was scheduled to remain in South Georgia for the remainder of the week, rendering him out of pocket for a TV interview. When Ceci called Joseph Gordon's home, his mother informed her that Joseph's father had just died. With this and school, he was too busy to be interviewed, making him unavailable as well.

Not easily deterred, Ceci planned to follow up with both Sean and Joseph for segments she had planned for the following week. As relentless as a credit card bill collector, Ceci was determined to interview both for *The Kelly File*.

Disturbed by the turn of events he witnessed on the TV, Lance Rector popped into Detective Michael Renfro's office early Friday morning with two pumpkin spice lattes from Starbucks, brewed by Patricia Easton. Handing one to Michael, Lance sat down quietly until the detective finished his telephone conversation. When he did, Michael said, "What a pleasant surprise." Holding up the latte, he nodded his head in appreciation, which Lance acknowledged with a grin.

Lance said, "What's going on, Michael?"

Knowing exactly what Lance was referring to, Michael announced, "We are proceeding with the case against William Steiger; that's what's going on."

Taking a sip of his latte, Lance said, "That's what I thought, but what are we going to do—you and I? Neither of us believes Steiger is guilty."

"The key word in your sentence is 'believe,' Lance. We may believe one thing, but we don't know for sure, do we?" Michael challenged.

"All right, so you're okay with letting an innocent man be railroaded for a murder he didn't commit?" Lance reasoned, non-confrontationally.

"I didn't say that, Lance," Michael replied, clearly conflicted by the direction of the conversation. "I intend to do my job—that's all; which, by the way, is to aid the district attorney in his prosecutorial efforts. That's what I am paid to do—you too!"

"Do whatever you want, Michael, but I'm not going to perjure myself—just to get Kenyatta elected governor. I'm not even going to vote for him. He's a narcissist," Lance added.

Anxious to deflect from Lance's troubling questions, Michael added playfully, "Some people might think you're a racist, Lance."

Responding in kind, Lance retorted, "Michael, everybody knows I'm a chocoholic," referring to Ring Man's current lover, an African-American.

Not wanting to pursue the subject, Michael returned to the original topic. "I'm not going to perjure myself either Lance, but at this point, I'm not willing to scuttle my career over a guy nicknamed Pencil; are you?"

Lance raised an eyebrow but didn't reply.

Continuing with his self-serving justification, Michael added, "Besides, the guy is guilty as hell of shooting Sabarisi. It was a gangland hit for God's sakes. I'm not going to lose any sleep over what happens to a burned-out alcoholic murderer." Looking at Rector coolly, as he drained his latte, Detective Renfro concluded, "I suggest you adopt a similar attitude."

CHAPTER TWELVE
"It Was a Zephyr"

On Friday morning, William Steiger was scheduled for arraignment in Superior Court, as was his fellow inmate, Ernesto Rodriquez, who had also been transported to jail from the emergency room on Sunday afternoon. Pencil's arraignment, however, was postponed due to a medical crisis. Not having alcohol while being incarcerated, which his body now required in large quantities, his system revolted to the abrupt withdrawal, and Pencil became incoherent. His behavior bordered on delirium tremens. Physically addicted to a quart of vodka per day or more, Pencil's withdrawal was severe, necessitating medication and vigilant monitoring.

People frequently die from withdrawal, which the authorities understood. Needing Pencil to serve their purposes, they wanted to be certain he wasn't one of the fatalities.

Pencil had become a celebrity at the Garnett Street Pre-Trial Detention Center. He was their most valuable prisoner. In a bizarre twist of fate, Pencil had arrived, not as America's Hero but as an American anti-Hero. In this role, which afforded him special consideration, he attained substantial notoriety. As someone never taken seriously, he desired fame, but infamy might also had a certain appeal. If his detoxification hadn't been so severe, he probably would have enjoyed the heightened attention, but he was too sick to notice.

The DA's office made certain to inform the guards they were to take special care of William Steiger—a charge they understood and accepted. He was Wilbur Kenyatta's ticket to the Governor's Mansion, and the DA wasn't about to permit any harm to befall the man who was going to put him there—not until after Pencil's conviction, anyway.

Ernesto Rodriquez's arraignment was another matter. As an illegal alien, he should have been held without bail and eventually shipped back to Mexico, but this isn't what happened. Instead, he was given a hearing—like a citizen, which he wasn't. His bail was set at $25,000, which was posted by his friends. As a result, Ernesto was released at 10:37 a.m., with his trial for carrying a concealed weapon set to begin six weeks later.

As Ernesto left the courtroom, he was nervous about what awaited him. There was a chance he might survive, but it wasn't a certainty. His friends might assume he had cut a deal, which ensured a death sentence would await him. It had happened to others.

In his line of work, this was the chance he took. Now that the die had been cast against him, however, he wanted to live. He wanted to have another chance. If there is such a thing as a jailhouse conversion, then he had had one. He wanted out of his life of crime.

Such a change of heart though, might prove fatal. This terrified him. As he walked out of the courthouse, he smelled the fresh air of freedom, and he loved it. Looking up the street, he saw a car headed toward him with three of his "bandito" brethren sitting inside. As soon as he saw them, he suspected he would not survive the day.

Slowing down, the driver motioned for Ernesto to walk over to the car, which he obediently started to do. Making a split-second decision that would inalterably seal his fate one way or the other, Ernesto stopped to talk to two policemen who were standing on the sidewalk, smoking cigarettes. Asking directions, the car that was waiting to pick up Ernesto was forced to make a right turn, when the heavy traffic behind them became impatient and started honking. Certain to be armed, the car's occupants didn't want to risk being stopped, especially in front of the jail.

The moment the car turned, Ernesto pointed to it and bolted at full speed, leaving the officers to wonder what he was doing. As they looked in the direction of the slow moving vehicle, Ernesto ran in the opposite direction, headed toward the MARTA Station, where a train had just stopped. Its destination was the heart of the city, where Ernesto thought he could get lost.

Jumping the turnstile, he raced into one of the passenger cars, just as the door closed. It was fortunate for him there were no MARTA cops watching. If there had been, he would have been arrested and gone straight back to jail. Thanking God for sparing him, he sat down, knowing he had dodged a bullet—at least for the time being.

A few seconds later, Ernesto saw the faces of two of the men who had been sent to pick him up, but they were too late. The train doors had already closed. As the train left the station, picking up speed quickly, it plunged into the subway system beneath the city. Metaphorically, this is precisely what Ernesto intended to do for the rest of his life—go underground.

When he reached Five Points, Ernesto switched trains and headed out of the city in a different direction. His goal was to disappear, knowing his life was over, if his friends ever saw him again. To be successful, he needed help, and he knew where he could get it. Making a call, he was told to be at the Starbucks at Barnes & Noble on Peachtree Street that Sunday evening at 6 p.m. With his life depending on it, Ernesto intended to keep the appointment.

On Friday afternoon, Luke Easton turned over and gave Melissa a tender kiss, as he reluctantly slipped out of bed. He needed to make a quick trip to his condo before heading to work for his evening shift. Melissa, who had been stroking his arm gently just before he kissed her, had been scheduled at the ER as well, but she used several of her vacation days to take some time off, knowing Joseph would be arriving in a few hours. Because of his father's death, she had no idea what the weekend would entail but, like a good Scout, she intended to be prepared. By not working, she had the flexibility to accommodate Joseph's needs, regardless of what they might be.

After buttoning his shirt, Luke sat back down on the bed and simply looked at Melissa. Knowing what "that look" meant, Melissa turned her head away from him.

Not content to let the matter slide, Luke spoke up. "We've discussed this repeatedly, Melissa. You know we have." Having said this, he just sat there, waiting for her to respond.

Finally turning back to him, exhaling audibly, she replied, "I know we have, Luke. It's just difficult for me. You know that."

"I do understand, but packing up my things every time Joseph comes makes me feel unimportant." Acknowledging this, his countenance assumed a sad expression.

"I don't want you to feel like that, Luke. You are important to me. You know you are."

"Then, the right thing to do is to tell Joseph we're going to be living together," he replied, matter-of-factly.

"You're right. It's not fair to keep this hidden. It makes me feel sneaky," she admitted. "When he gets here, I'll tell him you are moving in. I promise I will," she added, nervous about fulfilling her commitment.

"That's my girl," Luke replied, encouragingly. "I'm sure he already knows. He's not a fool. Even if he doesn't, it certainly shouldn't be a shock." Waiting for a long moment, he added, "Besides, he's living with Molly. What's the difference?"

"The difference is I'm his mother," she replied, with more than a hint of vexation, making Luke wish he had not asked the question.

"I'm sorry, Melissa. That was insensitive of me," he responded. After a long moment, while she looked at the ceiling with a clenched jaw, he added, "I know there's a difference. Let me take that back."

Knowing how silly that was, Melissa concluded, "I said I would tell him, and I will. That's all I have to say. Now, you had better hurry, or you'll be late for work."

"I wish you were coming with me," Luke replied, with a touch of whininess in his voice, which she couldn't stand. Her ex-husband whined constantly, and it exasperated her to the point of distraction. When Luke acted the same way, she was delighted she could send him home for a day or two, which was an option she was about to discard.

Hopping out of the bed naked, she headed for the shower, saying, "You had better get out of here before I change my mind."

Fearful she might be serious, he replied, "I'm gone. Call if you need me. If not, I'll talk to you early Sunday afternoon, just as soon as I wake up from my Saturday night shift, okay?"

Knowing verbatim what he was saying, she didn't bother listening or responding, choosing instead to turn on the shower to get the water warm.

✑

After stopping by his condo, Luke headed for Peachtree Medical. As he did, he thought about how much Melissa meant to him. She was the best part of his life, and he knew it. He understood Joseph was the most important person in hers, and he accepted this—sort of. Joseph was gone most of the time anyway. Nevertheless, Luke resented being a vagabond, forced to leave Melissa's bed every time Joseph came to town. This was not something he had ever been able to accept, nor would he.

This is the reason he pressured her to stop hiding things from her son. Joseph wasn't a kid anymore; he could handle the truth. As Luke continued to drive, he also thought about how well he had done on Megyn Kelly's show. She always called him Dr. Big Shot, which he had come to like—only because nobody knew how he acquired the name, though. Had people understood its origin, he wouldn't have liked it—not one bit. Just the thought of the incident continued to horrify him.

As he approached the hospital, his thoughts returned to Melissa—the best lover he had ever had. At first reticent, out of her ten-year deprivation and un-sated yearnings, she had abandoned her restraint, doing exactly what he liked, precisely the way he liked it. Although they had never discussed matrimony, the thought was beginning to enter his mind. He was keenly aware he would never find a better woman.

Smiling to himself, he was already thinking about their next time of intimacy, but that's all he would ever do—think about it. Little did he know, but as he entered the employee parking lot at Peachtree Medical, he had made love to Melissa for the last time.

As Joseph was driving south on I-75 from Nashville, having left Molly at school to study for a test, he headed for his home in North Atlanta, finally ready to have a heart-to-heart conversation with his mother. Sean was also headed to Atlanta, but from the opposite direction. Coming from Valdosta, it was slow going. He had to fight the bumper-to-bumper traffic on I-75, which was always horrendous near I-675 on Friday afternoons.

Marla-Dean had hoped to see him before leaving for the ER, where she was scheduled to work with Dr. Easton. Despite being frequently slow and methodical, she loved working with Luke—her hero. Marla-Dean was happier than she ever believed she would be, especially after having such a disastrous bout with alcoholism several years earlier. She owed all of this to Luke. By saving Sean's life two years earlier, she was now a wife, a mother, and a respected physician—the "trifecta." This was everything she required to make her feel like a complete woman.

Having had to breastfeed Connor an additional time before leaving, she was unable to eat at home, but with the cafeteria so close to the ER, this wasn't a problem. She knew she could check in, run to the cafeteria, and grab a quick bite.

Thirty minutes later, with the waiting room nearly empty, she was ravenous. So, she headed straight for the cafeteria. Buying a garden salad and a bowl of yogurt, Marla-Dean sat down to eat. As she was taking her first bite, Dr. Porthos walked by. When he did, she called out, "Gus, do you have a second? There's something I want to ask you?"

Still peeved, feeling "cheated" by the sale of his lake house, he wanted to ignore her, but he knew that was no way for a mature physician to act. Choosing to be an adult, he sat across from her, and smiled. With inquisitive eyes, he asked what she wanted?

Grateful he was not irritable, she said, "We went to the house last weekend and had a great time. I'm so pleased with the place. I really am."

Since her happiness came from his misfortune, her statement stung. So, he just smiled again—but this smile was obviously less than genuine.

Sensing his change in attitude, she dispensed with further small talk and came straight to the point. "Gus, last Saturday night, when the moon was full, I was sound asleep, but my husband was awakened by two people talking outside on the deck. Because it was so pleasant— with such a nice breeze—we left the sliding glass doors open."

When she said this, a knowing look came across Gus's face. She could have stopped right there because Gus knew what she was going to ask, but she didn't.

Instead, she continued, "Voices woke him up out of a sound sleep. There were two of them—a man's and a woman's. Sean said they were upset about something, but he couldn't understand what they were talking about, because they weren't speaking English."

Before she could continue, he interrupted her. "And you want to know if I have any idea what might have caused this, right?"

A little surprised at how quickly he discerned her intent, she replied, "Precisely. Do you know what it was?"

"It was a zephyr."

"A what?" she asked.

"A zephyr. That's a gentle breeze that blows from the west to the east. What Sean heard came from the house across the lake."

"No, that's not possible, Gus," she replied. "That house is much too far away for us to hear anything coming from there."

"I know. That's what I thought too. Normally, you would be right, Marla-Dean, but not in this case," he corrected her. "It definitely was from the house across the lake. I know it for a fact. It happened to us a couple of times. The first time I heard it, it scared me to death. I was certain someone was on the deck, ready to come in and slit our throats."

Laughing, Marla-Dean replied, "That's exactly how Sean felt— exactly. It scared him so much; he bought a shotgun for the place. Can you believe it?"

Joining in her laughter, he replied, "So, it scared the shit out of him, huh?"

"Yep, it sure did," she acknowledged, as both laughed heartily.

As he rose to leave, he added, "One more thing, Marla-Dean. It was Spanish. A couple of times, Darden understood what they were saying. She speaks fluent Spanish, you know?"

"No, I didn't know that, Gus," she said. "Thanks for clearing this up—a zephyr? If you learn something new every day, this is what I've learned for today."

As he walked away, he resumed his arrogant posture, thinking, *She could learn a lot from me!*

CHAPTER THIRTEEN
"The Other Guy—Poor Man"

By the time Joseph walked in the front door three hours later, Melissa was exhausted. Once Luke departed, she stripped her bed, washed and dried the sheets and towels, remade the bed, scrubbed two bathrooms, vacuumed, dusted, and cleaned the kitchen, erasing any trace of her lover's presence, especially his scent. Certain she hadn't missed anything; she was finally prepared for Joseph's arrival.

Nevertheless, when she first saw her son, she blushed, hopeful no telltale sign remained, revealing she had been making love earlier in the afternoon. Although she had enjoyed being passionate at the time, her conscience was bothering her—both as a Christian and as his mother. Living in sin was something she had yet to come to terms with.

In some ways, she envied Luke, who never seemed to be bothered about anything. Normally, she wouldn't have allowed him to be at the house so close to the time of her son's arrival, but she wouldn't have the opportunity to see him again until late Sunday. This is why she permitted it. Luke was the most ethical doctor she had ever seen, but when it came to relationships, his behavior wasn't nearly as high-minded as hers. It was almost like she was dealing with a different person when it came to their personal relationship. She couldn't quite figure it out.

Nevertheless, she had given in to his whining plea for them to spend the night together, which she now regretted. She was racked with guilt—certain it showed in some way. Feeling uncomfortable, as Joseph walked into the house, she hoped he wouldn't notice anything being amiss.

Joseph never noticed a thing, of course. What twenty-year-old guy would? It was the farthest thing from his mind. Instead, he was the one who felt guilty for being so deceitful for the past two years. He was far more concerned about how she would react to what he needed to say than any confession that might be on her mind.

Putting down his bag and truck keys, he hugged her and kissed her on the cheek. As she started to pull away, he held her tight, not letting go. Then, he began to cry—just like he had when he was a little boy. A good mother, Melissa's heart went out to her son. She had almost forgotten what this part of motherhood felt like, but she loved it. All moms do. Patting his back, exactly the way she had done since he was a toddler, she allowed him to cry on her shoulder uninterrupted for a long time.

Once finished, which not only washed away his pent up emotions but also his estrangement, he grabbed a paper napkin from the kitchen counter, wiped his eyes, and blew his nose. Taking a deep breath, he said, "Is there anything to eat around here. I'm starved."

Not surprised in the least by this dramatic change of direction, knowing him as well as she did, she just laughed. Answering his question, she said, "Now, what do you think? Of course there is. The refrigerator is full—just like it always is."

Smiling, he said, "Great. Let me go to the bathroom and wash up. Then, we'll eat, okay?"

"Absolutely. By the time you get back, I'll have a plate ready for you."

Ten minutes later, Joseph returned to find a huge plate of roast beef, mashed potatoes and gravy, string beans, sliced tomatoes that his mom had peeled, and cornbread waiting for him. Smiling, he said, "Yummy, the only thing missing is a piece of pecan pie with vanilla ice cream, but you've got that coming after I finish, don't you?"

"I'm not sure whether I do or not," she replied playfully, cherishing every minute of their time together. "I guess you'll just have to eat what I've put in front of you to find out, won't you?"

"Mom," he replied dramatically, "There will be no problem with that." Abandoning his smile, as his countenance seemed to shrink, he added, "I haven't eaten a good meal since Dad died."

"Then, it is time you did, son," she answered with maternal concern.

Sitting down, they blessed the food, and he dug in—just like old times, when neither had a care in the world . . . or a misgiving.

✑

Normally, after finishing a meal as hardy as the one he had just consumed, topped off with pie alamode, Joseph would be ready for a nap, but not this time. He had too much that needed to be said, and he wanted to get started. Looking at his mother, he asked, "Do you want me to help you with the dishes, or should I just start telling you the stuff you don't know?"

Having wanted the breach between them mended for nearly two years, she couldn't have cared less about the dirty kitchen. Smiling, she said, "The dishes can wait."

Nodding his head and taking a deep breath, he asked, "Do you remember when you came up in the fall of my freshman year? The time you surprised me, and I was upset with you because you did. Remember that?"

"Yes, I definitely remember that," she answered, still wounded by being rebuffed, which she never expected and certainly didn't deserve.

"That wasn't what you thought it was, Mom."

Puzzled, she just looked at him quizzically.

"I did that to protect you, or at least that's what I thought I was doing." He added, "I knew you wouldn't understand, but I couldn't help that."

"Protect me from what?" she asked.

'Mom, there's so much you don't know—so much I've kept from you. It's hard to know where to begin," he acknowledged.

Again, she just looked at him, curious but eager for him to continue.

So, he pressed forward. "Just before I started college at Belmont—the first time I went to visit Dad and his new wife, you remember that, right?"

"Of course," she replied, in a crisp tone he recognized instantly. It indicated she wasn't stupid, and he needed to stop stalling, come to the point, and say what was on his mind.

Complying with her insistent tone, which had a very familiar ring to it, Joseph said, "When I walked into Dad's house for the first time and met his pregnant wife, it was Joy. She had changed her name to Landria, but it was Joy."

"What!" Melissa exclaimed, jumping straight out of her seat.

"It was her, Mom. She was even wearing jeans that showed that snake tattoo."

"I don't believe it," Melissa said, nearly apoplectic with rage.

"Mom," he said, in a tranquil tone. "Please try and stay calm. I have a bunch more to tell you."

A bunch more, she thought. *How much more could there be?* Anxious to hear it, she took a deep breath, and calmed herself. Then, she sat back down, completely focused, and ready to listen to everything her son had to reveal.

"That's why I didn't want you to come to Nashville. That's the only reason. It was to protect Dad."

Thinking about it, she nodded, understanding what had happened from her son's perspective, which took the sting out of having been thwarted.

Returning to his story, Joseph said, "When Joy left Atlanta, she went to Nashville and hooked up with Dad. Why she chose him I still don't know, and I probably never will. Anyway, she was pregnant with my daughter, but she told Dad the child was his. Because Jo Ellen looks so much like me, she also looks like Dad, so it was easy for her to fool him."

"This is unbelievable," Melissa interjected.

"Well, there's a lot more that is just as unbelievable."

"I want to hear it all," she said, and she meant it.

Continuing, Joseph added, "Landria played it cool, acting like she had never met me. When she did, I felt like I had to along with it." Looking at his mom warily, he added, "Landria did try and seduce me again, but I wouldn't let her." Being resolute and forceful, he affirmed, "I promise I didn't!"

"I believe you, son," she acknowledged, accepting the truthfulness of what he had just stated.

"I told her I would keep her secret, just as long as she was a good wife to Dad and a good mother to Jo Ellen, which she was—at least as good as she is capable of being. All of this lasted until last weekend, when Dad died." Being very candid, he added, "When I got involved with her, all I wanted was to have sex—a little fun—just like all the rest of the guys in school. I never thought it would lead to a mess like this; and now Dad's dead because of it."

Joseph expected his mother to scold him at this point, but she didn't, which surprised him. He was very grateful she didn't.

With a quavering voice, he added, "This is all my fault, Mom, all of it." When he finished, the tears began to roll down his face, and he cried copiously for a long time. As he did, his mother held his hands, never loosened her grip, comforting him.

Although Joseph was mature for his age and now had a world of responsibility, in many ways, he was still a boy—a boy who needed his mother. Loving the tenderness of the moment, Melissa held him while he cried his eyes out for the second time of the evening.

A few minutes later, she got up and brewed them a pot of coffee. Then, she made Joseph a huge bowl of strawberry ice cream. She put it in front of her son, hoping it would settle him down. Saying he didn't want it, she told him to just take a bite anyway, which he did obediently. Once he did, he finished the bowl in less than five minutes.

Watching him gobble it down, Melissa smiled, making a mental note to thank Marla-Dean for sharing the secret of how valuable a bowl of strawberry ice cream can be.

When he finished, he wiped his mouth and told her of his dad's misgivings about the marriage, and about how his dad had made him the Executor of the estate. When he finished the story, Joseph sat there, drained. Melissa was also emotionally exhausted.

Looking at the clock, she said, "It's getting late. I've made your bed. Why don't you go upstairs and take a shower. I'll finish up in the kitchen. We can continue what you need to tell me in the morning." Standing, she started to clear the table. Looking at Joseph, she concluded, "A lot of puzzling things are beginning to make sense. Isn't it good to get everything out in the open?"

Nodding, he didn't say anything else except, "Good night." As he was walking up the stairs, he thought, *I'm just halfway through, but she's right. It is good to get things out in the open.*

The following morning, Joseph slept until 10 a.m., which isn't late for a twenty-year-old, especially one whose body clock was still on Central time. Melissa, however, had been up for hours, replaying in her mind what Joseph had divulged. His revelations filled in numerous gaps but, best of all, it had restored their communication; connecting them at a level she desired but had almost forgotten even existed. It was an answer to prayer that she had nearly lost hope would ever be fulfilled.

When he stumbled to the table, disheveled and groggy, barely conscious, she put a cup of coffee in front of him, complete with half &

half and three teaspoons of sugar—just the way he liked it. Long past telling him how bad sugar was for him, she wanted to make him feel at home. He drank it eagerly and asked for another, which she made promptly. After eggs, cheese grits, and an English muffin, slathered with butter and grape jelly, he had his third cup of coffee. Asking to be excused shortly thereafter, because he was a regular guy, he returned in fifteen minutes, ready to resume their conversation.

As he was about to speak, Melissa held up her hand, stopping him. Blushing, she looked at him and said, "Before you begin, there's something I need to tell you."

Taken aback, he just sat there, waiting for her to proceed.

Mortified by what she was about to say, her face turned scarlet red. Nevertheless, she continued resolutely. "As you know, I've been seeing Dr. Easton for quite a while. Although it may not lead to marriage, he wants to move in with me, and I've told him he can. I'm not asking for your permission, Joseph, but I do want you to know about this before it happens."

Once she said this, which was one of the most difficult things she had ever felt required to do, she looked at her son. She expected him to reply, but he didn't. Not knowing what his thoughts were, she assumed he thought she was nothing better than a tramp, which crushed her. Close to tears, feeling worthless and ashamed, she added, "I know this goes against the values I've taught you. I'm not completely settled with it myself. There is a part of me that's hesitant. But I can't find a good reason to say no, other than it's just wrong. Anyway, he does stay here a lot. You've been so honest with me. I want to be straightforward with you as well."

Admitting all of this was very difficult. Needing to deflect from her own sense of moral failure, she added, "Luke is a wonderful man and a great physician."

"I know that, Mom," Joseph interrupted. "I was on the bridge that night. I saw him singlehandedly save Sean's life."

Pleased that the first words spoken about the subject were not scolding, her self-loathing diminished. She was about to say something else, when Joseph raised his hand, stopping her. Looking her straight in the eye, he said, "Part of what I needed to tell you this morning is about Dr. Easton, Mom."

Stunned and surprised, she asked, "Why would you need to talk to me about Luke?"

"Because I lied to you the day we had the blowup about Landria—I mean Joy." Taking a breath, he continued, "You were right that day, Mom, but I couldn't admit it. It was just too hard for me to tell you the truth." Being forthright, he confessed, "I wasn't the only one she was having sex with. I couldn't be honest then, but I can now. I thought I loved her, but that's not what it was—not real love, anyway. It was more like she had some kind of possession of me—like she owned a piece of my soul. I was completely mesmerized by her and would have done anything she wanted. I mean it. As I think about it now, it scares me. Does this make sense to you, Mom?"

"Absolutely," she affirmed, terrified by the evil that had come so close to destroying her son, perhaps beyond repair. Responding thoughtfully, she added, "Most men never realize the power an unscrupulous woman like Joy—I mean Landria—can have over them, but you do, son. It's a terrible lesson to learn—a painful one too—but at least you've learned it."

"Thanks for understanding, Mom," he said. "I thought you would be critical and judgmental."

Smiling at the irony, she replied, "Hardly. The person I feel sorry for is the other guy—poor man. I can't imagine what happened to him, can you?"

"Yes, I can. In fact, I know who it was."

"Who?"

"It was Dr. Easton, Mom."

"What!" Melissa exploded. She was so shocked; she could barely take it in.

"It was Dr. Easton. He was the other guy."

"It couldn't have been, Joseph. He's never said a word to me about Joy, and he definitely would have. He doesn't even know her," she proffered defensively.

"Yes, he does. It was him, Mom. I know it was him. I'm not guessing. I know this for a fact," Joseph asserted.

"Son, I need to ask you a question, but I don't want you to be offended." Giving him a second to adjust, she asked, "You're not just saying this because Luke's moving in with me, are you?"

"No, I wish I was, Mom. I've kept this from you for a long time. I should have told you before. I know I should have, but I couldn't. I'm so sorry to have to tell you now."

Still unconvinced, Melissa just looked at him, silently asking for further explanation.

"His ex-wife knows about it," Joseph added. "It's one of the reasons they split up."

When Joseph mentioned this, the lights seemed to go on for Melissa. Admitting to herself the unthinkable, she realized her son was telling the truth. She remembered Patricia Easton had been sitting in the parking lot across from Joni P's, with her engine running, the night "The Shitter" died and Joy went missing. Patricia must have been waiting for Joy, intent on confronting her about the paternity of Joy's unborn child.

Shaking her head as she looked back at her son, Melissa said, "Oh my God, you're right." With this, her stomach lurched, and she ran to the bathroom, just making it to the commode in the nick of time. After throwing up, she rinsed her mouth, her face, and her eyes, and returned to the kitchen. Joseph, knowing from experience to leave her alone, just sat and waited for her patiently, as she placed dirty plates and flatware in the dishwasher.

Resuming her seat several minutes later, Melissa said, "Thank you for letting me know about this. I've been in the dark for so long. It's hard for me to take it all in; it's just so shocking."

"It's also why I didn't want you and Dr. Easton to come to Nashville,

Mom. What if he had seen Joy? There's no telling what would have happened, and I couldn't risk that."

Hearing this, Melissa's countenance shrank even further. As she began to comprehend things she had never even considered, she realized how badly she had been duped. Slumping in her chair as the tears began to flow, she admitted, "I feel like such a fool, but Luke never said a word to me about any of this—not one word."

"You're not a fool, Mom. If it's any consolation, I don't think he ever knew about Joy and me. In fact, I'm sure he didn't," Joseph explained, in an attempt to comfort her, but she wasn't in the mood for being consoled.

He started to say something else, but she stopped him. "Can this be enough for now, Joseph?" she asked, almost begging for him to stop. "I don't think I can take anymore right now."

"Sure Mom," he said, going to the refrigerator and pouring her a glass of iced tea. With her head hung down in despair, she accepted the glass of tea, setting it down to drink later.

Sensing she would prefer solitude, Joseph left quietly, returning to his room.

CHAPTER FOURTEEN
Her Best Friend Was a Crooked Cop

At 8:15 a.m., Marla-Dean pulled into her driveway, worn-out from her long night at the Peachtree Medical Emergency Room. Although neither Dr. Easton nor she had any complicated or memorable cases, it was a fatiguing shift nonetheless. Weekend nights always were. Walking into the kitchen from the garage, she heard Connor crying loudly, which both concerned and energized her. Putting her purse and keys down, she looked at Winky, who was trying her best to feed the infant with the milk Marla-Dean had pumped the evening before.

Taking Connor from her, Marla-Dean gave him her breast, and he settled down at once to nurse. Frazzled by Connor's unwillingness to eat, both Winky and Sean breathed a sigh of relief. Adding a commentary, Sean said, "Connor's Irish, Winky. Because the blood of the Emerald Isle flows through his veins, he always prefers the real thing to something fake. Who can blame him?"

Winky just looked at Marla-Dean who, despite being exhausted, had a smile on her face. Blushing a little, Winky smiled too, excusing herself to tend to the laundry.

After pouring a cup of coffee, Sean walked over to his wife and kissed her on the cheek, saying, "I missed you, darling. It's good to be back from South Georgia."

"I missed you too, Sean. Three days is a long time," she replied, as she burped Conner, switching sides for him to finish nursing. A minute later, she asked, "How did things go in Valdosta?"

"Fine, I doubt this case ever will come to trial." After taking a sip of coffee, he added, "I won't be leaving town again for quite some time."

Hearing this, Marla-Dean's shoulders relaxed. She was relieved he would be around. Before having Connor, neither had a clue how exhausting taking care of an infant would be—and they had a nanny! Marla-Dean couldn't imagine what she would do without Winky.

As Connor was finishing, Marla-Dean looked at Sean and asked, "Did the producer from The Kelly File reach you?"

"Sort of," he replied. "She called, but I was so busy I sent her an email, telling her I wouldn't be available until next week, if they still needed me. I haven't heard back, so I don't know what's going on."

"Everybody's talking about the Steiger case," Marla-Dean said.

"I know. It seems funny that we're a part of it, doesn't it? It seems almost surreal." Thinking for a moment, he continued, "I find it odd we have a connection with the suspect, don't you?"

"He's not the only connection we have," she replied, capturing his attention instantly. "At first I missed what our part was, but after Steiger was connected to Pretty Boy's shooting and it became the lead story on every channel, I started putting the pieces together."

Looking at her expectantly, he just raised his eyebrow, which was a signal for her to explain what she meant.

Returning his gaze, she added, "Not long ago, Mrs. Steiger came into the ER with a wrenched back. When I examined her, the first thing I noticed was she had severe bruising around her vagina."

"What in the world would cause that?" he exclaimed.

"Extremely rough sex," she answered matter-of-factly.

"Like being raped?" he asked.

"Yes, rape victims often have vaginal bruising, Sean."

"So, either Steiger or someone else raped her, and she ends up dead?"

"That's what I thought when I first saw the magnitude of the bruising, but she assured me the sex that caused her bruising was consensual."

"Consensual? You've got to be kidding?"

"I wish I was, but there's more, so listen," she admonished.

Taking a seat at the table, as directed, Sean gave her his undivided attention. Continuing, she said, "I asked her point blank, 'Did your ex-husband do this?' She told me flat-out that it wasn't him, and I believed her. Then she said, 'It was my boyfriend. He just likes it a little rough; that's all.' I remember those were her exact words because, having said them, she let me know she liked having sex that way. She said, it was 'no big deal.'"

"Well, she was wrong about that, wasn't she?" he asked rhetorically. "It was a big enough deal to have gotten her killed."

"Apparently, but that's not all, Sean."

He just looked at Marla-Dean and waited expectantly, engrossed by what she was telling him.

"The woman had bruises on her neck as well. She tried to cover them up with make-up, but they were too prominent for that to be effective." Putting Connor on her shoulder, she burped him a second time. Having filled his little tummy, Connor was ready for a nap; so was Marla-Dean.

As Sean was thinking about what his wife had disclosed, she stood to take Connor back to his room. Before leaving, she added, "Anne Morrow-Steiger was strangled to death. It's all over the news, but I think it was from being strangled while she was having rough sex with her boyfriend—not by being raped and murdered by her ex-husband."

"Let me get this straight. You think some guy killed her while he was screwing her?"

"Yes."

"And, instead of owning up to being a pervert, he made it look like her ex-husband murdered her?"

"Yes."

"And, you're telling me all of this because you think I should get involved. Is that right?"

"Exactly. By telling you this, I'm breaching patient confidentiality, but Anne Steiger is dead, and everybody thinks her ex-husband did it. Whatever William Steiger might or might not have done, there's one thing I do know for sure. He saved your life. Now, it's your turn to do something for him, don't you think?"

"Maybe I should," Sean replied thoughtfully, contemplating this possibility for the first time.

Smiling, in complete agreement with the direction of his musing, Marla-Dean concluded, "That's what I thought you would say, Mr. Charles."

Referring to the detective, Nick Charles from *The Thin Man* movies in the 1930s, she didn't add another word. Cooing to Connor as she walked out softly, she left Sean to think about what she had said.

Despite the Dawgs being on TV in the early afternoon, Sean had lost interest. He could do nothing but think about the case against William Steiger.

⌀

By mid-afternoon, Joseph still had not left his room, nor had he eaten another bite. From the bottom of the stairs, Melissa called, "Joseph," but there was no reply. Yelling a second time, there was still no response. Finally, screaming, "JO-SEFF!" His door finally opened.

"What?" he said, with a hint of indignation in his voice.

This exchange, which is the most exasperating part of being a mother, always infuriated Melissa—just like it does millions of moms across the fruited plain. It had for years. Calming down, by taking a deep breath, she said, "I've got to go out for a few hours. There's plenty to eat in the refrigerator, but don't eat too much. We're going out for dinner. You choose the place. Where do you want to go?"

Without hesitation, he replied, "Joni P's," which surprised her.

"Okay, you're the man around here," she replied. "If that's where you want to go, that's where we will go. I'll make a reservation for 6 p.m., and I'll pick you up at 5:30. Be ready!"

"Yes, ma'am," he answered, going back to his room, where he had been studying with music blaring in his earphones, just like he had done in high school.

When Marla-Dean awoke a little after 2 p.m., she expected to find Sean sitting in front of the TV engrossed in the Dawgs vs. South Carolina game, but he wasn't. Instead, he was in his office, and it looked as if he had been there for hours. Popping her head in, she asked, "Why aren't you watching the game?"

Looking at her over his glasses, with a knowing smile on his face, he replied, "I think you know the answer to that, Mrs. Charles."

Smiling wryly, she added, "Indeed I do, Mr. Charles. It's one of the reasons why I love you so much."

Breaking into a broad smile, he continued, "I've been reading everything I can about William Steiger but, before this week, there hasn't been that much to read. He has two kids at Auburn. He doesn't work because of chronic alcoholism, and he hasn't for years. He went to LSU. Other than that, there's very little about him, but I did discover his nickname. It's Pencil."

"Why would he have a name like that?" she questioned.

"Don't ask," he replied wryly.

"Hmmm, that's another reason I love you. If you're free an hour from now, Winky is taking Connor and Asta for a long walk around Memorial Park, and . . . Can you take a break?" she asked.

"Of course," he replied, delighted by the offer. Confused by the other part of what she had said though, he inquired, "What other reason?"

Replying sensuously, she answered, "No one would ever nickname you Pencil, Mr. Well Endowed."

⸾

While Sean and Marla-Dean were bantering playfully, the way loving married couples do, Melissa was knocking on the door of Luke Easton's condo. Having been awake for about an hour, Luke had already showered and shaved. Nevertheless, he was genuinely surprised when he opened the door and saw Melissa standing outside.

Delighted, he stepped aside, allowing her to enter. After shutting the door, he reached out to hug her but was instantly rebuffed. Confused, he asked what was wrong.

Once she was seated in his tastefully appointed living room, she looked at him and said, "Why have you never told me about Joy?"

Stunned, Luke was pierced to the core. Frightened, he couldn't think of a thing to say in response. Offering the best defense he could think of under the circumstances, he replied, "Melissa, that was a long time ago. I didn't think it was important; that's all."

"Not important! You were having an affair, cheating on your wife, and you didn't think that was important enough to tell me?" She challenged incredulously.

"Honey, it was nothing. It wasn't significant," he retorted as skillfully as a Democrat justifying the misuse of taxpayer funds.

"That 'nothing' is what caused your divorce, isn't it?" Rebuffing him further, she added, "Luke, we talked about your relationship with Patricia for hours—dozens of times—but you never said a word to me about this. Why? What kind of man would do that?"

"Melissa, it was just sex—nothing more," he said, trying to calm her down, but Melissa would have none of it.

"Nothing more?" she countered. "She told you she was carrying your child. I suppose that wasn't important either?"

Stunned, Luke could hardly breathe. Finally, he asked, "Who told you about all of this? Have you been talking to Patricia?" he demanded. Hopeful of regaining control of the situation, he became indignant and defensive.

"It doesn't matter how I found out," she retorted. "What does matter is you've lied to me since the beginning, while I've been completely honest with you. I even told you about my herpes, which was the most humiliating thing I've ever had to do in my entire life. I told you because I thought you needed to know everything."

"And I appreciated that you did, Melissa, you know that," he replied, abandoning his defensiveness.

"I went to such lengths to protect you, Luke. You'll never know all I went through to make sure you didn't get it," she said sorrowfully, nearly in tears.

Standing up, he paced for a while shaking his head, as he thought about what her newfound knowledge would mean. Becoming quite humble, he said, "I guess this means I won't be moving in any time soon, doesn't it?"

Looking at him like he had lost his mind, she replied, "Luke, we're done. There's nothing left between us—not a damn thing. I just came here to tell you in person; that's all."

"Melissa," he whined.

Holding up her hand in a gesture that stopped him cold, she concluded, "We're professionals who work in the same emergency room; that's it—nothing more." Understanding him well, she knew she had to draw firm boundaries, so she added, "You are no longer welcome at my home. Never call me; never email me; and never text me again about anything that isn't work related. Have I made myself clear?"

"Melissa, this will all blow over," he countered hopefully.

"No it will not, Luke. You've been deeply deceitful, and I will never trust you again. How could I?" she said rhetorically. Standing, she grabbed her purse and walked out of his house—and out of his life.

⁓

An hour later, after driving around crying, while listening to soothing Christian music, Melissa stopped, refreshed her make up, and pulled into her driveway. Then, she honked for Joseph. Less than a minute later, he stepped out, looking as handsome as a Hollywood celebrity. Getting in the car, she said, "I'm starved. How about you?"

"Always," he replied.

"Then, let's get something to eat," she said, backing out of the driveway.

When they entered Joni P's thirty minutes later, the crowd was sparse because it was early. This meant Joseph was able to pick the table he desired, which was the one he and Sean always occupied. As he looked at the menu, which he practically knew by heart, he missed Molly and wished she could have been there with them. If his heart already ached for her to be with him, and they had only been apart for one day, he wondered how he could possibly handle her moving off to attend law school at Stanford. California seemed so far away, and for good reason; it was.

After ordering, Melissa told Joseph she had broken off her relationship with Luke. When she explained what had happened, leaving out most of the details, Joseph felt terrible. He said, "Mom, you were happy with Dr. Easton, and I interfered. I hate that. It makes me feel terrible."

"No, son, you did the right thing." Looking at him, she added, "Never apologize for telling the truth. It's much better to have found out now, rather than later. It will be hard for a while, but it would have been much harder if we had been living together for a year or two. You understand this, don't you?"

"Yes, I do," he replied, and he did.

Their food came shortly thereafter, and they ate without further substantive conversation. Although Melissa said she was starving, she hardly ate a bite, which Joseph noticed but wisely didn't mention.

When they were through eating, while Joseph was looking at the desert menu, Melissa surveyed the restaurant. Being an hour later, the place was packed. Viewing the crowd, she said, "This is a great table, son. You can see what's going on all over the restaurant."

"That's why I picked it, Mom," he said purposefully. "This is the table Captain Baird sat at the night she saw Joy and me sitting at the bar."

Melissa looked at him with her mouth slightly pursed. Joseph pointed out the stools, where he and Joy had been sitting, as well as where Sean had been drinking at the other end of the horseshoe bar, practically hidden by a large plant.

When Joseph finished, she said, "I was so upset that night; but I'm delighted Barbara told me the truth—just like you have this weekend. I mean it, son."

"I'm glad, Mom, because there's one more important thing I need to tell you."

Slumping in her chair, she said, "Oh my God; what else?"

"It's about Captain Baird; she's not who you think she is," Joseph announced.

"Oh, if that's all it is, don't bother. I know about her. She's pretentious, shallow, and extremely vain. Everybody knows that, and I'm sure she's jealous of my relationship with Luke—my former relationship—that is. But she's harmless." Dismissing Joseph's concern before listening to what he had to say, Melissa prepared to pay the bill and leave.

Stopping her, Joseph said, "This doesn't have anything to do with her vanity, Mother. It's much worse than that."

Intrigued, Melissa put her purse down to listen.

Having gained her attention, Joseph continued. "That night, she sat in your seat. In my seat, her dinner guest was Pretty Boy Sabarisi—the drug dealer from New Orleans—the guy who shot Sean."

"What?" she exclaimed. "I don't believe it," Melissa protested, incredulously. "She's become a pillar of the church, and she's been my solid friend." Thinking for a minute, she added, "Besides, she was at Sean and Marla-Dean's wedding. If she had been involved with the man who shot him, do you think Sean would have invited her to his wedding?"

"Yes, I do, Mom. Sean's smart, and he knows to keep your friends close, but keep your enemies closer."

Impressed by how mature and wise her son was becoming, but still not prepared to accept that her best friend was a monster, Melissa reasoned, "You can't be certain about this, Joseph. How could you be?"

"Because Molly was their waitress, and she recognized the photo of Pretty Boy that Sean brought back from New Orleans the night he was shot." Now on a roll, Joseph added, "That's the reason Molly pulled me away from Captain Baird at the hospital when Sean was in surgery. She knew I was about to confront Captain Baird, which would have put my life in danger—Molly's too."

"Oh my God," Melissa said, as the lights went on for her a second time that day. Her response was as close to swearing as Joseph had ever heard from her. Normally, she never used God's name except in prayer.

Not yet finished, Joseph added, "Sean, Molly, and I made a pact not to speak about this to anybody. I doubt your friend Marla-Dean knows. Sean said that as long as he was 'out of the game,' Captain Baird would probably leave us alone, but if she knew how much we knew, our lives—Molly's and mine—would be in danger." After finishing, Joseph just sat there in silence for a long moment.

Finally, Melissa asked, "Is there more?"

"Yes," he acknowledged. "It isn't that she's just getting money from these drug kingpins, Mom. Sean is pretty sure she has been involved in murder."

As the blood drained from Melissa face, she asked, "Are you serious? Does he have any idea who she's killed?"

"He thinks there may have been a witness in a case he lost, and he's suspicious about how her husband died, when he left her all that money. Plus, the judge that was shot in his driveway." Looking at his mother, he added, "She's a bad lady, Mom. I've told you all of this because you need to get her out of your life, but you can't let her know the reason why. By confiding in you, I've put our lives in your hands, and I've broken my word to do so."

"I'm so glad you have," she admitted.

"You're playing with a cobra, Mom. Don't let her bite you." After telling his mother this, Joseph's gaze returned to the menu.

Melissa just sat there speechless, unable to process all that had happened in less than twenty-four hours. During this time, she had learned she son's lover had married her ex-husband; she was a grandmother; her boyfriend was a two-timing liar; and her best friend was a crooked cop and probably a murderess.

Shaking her head in disbelief, she questioned, "Is there anything else? Because if there is, I want to hear it right now."

"Just one thing," he said.

"Good Lord, what?" she asked impatiently.

"Is it okay if I get the 'Death by Chocolate Sundae' before we go?"

CHAPTER FIFTEEN

"She Looks Just Like You"

The following morning, as Joseph was finishing another sumptu-
ous breakfast before heading back to Nashville, his mother had
already asked him a gazillion questions, nearly all of which had never
occurred to her son. It is one of the major differences between men
and women. How women come up with the questions they do, puzzles
most men, but Joseph was still too young to have already figured this
out. Some guys never do.

He simply thought his mom was inordinately inquisitive—or
nosey—depending on the subject being discussed. While trying
to answer a question about Jo Ellen, who had been the focus of her
grandmother's inquisition, Joseph received a text message. Certain it
was from Molly, he opened it casually. Surprised it wasn't, he was even
more surprised to see that it was from Landria.

Looking at the screen, it said, "J, can u meet at 5? My house. We
need 2 plan."

Grateful and relieved to have heard from her, he replied, "K."

Closing his phone, he told his mom it was from Landria, a.k.a. Joy, and he needed to leave by 1:30 p.m. Realizing the importance of the text, Melissa told him they should probably just say goodbye, then and there. She was already dressed and ready for church. Knowing what she needed to accomplish, she wasn't certain she would make be able to it home before he needed to leave anyway.

Taking the dirty dishes to the sink to be washed, she turned to her son and confessed, "The day after Joy went missing, I was too hard on you. I know this now. It created a breach between us that I thought might be permanent, but now it feels like it's gone. It is gone, isn't it, Joseph?"

"Yes," was all he said in response.

"I'm so glad to have you back, son. I've missed you terribly." With tears welling in her eyes, she added, "You're turning out to be a better man than I had ever hoped, and I want you to know how proud I am of you."

Knowing how difficult it was for his mom to admit being wrong, Joseph didn't say a word. Instead, he just got up and gave her a big hug. When he did, she cried just as long and as hard as he had when he arrived Friday evening. So much had happened since then, it was difficult to believe that less than two days had passed.

When she finished, she said, "My make-up is all over the place. I'll have to start over, beginning with Murine for my red eyes."

"You look great, Mom," Joseph responded with a smile.

Becoming serious, she added, "There's just one more thing I need to address."

"What?"

"It's about Molly; I haven't given her the credit she deserves." Beginning to cry again, Melissa stated, "I'll be better to her from now on; I promise."

Genuinely touched, Joseph said, "I love you, Mom. You're the best mother a guy could ever have."

He was about to say more, but she stopped him, deflecting his validation, which she often did. "Thanks, son. I love you, too, but I've got to get moving. I don't want to start crying again. So, just go on; get out of here before I do."

"Yes, ma'am," he replied, laughing as he left the kitchen to return to his bedroom.

∽

An hour later, as the church regulars were chatting over coffee and donut holes before the Sunday morning service, Barbara Baird walked up to Melissa to say hello. As she reached Melissa, she sensed something wasn't quite right with her. Stopping abruptly, Barbara said, "Oh dear, things must not have gone well with Joseph. Is that what's troubling you, Melissa?"

"No, Barbara, his visit has been wonderful—actually, far better than I could have asked for."

"That's wonderful news. I'm so happy for you. But what is it, then?" Barbara pressed, which Melissa knew she would do—nosey bitch that she was.

Looking at her friend—the crooked cop—stoically, while harboring hidden contempt and derision, Melissa replied, "It's Luke. We've broken up, Barbara. Our relationship is over, and there is no possibility of reconciliation."

"Oh no! I'm so, so sorry," Barbara replied, showing outward concern, while being inwardly gleeful. Having been enamored with the physician for years, she had practically given up hope. Desirous of further details, she inquired, "Do you want to tell me what happened?"

"I've got a better idea," Melissa replied brusquely. "Why don't you ask him yourself? You've always been jealous of what Luke and I had. I could see it in your face. Now's your chance, Barbara; go for it. He's all yours." Unwilling to discuss the matter further, Melissa simply walked off to join another conversation, leaving Barbara behind.

Rebuked, Barbara just stood motionless, with her mouth wide open. Regaining her composure quickly, as always, Barbara resumed her warm and friendly demeanor. Thinking about this unexpected turn of events, Barbara's eyes took on a malevolent twinkle.

Already scheming, she said to herself, *Melissa has taken the gloves off. That two-faced bitch has finally shown her claws. I can see right through her. I've always been able to. Now that she's out of the way, I will make another play for Luke, and this time I'll get him.*

After rebuking Barbara, Melissa never ventured a backward glance. Having thought about what to do ever since Joseph confided in her, Melissa tried to figure out a way to extricate Barbara from her life, without creating suspicion. By pretending Luke had broken up with her, instead of her dropping him, Melissa became the scorned woman. Acting out of this role, she also played the part of a jealous lover, condemning Barbara to the position of an unwelcomed rival.

Melissa knew such a move would appeal to Barbara's vanity, accomplishing the nurse's goal. It would get Barbara out of her life, and the crooked cop would never know the real reason why. Melissa was proud of the way she handled the situation with Barbara. It was ingenious.

Knowing Luke would find Barbara's crush on him to be comical, Melissa didn't suspect she would be causing Luke a significant problem. Besides, he knew how to play women. He was a master at it. Just thinking about him being Joy's lover, as well as hers, infuriated and sickened her. That Joy had seduced her son made it even worse. Shaking her head, she said to herself, *We are no better than trailer park trash.*

Having such thoughts was unhealthy, which she recognized. It's why she needed to put all of this unpleasantness behind her. Going to church was a good place to start. Trying to be upbeat, she smiled, repeating to herself, *This is the first day of the rest of my life, and I'm going to seize it. Carpe diem, baby; carpe diem.*

～

Approaching Brentwood, just as soon as he turned off of I-24 onto the 440 Connector, Joseph thought about his daughter and all that was needed to take care of her. When he thought of bringing her with him to Atlanta to meet "her grandmother," he smiled and couldn't wait for that to happen. His mom would just love Jo Ellen. He knew this by the questions she had asked about the toddler.

By giving Landria a couple of days to simmer down, for the sake of their daughter, he was certain she would be more amenable to working with him. Although he knew about the funds she had stashed away, when she brained Pretty Boy several years earlier, Joseph assumed that Landria needed him more than she did.

But just like always, when it came to the motives of the woman with the snake tattoo, he didn't have a clue. Why she wanted to meet him that afternoon, when she knew he had to drive all the way back from Atlanta, he had no idea. At least, he would get to see Jo Ellen, even if it was just for a few minutes. Thinking about this pleased him.

As he turned on the street to his dad's house, he felt sad. Suddenly, he missed all of the years they were apart, and now he would never see him again. It didn't seem fair.

Making a determined effort to be strong for Jo Ellen's sake, Joseph pulled into the driveway promptly at 5 p.m., just like Landria had texted him to do. Walking to the front door, he saw a sealed envelope with his name on it, stuck in the door jam. Surprised, he opened it and found nothing but a key. Assuming it was to the front door, he tried it, and it worked.

Opening the door, he walked in. As he looked around, he saw that the place was completely empty, stripped of everything—furniture, rugs, lights, and artwork. There was nothing in the kitchen either. It was all gone, and so were Landria and Jo Ellen.

While he had been in Atlanta, Landria packed up everything and disappeared. Having done this numerous times before, Joseph shouldn't have been surprised, but he was. Having no idea what else to do, he just walked from one room to the next aimlessly, repeating the process several times, which increased his anxiety.

A few minutes later, as he started to leave, he received another text. It was from Landria. Opening the phone quickly to retrieve the message, it said; *Joseph, this is from Jo Ellen. "Today's episode of Sesame Street is brought to you by the letters F and U."*

That was all, but the implication was obvious. Landria had vanished into thin air, and it was her intention to keep him out of Jo Ellen's life. He was sure she had already transferred Pretty Boy's money. Since his dad had died, Joseph saw no need to keep the detective agency on retainer, which he now realized had been a big mistake. As cunning as she was, Landria had outsmarted him.

Heartbroken and defeated, he was unable to contain his emotions. Sitting on the front porch of his father's house, he cried his eyes out for the third time of the weekend. A few minutes later, worn and frazzled, he got into his truck and headed back to the university where Molly was waiting.

As he thought about the difference between Molly and Landria, he simply shook his head in amazement. While making the twenty-minute drive, he called his mom and told her what had happened. Like always, she asked a million questions to which he had no answers. Exhausted by the time he reached home, he said goodnight to his mother and hello to his girlfriend.

✑

While Joseph was discovering Landria's treachery in Nashville, Ernesto Rodriquez had been doing his best to hide from the men who wanted to kill him. Having little money and apprehensive about being discovered at some cheap motel, he went to a gay bar and allowed himself to be picked up by a nice older man. Spending several nights with the man, Ernesto knew he was safe and would not be discovered. He didn't really like what he was doing, but it worked. It was an idea he learned about while watching an old movie. The goal was to make himself invisible, and it worked.

He knew the gay man would make advances toward him, but he needed to hide, so he submitted, pretending to be gay himself. Ernesto hoped nobody would discover the truth about what he had done, since it was a mortal sin, but he reasoned it was a small price to pay for survival.

Still alive, he walked into the Starbucks at Barnes & Noble on Peachtree, promptly at 6 p.m., as he had been instructed. Just as soon as he entered the coffee shop, his contact handed him a large envelope, containing $10,000. He was told that was all the funds that were immediately available. The following week, he would be given $100,000 more. After that, he was on his own.

Grateful, Ernesto left Starbucks and headed back to the gay man's condo. Reasoning that he needed to hoard his funds, he decided to stay with the gay man for another week. What other choice did he have? Besides, the man was nice to him and, more than anything, Ernesto needed to hide in a safe place.

A few minutes after Ernesto walked out of the bookstore, Winky Weller walked in. Having taken care of Connor for two nights, while Marla-Dean worked at the hospital, Winky was given the night off. Hopeful she might run into the woman who had her cluster ring, Winky looked around the store expectantly, but she had no luck. Giving the ring away still bothered her. The longer the ring was gone, the more she missed it. Feeling stupid, she realized she shouldn't have parted with it. She had been much too impetuous.

Refusing to come to terms with her loss, she skulked around the store for quite a while, finally settling down to read a book of prayers, which was exactly what she needed. It was titled, *Prayers for Recovering People*, written by the guy who was Sean's sponsor—Jack Watts. Drinking a grande raspberry mocha latte, while she read, she relaxed for half an hour.

✑

Saturday night at the ER had been a little easier for both Dr. Kincannon and Dr. Easton but, for some reason, Luke was not very engaging. In fact, he seemed to be quite withdrawn, which concerned Marla-Dean. She asked if anything was bothering him, but he didn't want to discuss what it was.

When he left work early in the morning, he went home and straight to bed. Sleeping fitfully on-and-off, he finally got up in the late afternoon and cooked some eggs. After that, he turned on the TV and watched pro football, without paying much attention to the game.

He was depressed and he knew it. Kicking himself for holding out on Melissa, he realized their relationship was over. To make matters worse, he couldn't even be angry about it. He didn't blame her. How could he? She had every right to be offended, but that didn't take the sting out of the way he felt. If anything, it increased his pain.

Thinking a shower might help assuage his conscience and feelings of loneliness, by washing the pain from his body, he allowed the soothing water to run over him for a long time. Finally, toweling off, he went downstairs to watch *Sunday Night Football*. The Giants were playing the Patriots, which he hoped would take his mind off of his troubles.

When the doorbell rang at 9:30 p.m., his heart leapt. He was certain it was Melissa, and she had changed her mind. Grateful he had shaved and showered, he walked to the front door quickly and expectantly. When he opened the door, the person standing there wasn't the woman he had anticipated. Instead, it was a woman from his past.

"Hello, Luke," she said.

"Hello, Joy, " he responded.

"I was just passing through. I don't want to intrude or make any trouble for you, but I thought you might like to meet your daughter." Lifting a sleepy toddler, she said, "This is Ellen." Looking at Luke and then back at her daughter, she remarked, "Now that I see the two of you together, she looks just like you, Luke. Don't you think so?"

CHAPTER SIXTEEN
Like Manna in the Wilderness

Immediately after the funeral, when Landria told Joseph about the reading of his father's Will, he informed his stepmother he would make himself available anytime she needed him before noon on Friday. That's when he planned to leave for the weekend to see his mother in Atlanta. With this in mind, Landria scheduled the Will to be read on Wednesday afternoon. For her, the sooner the better, she needed the money.

After the Will had been read, when she fully understood how Joseph and his father had screwed her, she decided to implement an alternative strategy. Without the money from her deceased husband, she was not as rich or affluent as she deserved to be, but it would be enough. It would have to be.

Besides, she could always marry another rich fool. Finding a prosperous man to take care of her would be easy. She knew how to play the part of a desperate woman requiring a man to rescue her. Being the leading lady in a sequel to portraying Dwayne Gordon's dutiful wife wouldn't be difficult. She might even enjoy it, but she didn't have time to speculate that far into the future.

What she needed was to execute her revised plan swiftly and precisely—just like the woman always did on those old reruns of *Mission Impossible*—the show she loved to watch as a kid. The heroine always made fools out of men who thought they were smarter than she was—just like Landria did.

Unbeknownst to Joseph, while he was packing his car to leave, after his last class at noon on Friday, Landria was watching from a nearby parking lot. Just as soon as she saw him drive away, she called the movers and had them start packing. Paying a premium for this unusual request, they followed her instructions to the letter, promptly emptying the house in record time.

With Jo Ellen at the baby sitter's, it was much easier for Landria to accomplish her goal, although securing Dwayne's furnishings, which now belonged to Joseph, was not her primary purpose. It was actually quite far down on the list.

Pulling into the Panera Bread Restaurant near Vanderbilt, where she could access free wifi, she hacked into Joseph's computer, which she had been doing for months. Having his email address, she knew he used it as his user name for all of his apps. By trial and error, she figured out his password—Molly1. This discovery wasn't difficult, not with a trusting dolt like Joseph as her mark. He was so predictable. It was hardly a challenge. Once she obtained his password, which he used for everything, she had the keys to his life.

While her victim drove to Atlanta, oblivious to all that was happening in his absence, she cancelled the app that monitored her banking deposits and withdrawals. Once this was no longer functioning, she transferred her assets to another bank. Then, for safe measure, she split the assets into three different accounts, using three different banks. She reasoned that a girl could never be too careful.

While she was at it, she tried to hack into the funds from Dwayne's estate, but she had no luck. She was reluctant to do this anyway, knowing such a move could send her to prison. Being forced to screw

Dwayne for two years, while under Joseph's thumb and constant surveillance, she knew what being in prison was like, and she had no intention of being confined again.

Once she secured her funds and had two-and-a-half days to execute her plan, everything else was easy. She was much smarter than Joseph, despite his college education.

For Landria, since the reading of the Will, things had changed. Running away was no longer her primary purpose. She wanted more. She wanted to get even with the little prick that had made her life a living hell for nearly two years.

Her mistake had been marrying Dwayne in the first place. Why she thought it was a good idea still puzzled her, but that was in the past. She had weathered the storm. Her life was about to have a fresh start, and she savored the opportunity. But before her final goal could become a reality, she needed to get even with Joseph, and she knew exactly how to do it.

Two years earlier, when Joseph first came to Nashville, she had offered herself to him, but he turned her down flat, showing no interest or respect—not even an inkling. Nobody had ever treated her like that before, and she would never allow it to happen again either. *Who the hell did that little shit think he was anyway?* She ruminated spitefully.

But things were different now. She had the upper hand and, come hell or high water, she would never relinquish this position to Joseph Gordon again. By simply vanishing, depriving him of his daughter for the rest of his life, Landria realized that wouldn't be enough—not nearly enough. She needed to pull off something far more spectacular to exact the revenge that would make her even.

One time, when Molly had been at the house with Joseph in Brentwood, she mentioned that Joseph's mother was dating a doctor who had just become divorced. Because Joseph was careful to never divulge anything about Melissa, Landria suspected the doctor might be Luke, and she was right.

Once she had access to Joseph's computer, she went into his

Facebook page and looked at his friends. There—front and center—was the smiling face of Luke's whore, Melissa Gordon. Since Joseph and his mom were "Friends," Landria looked at Melissa's page, where there were numerous photos of Luke. The two of them were having fun—going to plays, football games, fancy dinners, and concerts at Chastain Park—all the things she wanted to do but couldn't, not and take care of her little brat. Added to this was all of the work required to satisfy the insatiable sexual needs of her pathetic husband. Thank God he was dead. She didn't miss him one bit. All she felt was relief that he was out of her life and would never return.

Finalizing her plans, she leased a house in Decatur, near Emory—one that was elegant but not ostentatious. By the time Joseph returned to Nashville on Sunday, she would already be in Atlanta, ready to proceed with phase two.

When Joseph found the house empty, he would think she disappeared again, but this was simply to mess with his head. The heartache her disappearance would create was just foreplay to what she intended for him. Her retribution would be sweet, and she planned to savor every moment of it. Just thinking about it made her tingle. Enjoying such thoughts—like the caresses of a new lover—she entertained her vengeful notions repeatedly.

Her plan included taking Luke away from Melissa. If Landria could accomplish this, and she knew she could, it would destroy Joseph's mother. Crushing Melissa would break her son's heart. It wouldn't even the score—not quite—but it would be a good start. She also toyed with the idea of insisting Joseph have sex with her, as a prerequisite for seeing his daughter. Landria liked this idea, insisting that he screw her first. It would create an unbearable conflict for him—one she would enjoy exacting. Just the thought of it was arousing, but she hadn't made a firm decision about this part of her plan—not yet.

∽

Once Landria discovered Luke's schedule, which wasn't difficult, she knew exactly what to do next. Showing up at his condo unannounced was a bold move, even for her, but it was necessary. By telling him Ellen was his daughter, she knew she would be granted immediate access.

Once inside, she would put Ellen down, so the two adults could talk, and that would be all she needed. Being alone with Luke for fifteen minutes, she would own him.

Her strategy worked to perfection, as she knew it would. She had Luke in bed in less than half an hour, which was exactly what she wanted. Feigning reluctance, which allowed him to be the aggressor, she accomplished exactly what she intended in record time, including her first legitimate orgasm in more than two years.

She suspected it might be easy, but she never believed it would be as easy as it was. The vixenish heroine from *Mission Impossible* would have been proud of her. Because having sex was part of her power play, she enjoyed it, but climaxing wasn't that important for her. Captivating Melissa's foolish boyfriend with her sexual prowess was.

For Landria, it was wonderful to be with a real man again, after the ordeal she had been forced to endure with Dwayne for so long. Falling asleep soon afterward, she slept until early the next morning. Her daughter, who had not slept in a comfortable bed for several nights was out like a light and slept like a log all night long.

Monday morning, Luke made breakfast for all of them. Having worked over the weekend, he had several days off and wanted to use them to get to know his daughter better. Having two college age girls by his first wife Patricia, Luke was good with kids, which pleased Landria as well as her toddler.

Leaving the breakfast cleanup for Landria, which she suggested, Luke headed out for the YMCA on Moores Mill Rd. for a quick workout before taking Ellen and her mom to the Atlanta Zoo. Because Landria had parked behind him in the driveway, he asked if he could use her car, which was blocking his. Handing him the keys, he kissed her on the cheek and left, just like a happily married couple.

As he drove, the despair Luke had experienced after Melissa ended their relationship, turned into euphoria. Seeing Joy—who wanted to be called Landria—at his front door the evening before was an answer to prayer. Devastated by Melissa's departure, he was lonely and needy, but then Landria showed up—out of the blue. She was like manna in the wilderness, making up for Melissa's departure.

But it was more than that. Luke had wondered why he had never heard from Landria again, but now he was clear about this as well. Not wanting to be a burden to him or to impact his marriage adversely, this virtuous woman left Atlanta to live in Niles, Michigan with her family. After Ellen was born, she wanted her child's father to be a part of her life. When she discovered he was divorced, she headed south to introduce him to Ellen, and he was delighted she had done so.

What would come from it, he wasn't certain. As he walked into the Y for his workout, with Landria and Ellen at his condo, he liked the way it made him feel. Landria definitely filled the void left by Melissa.

Besides, Ellen was as cute and as smart as she could be, which delighted him. Landria kept telling him how much the two of them resembled one another, but he hadn't seen it yet. Since he was the only person having sex with her at the time Ellen was conceived, she had to be his daughter. He knew that. He also knew the similarities between father and daughter would manifest themselves in time. He was certain of it. As he began pumping iron, he looked forward to spending more time with the two of them. His heart was still with Melissa, but his other appendages, now fully satisfied, were with Landria.

By the time Ernesto arrived at his friend's house, it was nearly 8 p.m. on Sunday evening. He had walked the entire way to Ansley Park, which was several miles, using secondary streets when possible to maximize his obscurity. Upon arrival, he saw that his new friend had been busy in his absence. Having nothing but the clothes he had been wearing when the accident occurred on I-285 a week earlier, Ernesto had been borrowing some of his friend's clothes ever since. Hoping Ernesto's stay might prove to be long-term, the man purchased several things for Ernesto to wear—all chic and stylish—fitting the trim, handsome Mexican perfectly.

Surprised and touched by the man's generosity, Ernesto wanted to repay his kindness, and he knew exactly how to do so. Taking his friend's hand, Ernesto led the man into the bedroom.

Being with him was something Ernesto no longer had to force himself to endure. What that said about him, other than it would send him to hell, Ernesto wasn't sure. That theft, drug running, and murder would also send him to hell was something that no longer troubled Ernesto. His conscience being seared, he hadn't thought about those mortal sins for years, but being with another man was different. Raised Catholic in Mexico, it definitely made him feel guilty. Worst of all, actively participating in gay sex was becoming easier each time. He still preferred women, of course, but being with a man who had been so generous, supportive, and caring was no longer repulsive to Ernesto.

Perhaps the man saw something in his guest Ernesto refused to see in himself. The Mexican wasn't sure. Although he was beginning to be confused about his sexual identity, at least he was alive and safe. For that, he was grateful.

After showering, the man, whose name was Daniel, picked out an outfit for Ernesto and told him they were going clubbing for the evening. Terrified of being seen in public, Ernesto balked. Sensing something was amiss; the man sat down on the couch, took Ernesto's hand, and asked why he needed to hide.

Pulling his hand away, which was too girly for Ernesto, he took a chance and outlined a sketchy summary of his past. Suspecting the man would be appalled and might even throw him out; he was surprised by Daniel's reaction. That Ernesto had been involved in organized crime for years didn't offend Daniel at all. It turned him on, which Ernesto could easily see.

Having taken a Viagra before Ernesto arrived, knowing his generosity would lead to intimacy, the forty-five-year-old man intended to be prepared, and he was. As Ernesto became increasingly revelatory, the man became aroused again, and the two had sex a second time, which didn't require a pill for Ernesto, who was quite a bit younger. This time, he was as desirous as his friend, who had come to terms with who he was long ago.

Instead of being fearful of Ernesto and his mob friends, the man loved being with someone that was so dark and mysterious. Ernesto's tales, which were real, were the most exciting thing Daniel had ever heard. When Ernesto told him about meeting his contact earlier in the evening, the Mexican showed him a wad of $100 bills that resembled a half roll of toilet paper.

Becoming thoughtful, the man took the money, stripped three bills from the wad and handed them to Ernesto. Then, Daniel asked if he should keep the remainder of the money in the safe. Liking the idea, Ernesto nodded that he would like for Daniel to do that.

With the money secure, Ernesto ended his tale by informing his friend that—like all gangsters—he had a nickname.

Becoming gleeful, Daniel's eyes lit up. He actually clapped like Liberace. Squealing with delight, he said, "Oh, how exciting. I can't wait to hear what it is. Tell me; tell me; tell me!"

Smiling, a little embarrassed by how ridiculous his nickname sounded, Ernesto admitted, "It's Tweedle-Dum."

Tickled, the man couldn't help himself. He laughed out loud, and for quite a while. "And I suppose Tweedle-Dee is the person who is after you, right?"

Instantly serious, Ernesto's smile vanished. "Yes, along with several others," he responded truthfully.

Realizing the mood had changed, Daniel's countenance changed as well. Replying, he promised, "Nobody is going to kill you Ernesto—

not as long as I'm around. If it's okay with you, I'm going to get the ball rolling. I want to take care of you permanently. I'll call a friend of mine—my former partner—to see what needs to be done to get you into the witness protection program. With what you know and can divulge, you're a perfect candidate for it."

Grateful for the help, which he needed, Ernesto smiled and nodded his assent. A minute later, his friend picked up the phone and hit five on his instant contact list.

After a long moment, a man answered. Responding, Ernesto's friend said, "Lance, can you come right over? There's someone you need to meet. It's urgent."

Curious, suspecting it might be important, Lance Rector replied, "Absolutely, I'll be right there."

In less than five minutes, Lance was out the door, headed to his former lover's house—the lover who gave him the idea of putting three rings around his penis to enhance his sexual gratification two years earlier.

CHAPTER SEVENTEEN

A "Gay Bandito Named Tweedle-Dum"

With Ellen, who was no longer called Jo Ellen after her biological father, sitting in the living room nursing her thumb, engrossed in *Sesame Street*, Landria was busy in the kitchen cleaning up. Delighted Luke had given her the chore, while he was at the Y working out, it provided her with an opportunity to rummage through his belongings with impunity. She loved snooping around while she was cleaning up. Appraising each item, one-by-one, she was deciding what she liked and what she didn't.

She certainly wasn't interested in blending families by having anything to do with Luke's daughters, but she was interested in blending accessories. She particularly liked Luke's cutlery and dishes, which surpassed the quality of those she had taken from Dwayne's house. As she was putting things away, she made a mental note to give Goodwill what she didn't want. She liked being charitable with the possessions of others. It made her feel good about herself—noble and benevolent woman that she was. But, she also intended to keep all of the receipts. They would provide her with tax deductions for each of

Luke and Dwayne's unwanted belongings.

While doing her best to figure out how to operate Luke's Italian espresso machine, which she simply adored, the front doorbell rang, startling her. Before leaving, Luke hadn't mentioned that somebody might drop by.

Walking to the door, she opened it. Stunned by who she saw, she just stood there for a long moment staring at the woman, with her mouth wide open.

Equally startled, the other woman returned Landria's stare. It was Barbara Baird. She had been driving downtown for a meeting with representatives from the DA's office, Atlanta law enforcement, and the FBI, concerning the William Steiger case. On her way, she stopped by Publix to purchase a fresh fruit basket for Luke. Her plan was to set it on his porch, along with a note, indicating how sorry she was to hear about his break up with Melissa. It was also a subtle way of letting Luke know she was there for him when he needed her. Seeing his car in the driveway and looking her best, she made a split-second decision to ring the bell, say hello, and hand him the basket in person.

When she saw the snake-tattooed vixen standing in front of her, Barbara nearly pulled a Pencil and had difficulty not wetting herself.

As both women stared knives at each other for a long moment, Barbara Baird was the first to speak. "Hello Joy," she said.

"My name is Landria. I remember you. You followed me into the ladies' room at Joni P's a long time ago." Appraising the woman with cold contempt, Landria added, "I could never forget you, but I don't know your name. What is it, anyway?"

"It's Barbara Baird—Captain Barbara Baird of the Etowah Police Department," she said, proffering her pedigree.

"Oh, I knew you were a cop. I recognized that the second you walked into the restroom," she sneered contemptuously—like being a policewoman was worse than having dog feces on your shoe. "Does Luke know you planned to stop by?"

Instantly defensive, which gave Landria the upper hand, Barbara replied apologetically, "Well, not exactly. I just wanted to drop off this basket of fruit. I know how upset Luke must be about his break-up with Melissa."

When Landria heard this, it was her turn to be surprised, which Barbara spotted, returning the upper hand to the police captain. Barbara added, "Oh, I can see you didn't know about that. Well, I didn't suspect you would. I doubt Luke would confide something like that with a woman like you, would he?"

Intent on infuriating Landria, Barbara went straight for the jugular, and it worked. Although Landria remained cool on the outside, she was definitely shaken. Responding in kind, she admitted, "No, as a matter of fact he hasn't, but I just arrived last night. We've shared a lot since then, but not that."

Upping the ante, Barbara sneered, saying, "I'm sure you have. By the way, do you still have that trashy snake tattoo slinking out of you-know-where?"

Responding instantly, Landria said, "Why don't you ask Luke about that, Captain Baird? My snake has always pleased him, but you wouldn't know about that, would you?" Looking at Barbara with mocking condescension, while maintaining a syrupy smile, Landria added, "I know what you want, but you'll never get it. What in the world would make you think that was even a possibility? You're old, wrinkled, and sooooo fake—Luke would never have anything to do with a woman like you."

Watching Barbara's reaction, Landria giggled, like a pretty cheerleader chiding a homely classmate. Landria's mirth stung Barbara worse than the insult.

Knowing there was some truth to what Landria had said, Barbara just stood there speechless. Wounded, apoplectic with rage, with her teeth clenched and her cheeks quivering, she couldn't think of a thing to say in rebuttal.

Not yet done, Landria added, "Of course, Luke is a doctor. I suppose he could write himself a prescription for a massive dose of Viagra. He would need half-a-dozen pills to get it up for a 'Two-Bagger' like you."

The two rivals continued to stare at one another for several seconds without saying a word. Finally breaking the silence, Landria concluded, "If that's all you want, I've got to get back inside and tend to Luke's daughter."

"Luke's daughter?"

"Yes, didn't you know? Of course you wouldn't, would you? Luke would never share something like that with a woman like you." Waiting for a long moment to allow her stinging barb to sink in, Landria added, "If you want to set your basket on the porch when you leave, that will be fine. I'll be sure to throw it in the trash later." With that, Landria walked inside and gently closed the door on Barbara, leaving the woman standing there, stripped of her dignity, holding an unwanted basket of fruit.

⌒∕∕∕

While Barbara Baird and Landria were engaged in verbal combat, Lance Rector walked into Detective Michael Renfro's office holding two pumpkin spice lattes. Taking one from Lance, Michael said, "If we keep meeting like this, your boyfriend might get jealous."

Without missing a beat, Lance replied, "Oh, there's no possibility of that, Detective Renfro. He knows I can do much better than you."

When Michael heard this, he laughed, nearly spilling his latte.

Looking at the detective, Lance's tone became serious. "I've got more on the Steiger case, Michael, and you're not going to believe what it is."

"Really?" Renfro asked, sitting down to enjoy his drink. "You've got my undivided attention—for at least as long as it takes to drink this latte—that is." Holding up the beverage, Renfro added, "Thanks, by the way."

"You're welcome," Lance replied. Getting straight to the point, he began. "Last night, I met one of the two men who staged Steiger's apartment to look like a murder scene. He knows exactly what happened, and he's willing to talk—naming names. Before he does, he wants our assurance he will be put in the Witness Protection Program."

Flabbergasted, Renfro put his latte down and focused intently on what Lance was saying.

Continuing, Lance added, "He wouldn't provide specifics, but he told my friend everything. We talked for a long time. I think he's credible."

Michael nodded, signaling for Lance to continue.

"He's hiding, but if we can get him a deal, he is willing to come forward with everything. What he knows will blow this case wide open, and it will end Kenyatta's run for governor before it begins. I can't make things happen around here, Michael, but you can. I'm just a CSI tech. You're a detective. I need your help with this."

"I'll have to take it upstairs, Lance. You know that? It's all I can do."

"I know, Michael, but will you try?"

Nodding his head that he would, the detective asked, "Is the guy safe?"

"Yes, he's close by, staying with my friend in Ansley Park—well out of the reach of those looking for him." Lance added, "The guy has someone from inside the gang helping him, but that won't be enough. He needs the Feds to protect him and, since this involves interstate drugs, the DEA or FBI needs to be contacted. Isn't that right?"

"That's correct, but like I said, I'll need to take this upstairs. Fortunately, I can do it today. They are having a high powered meeting about Steiger with all of the big wigs later this morning." Looking at Lance, he asked, "What's the guy's name?"

Tweedle-Dum," Lance acknowledged, as Renfro's eyebrows furrowed.

"Tweedle-Dum?"

"That's right," Lance replied. "Because he's scared, it's the only name he would provide. He thinks that if he gave his real name, the police would start looking for him, and he's right. They would."

"Okay, Lance. I'll look into it."

"Thanks, Michael. We both know this is a setup. Steiger may have killed Pretty Boy, but he certainly didn't kill his ex-wife. You know that as well as I do," Lance concluded.

Nodding his head in agreement with Lance's statement, the meeting ended.

When Lance left, the CSI tech felt like everything was finally under control, but Renfro knew this was wishful thinking. Wilbur Kenyatta wasn't about to watch his gubernatorial aspirations be dashed to the ground by an informant named Tweedle-Dum.

At the same time, Renfro knew Lance was right. Steiger probably killed Sabarisi—for which he deserved a medal—but he definitely didn't kill his ex-wife.

Proving he didn't, however, would be difficult for the suspect. What Steiger needed was a topnotch attorney—not a public defender. Too bad Pencil was broke and couldn't afford one.

After being out of town for most of the previous week, Sean Kincannon walked into the Public Defender's Office in downtown Atlanta and asked to speak with the person assigned to represent William Steiger. Being directed to the office of Dana Wallis, Sean knocked on her door and was granted admittance immediately.

After a few minutes of pleasantries, he came to the point. "Ms. Wallis, I have come to offer my services, pro bono, to defend William Steiger, if he is interested."

"Call me Dana, Sean," she replied pleasantly. "I'm not sure you know what you're getting yourself into, but cbefore we go any further, let me give you the rundown. Is that okay with you?"

"That would be wonderful, Dana," Sean replied cautiously, always nervous about stepping on the toes of another attorney.

"Normally, I would resent a big time lawyer like you sticking his nose in here—like I don't know what in the hell I'm doing—but not this time," she said, dispensing with niceties.

Surprised by her boldness, Sean liked the young lady and smiled, knowing exactly how she felt.

Returning his smile, she asked, "Before I get started, may I ask you why you want to defend Steiger for free?"

"You may," Sean replied forthrightly. "I was the man Pretty Boy Sabarisi shot on the bridge that night—the guy Steiger is charged with executing. That means if Steiger did shoot Sabarisi, the accused definitely saved my life."

When Sean said this, Dana's mouth dropped and her entire demeanor changed. She replied, "Pardon my ignorance, Sean. I really haven't had time to dig into this case the way I need to. When the incident with Sabarisi occurred, I was still in law school at the University of Tennessee, and I never heard about the details of what happened—not until recently."

Thinking this was precisely the reason Steiger needed him, Sean fudged a little when he replied, "It was only a big news story around here, Dana."

"Well, what you just said changes everything, doesn't it?" she replied warmly. "Sean, I admire you for doing this—for stepping up to the plate like this. Steiger needs someone like you. I just don't have enough clout to help him, but you might."

As she informed him of what she had gleaned from the case file, Sean listened, paying close attention to everything she had to say.

"Here's the way I see it," she said. "Do you mind me being blunt, Sean?"

"Not at all. I'm used to it," he added, referring to what living with Marla-Dean was like.

"Okay then. Wilbur Kenyatta already has Pencil—that's Steiger's nickname—tried, convicted, and sentenced to death. Kenyatta wants him to be guilty. No, it's more than that; he *needs* for him to be guilty. He's using Pencil as a way to prove he's a candidate that can be tough on crime. But so far, nothing has been based on having a fair trial, where Pencil is presumed innocent. Kenyatta's prosecuting this case, according to what the polls say the people want, which makes me sick. It's all because of Kenyatta's obsession with being the first black governor in the Deep South. Using Pencil like this really bothers me, Sean. The worst thing is, it will probably work."

Sean nodded, sharing her assessment about Steiger's chances, as well as her indignation about him being railroaded.

"Besides, Pencil is his own worst enemy. The first time I talked to him, he asked me if I watched Megyn Kelly and Greta Van Susteren on TV. When I said I didn't, he refused to say much. Until you walked in here a few minutes ago, I've been his only chance to survive, and he practically refuses to discuss the case with me. What kind of fool would do something like that?"

Sean just shook his head. He was as bewildered about Pencil's reasoning as Dana.

"Without getting any help from Pencil, my strategy has been focused on having him declared mentally incompetent. It seems like this is his only hope," she added.

"Thanks, Dana," Sean said. "From what I've read, I agree with your reasoning completely, but I would like to talk to Steiger. Can you check with him and see if he will accept my representation?"

"Certainly," she replied professionally. "I'll see to it right away, Sean." Their meeting ended soon thereafter.

True to his word, Detective Michael Renfro repeated the information he had been given by Lance Rector. Not having anything concrete to substantiate his assertions, the officials in charge didn't pay as much attention to Renfro as he had hoped they would. Essentially, they dismissed what he had to offer, saying the case was solid and they doubted a gay man could be part of a Mexican gang anyway. Nobody, including the FBI agent, had ever heard of a "gay bandito named Twee-dle-Dum," but they did thank Renfro for providing comic relief to a serious meeting.

With nothing left to do, at least for the moment, Renfro left with his tail tucked between his legs, wishing it had been Lance who made a fool out of himself instead of him.

Because of her involvement with the case against Sabarisi, Captain Barbara Baird was present. Still replaying her humiliation at the hands of "that snake tattooed whore," Barbara hadn't paid much attention to what had been said in the meeting. When Renfro interrupted, however, with his tale of a witness named Tweedle-Dum, who wanted to cut a deal, she laughed mockingly with the rest, but her humorous reaction was a ruse. She was paying rapt attention to Renfro. Although her associates dismissed the detective's information outright, forgetting it quickly, she listened intently to every word he said, committing each detail to memory.

When the meeting ended, she drove to the nearest Publix Shopping Center. Opening the trunk of her new Jaguar, she reached into the spare tire well and retrieved one of her numerous, carefully hidden throwaway phones. Dialing a number from memory, someone answered immediately, but never spoke. Repeating everything she had heard from Renfro, including the name of Lance Rector, the CSI tech in contact with Tweedle-Dum, she brought the gang up to speed. After delivering the information, she disconnected, dismantled the phone, and dumped its parts into three different trashcans, wiping her fingerprints off of each piece as she did.

On the other end, Amiglio's associate repeated the information to the drug lord, telling him nearly word-for-word what he heard from Captain Baird. Grateful, Amiglio Sabata immediately had his men stop searching in the Mexican areas of Atlanta. Tweedle-Dum was cleverer than his name indicated. Amiglio would never have thought to search for him in a gay area of town.

Now, instead of looking for Ernesto in a city of 6.5 million, the focus would be narrowed to an area where less than fifty thousand people lived. Before calling Ricardo Castillo—Tweedle-Dee—who was in charge of the hunt, Amiglio thought about who might be the inside person helping Ernesto? *Who would be willing to risk his life to save Tweedle-Dum*, Amiglio wondered?

A minute later, dialing Castillo, Amiglio gave his subordinate all the pertinent information, including the name of Lance Rector. Amiglio was careful, however, to leave out the part about Ernesto being helped by someone within his organization. Amiglio kept this piece of information to himself. Already wary, he realized his operation was in peril—all because of that damn slut he couldn't stop screwing until it was too late. He cursed himself for having been so intemperate.

When the situation was resolved, meaning when Ernesto was found and eliminated, Amiglio thought he might get some counseling. After all, Tony Soprano received therapy. Amiglio saw it on TV, and Tony was able to keep it quiet. Why couldn't he? Just as quickly, he dismissed the idea with a laugh! Amiglio Sabata whining to a shrink—it would never happen.

Having lived most of his stateside life in New Orleans, Ricardo Castillo had never heard of Ansley Park, but he soon became familiar with the area, especially with the gay section. By focusing his attention there, he narrowed the search to a small spot, where just a few thousand men lived. He also put a tail on Rector.

Thinking about Ernesto giving blowjobs made Castillo laugh. He wondered if the shoe had been on the other foot, could he have done the same thing? No, he decided. Just the thought of getting that close to a man's genitals was revolting. Besides, it was a mortal sin, Castillo reasoned, as he continued searching for Tweedle-Dum—intent on killing him.

After her short, tense conversation with Amiglio's contact person, Barbara Baird shook her head. Why these Mexican gangsters couldn't keep it in their pants was something she would never understand. First Pretty Boy and now Amiglio. Once again, her world was in danger of collapsing—all because of the dalliance of another sexually dysfunctional gangster.

Infuriated and apprehensive, Barbara went into Publix and bought two bottles of wine. As rough as her day had been—first with Landria and then with Amiglio—she intended to drain one bottle of Chablis, keeping the second on hand for backup—just in case the first one didn't accomplish the required job.

CHAPTER EIGHTEEN
"I'm Going to Have a DNA Test"

Sweaty when he returned from the YMCA, but with chiseled muscles from pumping iron, Landria was stirred by what she saw, especially after having to endure two years of a flaccid buffoon grinding away on top of her every night. Smiling at Luke as he walked up, she told him about her encounter with Barbara Baird, leaving out the part about how the two women originally met in the ladies' room at Joni P's. She allowed that to slide for obvious reasons.

Remarking that he wasn't surprised Barbara had been so brazen, Luke apologized to Landria for having to undergo such an unpleasant experience. When she told him she had called Barbara a "'Two-Bagger' to her face," Luke laughed out loud. That's just the type of humor a guy like Luke would enjoy. From then on, when they spoke of Barbara, they referred to her as "Two-Bagger" Baird, enjoying a hearty laugh each time—all at Barbara's expense, of course.

Excusing himself, Luke left to clean up. While he was in the shower, Landria put Ellen down for her morning nap. When Luke finished and was drying off, he walked into the bedroom, where Landria was waiting for him. He was surprised, but obviously delighted.

Lifting the covers, she said, "Ellen's asleep. After my horrible ordeal with that wretched woman, I need some comfort, Luke."

Dropping his towel on the floor, which Melissa would never have allowed but didn't seem to bother Landria in the slightest, he joined her. Drawing near, he kissed her. Ready to continue, she stopped him. "That's not the kind of comfort I need right now, darling," she said. Then, she gently guided his head to the spot where the snake tattoo originated.

Enjoying every moment, being completely obedient, he comforted Landria precisely the way she desired. It didn't take long for her to forget her unpleasant experience with Two-Bagger Baird.

Several minutes later, with an additional goal to be achieved once she was sated, Landria turned to Luke and said, "I've secured a fine home close to Emory. It's just as close to Peachtree Medical as your condo, but in a different direction; that's all. If you would like to join your daughter and me, we would love to have you move in with us. Would you consider this, Luke?"

Knowing how much he hated being alone, Luke jumped at the offer, telling Landria he had planned to move out of his condo anyway, having already rented it. He was careful, however, to leave out that his original plan was to move in with Melissa.

Having figured this out from her conversation with Two-Bagger Baird, Landria didn't mention it either. Instead, she smiled coquettishly, "Wonderful. Now that we've settled this, let me do something to take care of you."

After both had been satisfied, as Ellen was beginning to stir, Landria walked into the bathroom and picked up Luke's hairbrush, pulling several follicles from it. Just as he was about to ask what she was doing, Landria turned to him and said, "I'm going to have a DNA test performed to verify that Ellen is your daughter."

"Landria, you don't have to do that," Luke protested, but Landria cut him off with an insistent look.

"Yes I do, darling," she said. "A DNA test will settle any doubts you have or might ever have." Putting the strands in a Ziploc bag, she sealed it, kissed him on the cheek, and left to tend to his daughter.

Later in the day, Landria drove to her new home, where nearly everything had already been unpacked by the movers. Going into the master bathroom, she opened a box containing Dwayne's toiletries. She had intended to discard them but was glad she hadn't. Taking some loose strands from his hairbrush, she put them in a second Ziploc bag, discarding the original, which contained Luke's hair. Knowing Dwayne and Joseph had nearly the same DNA from an episode of CSI, she had an idea about how to deceive her sex-craved doctor.

As she thought about how nicely her plan was progressing, she felt satisfied with all she had accomplished in such a short period of time. Putting the hair sample in her purse, she smiled. Her deceased husband was still proving to be useful.

Driving off, she left the movers to finish their work. Returning to Luke's condo, she opened the door with the key he had already given her. Stepping inside, she began assessing his furnishings with a much keener eye, making numerous mental decisions about what to keep as she did.

c✗∂

Several weeks later, Luke developed a nasty sore on his lip. Having it checked out, his suspicions were confirmed. He had contracted genital herpes, given to him by Landria, who received it from her husband precisely the way he had infected his first wife, Melissa, years earlier. From the grave, although Dwayne Gordon had no way of knowing it, he continued to impact the living with the disease he received through his infidelity to Melissa years earlier. His STD was a gift that kept on giving, and Luke Easton was simply its latest recipient.

When Landria noticed the sore, she just shook her head compassionately and said, "I can't believe that bitch, Melissa. What an awful going away present she gave you. I'm so sorry Luke, but it will be all right. We'll just have to deal with it; that's all."

By mid-afternoon, Sean still had not heard from Dana Wallis, which made him wonder if the defendant had rejected his offer. Just as he was about to make plans to commit his time in a different way, which would have precluded helping Pencil, Sean's cell phone rang. Answering, he said, "Hello."

"Hi Sean, it's Dana."

"I was beginning to wonder if I was going to hear from you."

"Sorry about that," she said apologetically. "I couldn't get out of the office to see Mr. Steiger as fast as I thought, but I just spoke with him. I'm pretty sure he wants you to represent him."

"That's great news, Dana. I really appreciate your help. I mean it. If I can do anything for you down the road, let me know. When the time comes, you can count on me," he added sincerely.

"Maybe there's something you can do right now?" she suggested.

Intrigued, Sean asserted, "Just name it."

"You could find me a decent boyfriend—one that doesn't lie or cheat," she added, laughing.

Responding in like manner, he acknowledged, "There aren't many of those out there, are there?"

"Tell me about it," she responded, discouraged but still laughing.

Twenty minutes later, Sean was in his car, headed for the Garnett Street Pre-Trial Detention Center, where William Steiger had been remanded for the murders of Anne Morrow-Steiger and Pretty Boy Sabarisi.

About the time Sean started driving downtown, Lance finally had a moment to return Detective Renfro's call. The CSI tech had been at the scene of another gruesome murder. A Middle Eastern illegal alien had beheaded his wife for looking at another man. In his country of origin, where Sharia Law ruled, honor killings were routine and never prosecuted. Although certain to be downplayed by the media, having murdered his wife in Georgia, the man was likely to pay for the reinstatement of his honor by spending the rest of his life in a maximum-security prison, paid for by the citizens of the state of Georgia.

Once Lance had the detective on the line, he asked, "What did you find out, Michael?"

"Nothing, absolutely nothing. In fact, they laughed at me, Lance!"

"Hmmm, I was afraid that might happen."

"For us to make any progress with this, I'll need something more tangible from your informant, maybe something he can verify from the crime scene—a piece of information not reported in the news, something like that." Being firm, Renfro added, "Before I'm willing to make a fool out of myself again, I'll need information that is irrefutable. If this guy can't provide it, or is unwilling to do so, he's on his own."

"I understand, Michael." Lance answered. "I'm certain there is plenty of information Tweedle-Dum can provide. I'll get right on it; I promise." Sympathizing with what happened to the detective, Lance added, "I'm sorry I sent you up there with your pants down, Michael. As obsessed as Kenyatta is with getting a conviction, I should have known this would happen."

"I'm not blaming you. You did the right thing," Michael replied, somewhat mollified, as he hung up.

Not nearly through with gathering the evidence from the honor killing, Lance busied himself at the crime scene once again. He knew it would be late evening before he would have an opportunity to call Daniel and set up another meeting with Tweedle-Dum.

Arriving at the jail, Sean was taken to a room where William Steiger was sitting in a chair, manacled to the floor, waiting for him. Although being closely monitored, his detoxification was progressing nicely, which pleased Kenyatta's handlers.

Staring at Sean as he entered the room—before the attorney could sit down—America's Hero asked, "What's your favorite news commentary show?"

Stopping in his tracks, feigning surprise, Sean replied, Bill O'Reilly. I like Megyn Kelly and Sean Hannity too, but I can't stay awake for them most of the time. Why do you ask?" Sean replied, as if he had been surprised by the question.

Sean reasoned that if he had blurted out either Megyn or Greta's name, Pencil might have been suspicious and assumed he had been tipped off by Dana. Therefore, he chose an alternative course—one he hoped would seem credible to Steiger.

Pencil replied, "I don't like O'Reilly; he's too liberal for me, but I do like Megyn Kelly, Hannity and Greta."

"Mr. Steiger, I have a three-month-old son who gets up at 6 a.m. By the time Megyn Kelly or Sean Hannity come on, I've usually turned off the TV, but I do watch Greta sometimes."

Satisfied, Pencil changed the direction of the conversation. "So, you're the guy Sabarisi shot on the bridge that night?"

"Yes, I am," Sean acknowledged. "Before you say anything else, I need to know if you want me to represent you. That way, anything you say is considered privileged and will stay between us. Do you want me to represent you?"

Playing a little hard to get, Pencil appraised Sean for a good while. Then, he asked, "So, you played football for Vince Dooley?"

Not expecting this, Sean smiled, and said, "Damn right I did. It's better to be a Bulldog than an LSU Tiger!"

Taken aback, Pencil was stunned for a brief moment. Then, roaring with laughter, he replied, "If you can get me out of here, we can discuss that at length." As both men laughed, bonding in a way that guys do about sports—a concept women rarely understand—Pencil finally answered, "Yes, I want you to represent me. That girl doesn't know shit from Shinola about SEC football or about politics." With a knowing smile, he added, "How could she? She went to Tennessee. With you, at least I've got a fighting chance."

Taking off his coat and opening his legal-pad to jot down some notes, Sean asked Steiger to tell him exactly what happened on both nights, beginning with the first shooting.

Not having to be asked twice, Pencil proceeded, beginning with his friendship with Terrance Bruce, who was murdered by the President's men, all of whom were in cahoots with the Illuminati.

When Sean heard this, he put his pen down, thinking Steiger was not mentally competent to stand trial.

Proceeding from there, Pencil relayed to Sean how Joseph Gordon was on the bridge when Terrance Bruce's body was discovered—thanks to Pencil's anonymous call—and how concerned the young man had been about who the victim was. Sensing something was amiss; Pencil began to follow Joseph. That's when the suspect first saw Pretty Boy Sabarisi.

A while later, Pencil ran into Pretty Boy a second time—at a gas station. The man had a customized case in the back seat of his car, which Pencil was certain contained a sniper rifle. The following day, when Pencil read about Judge Bellew being murdered, Pencil was certain Pretty Boy had done it.

Picking up his pen, Sean began to make notes again; fascinated by the story he was hearing. For the moment at least, Pencil seemed quite lucid.

The night Sean was shot, Pencil had followed Joseph to Joni P's. America's Hero was waiting for Joseph to come out, when he saw Pretty Boy walk past his car. Leaving out that he was so scared he pissed his pants, Pencil related how the sniper walked up the outside stairwell of the high-rise apartment and hoisted himself onto the roof, using a small rope ladder.

When Pencil said this, Sean knew this diminutive derelict had saved his life. The rope ladder was a detail left out of the narrative by the police to keep screwballs from coming forward to take credit for shooting Pretty Boy.

Continuing, Pencil described how he followed the man and eventually confronted him, again leaving out that he had wet himself a second time. Admitting he shot Pretty Boy twice, once in the abdomen and a second time "right between the eyes," he said he was proud of what he had done.

Finally interrupting, Sean replied, "Obviously, I'm glad you did." Looking at the man in a different light, Sean added, "Thank you Mr. Steiger. Your heroism saved my life. I'm proud to represent you," Sean added. He showed his game face, which was strong, confident, and determined, while at the same time revealing vulnerability through gratitude and compassion.

Hearing this and seeing the respectful kindness Sean was professing, Pencil was stunned. He knew he had been a hero that night, but nobody had ever validated him for what he had done—not Megyn, not Greta, not Anne, not his kids, not anybody—but now Sean had. Because it was unexpected, Pencil's emotions became too much for him, and he started to sob. By doing so, he knew he wasn't being very manly, but he couldn't help himself.

Sean's eyes also misted, as he shed a tear. Finally, Sean called for a guard, asking if the defendant could be given a glass of water. Seeing the situation, the guard asked if Sean would prefer that he bring the defendant a Coke?

Surprised by the guard's magnanimous generosity, Sean said he would like that. Less than a minute later, the guard returned with two Cokes and an unopened box of Kleenex. Kenyatta had insisted Steiger be treated well, which the guards understood and had genuinely done their best to accommodate. Handing Pencil a tissue and then a Coke, the defendant regained his composure quickly.

Thanking the guard for his kindness, which gracious heroes always do, Pencil returned to his narrative. Believing Megyn Kelly would single him out of the crowd as a national hero the night she broadcasted from the bridge across from Joni P's, Pencil was crushed when she hadn't.

Listening to this part of Pencil's narrative, Sean returned to his earlier assessment. Steiger was not sane. Intent on refocusing the defendant's monologue, Sean said, "Mr. Steiger, we can go over the part about Megyn and Greta touching her hair later. For now, please skip the part about the Illuminati and move forward to the night your ex-wife was found dead at your apartment."

Doing as he had been instructed, Pencil liked that Sean was a "take charge" kind of guy. America's Hero was certain Megyn Kelly had been responsible for connecting the two of them. She knew Pencil's true value and intended to rescue her clandestine operative from the hands of the President and the Illuminati.

Continuing, Pencil fast-forwarded his narrative, saying, "Sean, I really don't know what happened. I don't even know how Anne got into my apartment, but I would never harm a hair on her head. She was an angel and, despite everything, I still loved her. We were close to getting back together. Did you know that?"

Suspecting this was untrue, Sean asked, "Can you tell me the specifics of what actually happened?"

Pencil replied, "I don't remember a thing until two cops threw me to the floor. I couldn't see. I thought they had blindfolded me, but that's not what it was. Someone put Anne's black silk panties over my eyes. Can you believe that? The elastic was tight, so I couldn't see a thing and had to breathe through my mouth."

"The police report says they found more of her panties in your drawer. How did they get there?"

"I have no idea," he whined.

Having none of this, Sean interrupted, "Mr. Steiger, if I'm going to represent you, you must tell me the truth—even the things that make you look bad. You can't lie to me about anything. Do you understand?"

"Yes, I do," he replied pitifully, caught red-handed. After taking a long moment to reflect, Pencil admitted what he had done. "All right, I took the panties from Anne's drawer the night I got the pistol from her house—the house that used to be mine."

By the way he said this, Sean recognized how bitter Pencil was about having lost his home through the divorce. Because this gave Pencil a motive to kill Anne, Sean was bothered.

Oblivious to what Sean was thinking, Pencil added indignantly, "Megyn Kelly insisted I retrieve the gun. I know that for a fact."

Learning to differentiate between what was real and what was delusional proved to be very difficult for Sean. His brain was working overtime to sort it all out.

Looking at the defendant, Sean responded, "The detail about the panties is important. It means Anne must have told the real murderer about you taking her underwear and putting them over your face. This means she must have known the man pretty well. That's not something a woman would divulge in casual conversation or to a boyfriend she didn't know pretty well."

Hearing this, Pencil was impressed. America's greatest detective hadn't thought of that, but the man sent by Megyn Kelly had. Knowing he was in good hands, Pencil made an internal commitment to be honest with Sean about everything—everything except for pissing his pants, of course. He would take that detail to his grave.

Looking at Sean, Pencil said, "I'm sorry, but that's all I know about Anne being in my apartment. But I didn't kill her, Sean. I didn't have anything to do with it." Focusing intently on his lawyer, Pencil added, "I did kill Pretty Boy, but I never would have killed Anne."

"I believe you," Sean said, standing to leave. He added, "We have a lot to do, and we need to do it quickly."

"When will you come back?" Pencil asked in his whiny voice.

"I'm not sure, but I will stay in touch. Until I return, be sure to stay put," he added with a smile.

Surprised by Sean's final words, Pencil laughed until he thought he might wet himself. As the guards took him back to his cell, Pencil sent a telepathic signal to Megyn Kelly, thanking her for sending Sean his way. Although he didn't have his UGA football helmet on for transmission, he felt pretty sure she would receive it anyway.

∞

After finishing a grueling day at the crime scene where the woman was decapitated, Lance left a message on his friend, Daniel's phone, telling him they needed to meet the following day, and Tweedle-Dum was required to attend. Disconnecting, Lance showered and collapsed into bed, totally exhausted.

Having worked late himself, Daniel didn't retrieve Lance's message until he arrived home. Looking at Ernesto, he told him they needed to meet with Lance the following day. Terrified, Tweedle-Dum balked, saying he had no intention of leaving the house until he was certain of police protection. Understanding Ernesto's fear, Daniel said he would meet with Lance and make all the arrangements.

Genuinely grateful, Ernesto hugged his friend. Then, he led the man into the bedroom once again. Lying on his stomach after disrobing, Ernesto opened himself up, no longer being reluctant. Trusting his friend completely, knowing his life depended on him; the "gay bandito" enjoyed the comfort, as he deepened his bonds with Daniel.

When all of the madness surrounding his life was over, Ernesto intended to be with a woman again—that was for sure. For the time being though, he intended to fulfill his friend's desires. What Ernesto didn't know was this act of gay intercourse would be the last sexual act he would ever experience, whether with a male or with a female.

∞

While Ernesto was satisfying his friend's needs, across town, Sean Kincannon was busy studying the police report, including the evidence obtained at the crime scene. Reading the material through the eyes of a skilled litigator, he was amazed. Based on his review, it seemed clear

Anne Morrow-Steiger had been murdered elsewhere, and Pencil's apartment had been staged to look like the crime scene. Impressed with the work of Atlanta's CSI unit, based on the evidence, Sean knew even a poor litigator could obtain an acquittal.

Yawning, fatigued after a long day, he headed for bed. While he was brushing his teeth, he made a decision. He decided to fight fire with fire. If Wilbur Kenyatta wanted to try this case in the media, so would he. Kissing Marla-Dean on the cheek goodnight, he said, "I'm going to hold a press conference tomorrow, and I think it will air nationwide."

Fading fast, Marla-Dean responded, "That's nice," as she fell asleep, oblivious to what her husband had just said.

CHAPTER NINETEEN

Intent on Making a Grand Entrance

The following morning, foregoing a stop at Starbucks, Sean arrived at his office earlier than usual. Directing his assistant, Margie, to alert the media that he was holding a press conference in the afternoon, Sean intended to announce his representation of William Steiger, who was charged with murdering his ex-wife, Anne Morrow-Steiger, and the gangster commonly known as Pretty Boy Sabarisi. Because of the media's attention, fueled by the campaign to elect Wilbur Kenyatta governor, Sean assumed there would be a modicum of interest in his news conference. After all, it would feature the defense laying down the gauntlet, but Sean wanted more attention than this.

To achieve it, he gave his assistant specific, detailed instructions concerning what she was to say to pique media interest. He told her to remind each member of the press that Steiger's attorney, Sean Kincannon, had been the target of Pretty Boy Sabarisi's failed assassination attempt. Sean suspected that with this added element of interest, attendance at the news conference would increase, perhaps substantially.

Loving the idea, as well as the challenge, Margie followed Sean's instructions to the letter. As soon as the first TV station agreed to attend, others followed suit swiftly, similar to the way teens blindly embrace a new fashion trend.

Because Wilbur Kenyatta had chosen to hold his press conference in front of the state capitol—to make him appear more gubernatorial—Sean decided to follow suit, not for political reasons, but as an affront and a challenge to the prosecution. Sean didn't like the way Steiger was being railroaded—all in an attempt to increase Kenyatta's popularity with the electorate.

Kenyatta's purpose and motivation were wrong, and Sean planned to correct the situation by pushing back vigorously. For an ethical purist like Sean, Wilbur Kenyatta had crossed the line, and Sean intended to step on the man's toes to rectify things.

Being a warm fall day, Sean scheduled his announcement for 2 p.m., which would allow sufficient time for newsrooms to edit his remarks before airing them on the local evening news. If he had made his announcement later in the afternoon, his coverage would have decreased substantially. Remembering this from his days as a prosecutor, Sean intended to make full use of the press to help Pencil's cause. Knowing the importance of obtaining positive coverage, Sean sought all the publicity he could get.

With any luck, he hoped a national show or two might pick it up, perhaps even the *Today* show or *Fox and Friends*, Marla-Dean's favorite. She watched Elizabeth Hasselbeck religiously, while breastfeeding Connor.

After providing Margie with instructions, Sean returned home and spent the remainder of the morning reviewing the material relevant to the case from his home office. Popping her head in, Marla-Dean appraised her husband's appearance with a discerning eye. Insisting he look his best, she scheduled a trimming for his thick, wavy, salt-and-pepper hair, suspecting the camera might make his hair appear bushy and unkempt. She was certain thirty minutes with Daniel at

Carcia—where she had been having his hair cut for years—would remedy any potential problem. Although Sean's day was full, he knew better than to argue with her about such matters.

While having his hair trimmed, Daniel and he chatted amiably, never coming close to discussing matters of substance, which might have changed subsequent events.

After his appointment, Sean raced home and took a shower, washing his hair thoroughly. Like all little boys, he hated having freshly cut hair down his back. It itched and would have driven him crazy.

By 1:15 p.m., he was ready. Smiling confidently at his wife as he left, she said, "I'm so proud of you, Sean," which made him feel like he was an armored knight headed out to slay a dragon.

⁊

As Sean was leaving for his press conference, Daniel walked into R. Thomas's natural food restaurant on Peachtree, located in midtown. Seeing that Lance was already seated, he walked to the table to greet him.

Looking peevish, Lance inquired, "Where is Tweedle-Dum? I told you specifically to bring him with you. I've put myself on the line for you, Daniel, and this is the thanks I get? You know I wanted him to attend this meeting."

"I know you did, Lance," his former partner replied, knowing from experience Lance was just getting started with his tirade. According to Daniel, it was the main reason they broke up. Having hurried from the salon where he had just finished trimming Sean Kincannon's hair, Daniel was equally frazzled.

"Then, why isn't he here?" Lance demanded.

"Because he's scared shitless, Lance. That's why. There are people after him, for God's sake. They intend to kill him, and he knows it. He refuses to leave the house until some kind of deal has been worked out. You can understand that, can't you?"

Pissed that he had wasted his time for a meaningless rendezvous, Lance asked, "Why didn't you just call me and tell me this? We could have set up a time for me to come by your house later. It's not like I don't know where you live." Calming down somewhat, he added, "Daniel, you have no idea how swamped I am."

"I'm sorry, Lance. I really am, but I promised Tweedle-Dum I would handle this for him," Daniel added, defensively.

"All right, but I don't have time to go to your place right now. When should I come?"

"What about early this evening? Would that be all right? Say seven o'clock?" Daniel asked.

"That will work," Lance agreed. Having the waiter put his vegetable plate in a to-go box, he ended the meeting abruptly.

Not having time to eat, Daniel drove home to tell Ernesto what was happening before he headed back to the salon for his 3:30 p.m. appointment. He knew he could have just called, but he wanted to check on Ernesto to make certain everything was okay. Daniel was a bit controlling, which is why he and Lance broke up, if you were to believe the CSI tech's side of the story.

Arriving home a few minutes later, Daniel explained what would transpire that evening. Ernesto, the "gay bandito," was relieved things would get moving quickly, and he would be safe. At the front door, as Daniel was leaving, Ernesto hugged his benefactor long, hard, and tight, with both of his hands solidly gripping the man's derriere, drawing him near, which the hairdresser loved. Although aroused, a moment later, Daniel scurried to his car to return to the salon.

Ernesto felt bad about refusing to leave the house for the luncheon, especially since he was about to leave for an appointment in a few minutes anyway. It was a meeting Daniel didn't know about, and Ernesto wanted to keep it that way, at least for the time being. Earlier in the day, Ernesto had heard from his contact, who was prepared to give him the $100,000. They had agreed to meet at the same Barnes & Noble, exactly like they had the first time. Their meeting was set for 5 p.m.

Knowing the contact would last just long enough for the money to be handed off, Ernesto was confident he would be back in plenty of time to make the 7 p.m. meeting with Lance and Daniel, even though it was a long walk. Daniel wouldn't even realize he had left until Ernesto handed him the additional funds to be put in the safe later in the evening.

Feeling guilty for having caused so much trouble, Ernesto planned to keep his clandestine meeting a secret all along. It would have made Daniel upset, which he didn't want, but he knew how to make it up to him.

Regardless of whether or not Daniel would be upset, Ernesto had to go. He had no alternative. His long-term survival depended on obtaining the money, and he knew it.

What Daniel didn't know, and never suspected, was that he had been followed from R. Thomas by one of Amiglio's men. Members of Sabata's organization had been tailing Lance ever since receiving Captain Baird's tipoff, alerting them to Ernesto's whereabouts.

When Lance met with Daniel, one car followed the CSI tech, while the second followed the other man. Being patient and cautious, the car following Daniel parked up the street while the hairdresser was in the house. When the man left a short time later, Ricardo Castillo, aka Tweedle-Dee, spotted his former partner in crime. When he saw Ernesto, he couldn't believe what he was witnessing. Ernesto was actually hugging the man at the front door—not like guys hug after a soccer game, but like a guy would hug his girlfriend—with his hands grabbing the man's ass. Ricardo just shook his head in contemptuous disbelief.

Having accomplished the goal of finding Ernesto, his former-accomplice felt satisfied. Nevertheless, he still found it difficult to believe that Ernesto was having sex with a man.

Making a quick call with his disposable phone, Castillo said, "Got him." Disconnecting immediately, he watched Daniel drive off. No longer important, Castillo allowed Tweedle-Dum's lover to go on his merry way. As the man drove past, without turning his head toward the crouching gangster, Castillo smiled. He knew that fag wouldn't be getting any more blowjobs from Tweedle-Dum. Those days were over.

∽

Having nursed a wicked hangover all morning, shortly after eating a sparse lunch, Barbara Baird began to feel normal again. The night before, one bottle of Chablis hadn't done the trick for her, so she drank a great deal of the second one. The alcohol helped numb her humiliation, but not completely. Still vexed, she decided to call Melissa.

When the head nurse's phone vibrated at the ER, Melissa checked to see who was calling. When "Barbara" flashed on the screen, Melissa's first instinct was to ignore the call, but she couldn't. Maintaining her deception was essential to ensure Joseph's safety, so she answered frostily, "Hello, Barbara."

"Melissa, I know you're not really interested in talking to me. I wouldn't have called if it wasn't important, but there's something I think you should know," Barbara announced.

"I'm listening," Melissa responded.

A little embarrassed to admit what she had done, Barbara continued nonetheless. "Yesterday morning, as I was headed downtown for a meeting, I stopped by Luke's condo with a fruit basket—just to cheer him up," she said nervously, hoping Melissa wouldn't hang up.

Melissa didn't respond, but it was obvious Barbara had piqued her former-friend's curiosity. Continuing, Barbara announced, "When I saw Luke's car parked in the driveway, I decided to ring the bell, rather than just leave the fruit basket on his porch." With no response from Melissa, which Barbara didn't expect, she added, "When I did, you'll never guess who answered the door?"

Barbara waited expectantly, hoping Melissa would ask who it was, but there was nothing but silence on the other end. Persevering, Barbara announced, "Melissa, it was Joy—the woman with the snake tattoo—the woman who seduced Joseph a couple of years ago."

"What?" Melissa exploded, now fully engaged.

"It was her, Melissa, standing right there in front of me with Luke's 'daughter' watching TV in the living room." Barbara added, "I didn't get a good look at the child, but I saw a toddler sitting on the couch, watching cartoons or something."

"I don't believe it," Melissa replied out of surprise—not out of disbelief.

"It was her, Melissa. I know it was. She called herself Lenora or something like that," Barbara added.

"Landria," Melissa corrected, knowing instantly she had made a mistake.

Allowing Melissa's correction to pass, but keeping it in the back of her mind, Barbara continued the conversation by saying; "It was such a humiliating experience, Melissa. It really was."

Knowing Barbara wanted sympathy, which she was not about to provide, Melissa cut her off, saying, "I'm on duty, Barbara. I have to go. Thanks for calling." With that and nothing else, she disconnected.

Barbara, who was just warming up, was offended but, without recourse, she closed her cell, muttering obscenities about what a heartless bitch Melissa really was.

Arriving at the state capitol early, Sean stayed in his car, fully intent on making a grand entrance to his press conference. When he was a prosecutor, he hated it when defense attorneys strutted up to the cameras. They seemed so pompous, phony, and arrogant. Having a swagger, they always seemed to be inordinately consumed with themselves. Worst of all, nearly all of them wore their hair in ponytails. What that was all about Sean still had never figured out. If he started to grow one, Marla-Dean wouldn't put up with it—not for one minute. Neither would his hairdresser, Daniel.

Now that he was a defense attorney, and the proverbial shoe was on the other foot, the pomp seemed to come more naturally. He fully intended to exploit it to his client's advantage. When the time seemed perfect, Sean sauntered up to the podium, which his assistant, Margie, had commandeered from another attorney's office for the occasion.

The defense attorney suspected his press conference would be well attended, but he really had no idea what awaited him. In addition to the local affiliates and radio stations, CNN and FOX News attended, as well as reporters from the *Atlanta Journal* and *Constitution*. Looking dapper and well groomed—thanks to Marla-Dean and Daniel—Sean surveyed the twenty-five faces that awaited.

Taking command, Sean announced, "Good afternoon ladies and gentlemen. Thank you for coming. I want to announce that I have agreed to defend William Steiger, who has been falsely accused of murdering his ex-wife, Anne Morrow-Steiger, and the gangster commonly known as Pretty Boy Sabarisi. As to the charge, Mr. Steiger is no guiltier of murder than you or I. The charges are unfounded, which the prosecution knows full well. In fact, the government should never have charged my client in the first place. Mr. Steiger is innocent of any wrongdoing, and we intend to prove it."

Pausing for a moment to make eye contact with each of the rolling cameras, Sean continued. "My client, Mr. Steiger, has been set up to take the fall for someone else, which we intend to prove, despite the fact that the burden of proof rests with the prosecution. At least, that's the way it's supposed to work but, in this case, it isn't working like that at all."

Fully intent on dealing the political aspirations of his opponent a blow, Sean pointed his finger toward the state capitol and asserted, "The District Attorney, Wilbur Kenyatta, in an effort to generate political support for his gubernatorial bid, has filed charges he knows cannot be substantiated—not based on the relevant facts. His actions are motivated by his lust for political gain, and it all comes at the expense of an innocent man. Ladies and gentlemen, I will not allow this miscarriage of justice to happen. Truth will prevail, of that, I can assure you. This is why I am standing here before you today— to ensure that justice triumphs, my client is vindicated, and his good name is restored."

Concluding Sean announced, "Make no mistake about it, Mr. Steiger is not going to prison for the rest of his life, just to ensure that Wilbur Kenyatta becomes the next Governor of the great state of Georgia." Pausing for a moment, after having completed his statement, Sean said, "Thank you for listening. If there are any questions, I will be happy to answer them."

Thrilled by Kincannon's blunt boldness, the press, always loving a conflict, asked numerous questions for the following twenty minutes. Sean answered each candidly and to the best of his knowledge, often repeating himself in the process. When the hubbub finally died down, he stepped away from the lectern and walked away, looking like a victorious hero sauntering off into the sunset at the end of a movie.

Later, inside the jail, the guards allowed the defendant to watch the clip of the news conference that was aired that evening on the 6 p.m. local news. Mesmerized as he watched it, along with the way Morse Diggs reported it, Pencil had a difficult time sitting still. Finally, America's Hero was getting the notoriety and attention he deserved. After dinner, as he was led back to his cell, he started thinking about the statue that would be made of him and the street that would bear his name. He hadn't thought about either of those things for a long, long time, but now that was all he thought about, as he drifted off to sleep.

CHAPTER TWENTY
"She Uses Sex Like It's a Commodity"

Remembering Joseph was taking an important test in the early afternoon, Melissa waited until her shift was finished before informing him about her disturbing but enlightening exchange with Barbara Baird. Knowing the conversation would be intense; she decided to drive home before calling. When she did, it was shortly after 4 p.m.

Answering immediately, Joseph said, "Hi, Mom."

"How did your test go," she asked cheerfully, delighted to be talking to him regularly once again.

"I aced it. I wasn't really worried; it's an easy class." Changing the subject, he said, "I haven't been able to discover anything about where Landria took Jo Ellen, I can't believe this has happened, but I'm not going to give up looking for my daughter. I'll never give up, Mom."

"That's why I'm calling, son," Melissa interrupted. "I've stumbled upon something."

Stunned, he replied, "You Have? What?"

Not having to be coaxed, Melissa related the conversation she had earlier in the day with Barbara Baird. Listening intently, Joseph didn't interrupt even once.

When Melissa completed her long narration, Joseph asked, "So, Landria is in Atlanta? She's living in Atlanta? Are you sure?"

"Apparently she is, Joseph, at least for now. What really surprises me is that she's already living with Luke. I'm sure Barbara was telling me the truth. She was enjoying herself too much for it to be a lie. She loved hurting me, which it did. I'm having a hard time with this, son. Everything has happened so fast," she said, as her voice cracked, and she came close to crying.

"I know, Mom. I'm so sorry," he said, consolingly.

Fighting back tears, she continued. "Joseph, I'm having to rethink many things I once believed about Luke. I trusted him completely, but now this. It stings, son. It really does; it's just too much to handle all at once. When I get off the phone, I'm going to have a good cry," she admitted.

Melissa had never before spoken this straightforwardly to Joseph. For him, it signaled that she was treating him like an adult for the first time, which he loved. Her candor surprised him, but he definitely welcomed it. After she finished, neither spoke for quite a while, but neither felt awkward. Both had so many emotions to process that remaining silent seemed appropriate.

Just a few days before, Luke had been planning to move in with Melissa. Now, he was living with another woman—that snake tattooed bitch who had not only seduced her son but also her ex-husband. Dealing with such a bizarre set of circumstances was difficult for Melissa. It was equally difficult for Joseph.

As Melissa continued to think about it, she didn't think she had ever heard of anything quite so trashy as this in her entire life, and it was happening in her own family. She was glad her mother wasn't alive. Melissa would never have heard the end of it.

The situation not only felt icky but it also felt incestuous. To say Melissa was not a happy camper would have been a massive understatement.

Finally breaking the silence, Joseph speculated, "I don't get it, Mom. If Landria wanted to disappear, why would she move back to Atlanta?" Thinking about it for a moment, he added, "And why would she reconnect with Dr. Easton? Doesn't that seem a little odd to you?"

"It certainly does. Perhaps disappearing wasn't her real intent," Melissa replied insightfully. " Maybe, she just wanted to mess with your head—to rattle you by leaving the way she did."

"I was just wondering the same thing. I think you're right. I don't believe being with Dr. Easton is that important to her. She just wants to hurt me," he said, coming to a conclusion that few young men would have the maturity to deduce.

Committed to getting to the bottom of things, Melissa said, "Joseph, tell me what you know about Landria. Start from the beginning, and don't leave out any details. Don't worry about hurting my feelings. This is very important. I need full disclosure." She asked, "Can you do that, son?"

"Definitely," he replied, relieved to have the opportunity to finally put the rest of pieces of the puzzle on the table. "Most of what I know is from Sean. He did some serious digging. Landria's real name is Lulu Bobo, and she was born in Ty Ty, Georgia."

"What? You're kidding me?" Melissa interrupted in disbelief—just like everybody else did.

In spite of the seriousness of the conversation, Joseph laughed. "When I heard it the first time, it surprised me too." Continuing with what he knew, Joseph told Melissa about Landria's mother, two sisters, and uncle, all living in a double wide in Ty Ty, between Tifton and Sylvester. Fulfilling his commitment to be completely candid, he told her about the uncle's molestation of Landria, including how she ran away after belting the guy in the head with a cast iron frying pan, leaving him unconscious and close to dead, in a puddle of blood.

When Joseph mentioned this, Melissa interrupted him. "Oh my goodness," she acknowledged. "Knowing these details changes everything."

"Why?"

"It means we are probably dealing with a 'borderline'—maybe worse," she replied.

"A borderline?" he questioned. "What's a borderline?"

"It's called a borderline personality disorder, and it's a serious mental and emotional imbalance," Melissa explained. "Knowing this confirms what I've suspected. She's a pathological liar, and she uses sex like it's a commodity. She's also terrified of abandonment. These are common characteristics of BPD. She's a very sick woman, Joseph."

"So, it's more than her just being mean and hateful?" he asked rhetorically. "Then, how do we deal with it?"

"That's a great question. There isn't an easy answer," Melissa asserted. "But, it does explain her irrationality. You see, Joseph, she doesn't see things the way other people do—the way you and I would, for example. She looks at life from the prism of her twisted, tormented reality. Being in a relationship with a woman like this is like walking on eggshells. Worst of all, she will never change; she can't."

"That's exactly what Dad said—his life was like 'walking on eggshells.' Can't she get help?" Joseph asked.

"Sure, the problem is she doesn't think there's anything wrong with her. You're the one with the problem—not her," Melissa explained. "Borderlines never change, which means dealing with her about Jo Ellen's welfare is going to be very dicey."

"I know. What a mess." Joseph concluded. "I actually feel sorry for Dr. Easton, don't you?"

After thinking about it for a long moment, Melissa replied, "No. No, I don't. He's simply reaping what he has sown. So are we, Joseph."

࿊

When Ernesto walked out of Daniel's house at 4 p.m., knowing he had quite a hike to Barnes & Noble and back, he wore sneakers. Being careful to lock the door, he headed down the street cautiously, planning his route as he did. Determined to use as many back roads as possible, he tried to think of all the things he could do to keep from being spotted. He thought about calling a cab, but that might be dangerous. The only thing that made him feel safe was knowing Amiglio's men would be searching for him in the Mexican areas of Atlanta and not in the gay areas.

He felt pretty good about all the precautions he had taken. As he rounded the first corner, however, a man stepped out from behind a large tree, hidden by thick shrubs, and tasered him. Ernesto never saw it coming. Dropping to the ground like a stone, the man grabbed Ernesto under both arms and began dragging him toward the street—just as a panel truck pulled up. Hoisting Ernesto inside, aided by two others, the door shut quickly, and the truck drove off at a normal rate of speed. From start to finish, the kidnapping required less than fifteen seconds. It was done so quickly nobody witnessed a thing.

Securing Ernesto in the vehicle, the truck merged onto the surface street, blending into traffic, and drove off. Thirty minutes later, it pulled into an abandoned warehouse, where Amiglio Sabata was waiting to greet the gay bandito.

As Ernesto's senses began to return, he felt the rough, grooved steel floor of the truck-bed beneath him, which was particularly uncomfortable. At first, he couldn't figure out what had happened. Everything seemed blurry and foggy, but then—in a moment of clarity—he understood. It was at that precise instant Tweedle-Dum knew his life was over.

As he was lying there, stark terror consumed him. He started shivering, despite the summer heat and the stale air in the truck with its air conditioning turned off.

A few minutes later, he was pulled from the vehicle, stripped naked, placed face down on his stomach, and tied to four posts. He resembled a starfish out of water. Although he didn't know what was about to happen, he knew it wouldn't be pleasant.

Then, someone talked to him. It was his old accomplice, Ricardo Castillo. "Hello, Ernesto. Are you awake? Do you know who this is?"

"Si, it's you, my lifelong friend, Tweedle-Dee," Ernesto replied; in a weak attempt to regain the allegiance of his former ally.

"That's right. It's Tweedle-Dee, your old friend. But you've been a bad boy, Ernesto. You know that, don't you?"

"Yes, Ricardo, I know that. I'm so sorry. It will never happen again," Ernesto promised in a pleading tone.

"I know it won't," Ricardo replied confidently. "What do you think your punishment should be for being such a bad boy, Ernesto?"

"Please, for the love of God, Ricardo, be merciful," Ernesto pleaded, knowing the consequences of his betrayal were imminent.

"Of course, I'll be merciful, my old friend. What else would I be?" he asked. "I understand you've become gay—that you like to suck cocks and take it up the ass. Is that true, amigo?"

"No, Ricardo, no. I am not gay. I was just pretending so that I could hide. That's all," Ernesto replied pitifully.

"Are you sure, Ernesto?"

"Si, mi amigo; I'm sure." Terrified, Tweedle-Dum was doing his best to remain calm, but it was becoming increasingly difficult. Being blindfolded added to his apprehension.

"I have to be honest with you, amigo. I'm not convinced. I think I'll have to see for myself."

With that, Amiglio's men began to torture Ernesto, nearly killing him in the process. Finally finished, Ernesto was left to lie there, as his tormentors went outside to laugh about what they had done, smoking and having a soft drink as they did.

Exhausted and incapable of taking anything more than shallow breaths, Ernesto wanted to sleep or to try and make himself more comfortable, but he couldn't. His limbs were stretched in four different directions, and he felt something warm beneath him, which he was certain was his own blood.

While lying there, waiting to be murdered, he heard the footsteps of a large man wearing leather shoes, walking toward him.

"Hello, Tweedle-Dum," Amiglio Sabata said pleasantly.

Recognizing the voice, Ernesto began to cry, pleading his case. "Amiglio, I'm sorry. Please don't kill me. If you spare me, I'll be your most trusted servant for the rest of my life. I promise I will."

"Silence, you mongrel," Amiglio commanded. Ernesto obeyed instantly, although he continued to whimper. Bending close to Ernesto's ear, Amiglio said, "You have one chance, and here it is. Tell me who your contact person is on the inside? If you do, there will be no more torture. We will kill you quickly and mercifully. I promise."

Crying, Ernesto knew his fate was sealed, but unwilling to endure further torture, he confessed, "It is your wife, Amiglio. It's Gabriela."

"What?" Amiglio said, standing straight up in disbelief. "You lying fag. You missed your chance." Turning to the men outside, Amiglio yelled, "Hombres, aqui."

Instantly, they stepped on their cigarette butts and hastened back.

Knowing what was about to happen, Ernesto panicked, yelling, "I'm telling you the truth, Amiglio. I'm supposed to meet her at five o'clock this afternoon to get some money and disappear."

Curious, Amiglio held up his hand for the men to stop, which they did. Bending down, he asked, "Where are you supposed to meet her?"

"At the Starbucks at Barnes & Noble on Peachtree Street in Buckhead," Ernesto admitted, truthfully.

Activating the GPS app on his iPhone, Amiglio put in the code for Gabriela's Mercedes. The app allowed him to know where she was at all times, if he needed her, which he never did. It showed her car parked at 3300 Peachtree Rd., adjacent to the Barnes & Noble bookstore. Looking at his watch, he saw that it was 5:15 p.m.

Turning his attention to Tweedle-Dum, he said, "Thank you, Ernesto. You were telling me the truth after all, and I will keep my word. Your suffering is over. Sleep well, mi amigo."

With that, one of the men was called and a hefty dose of Diazepam was injected into an exposed vein on Ernesto's arm. Immediately, the man fell into a deep sleep, from which he never awakened.

✑

Once Sean's press conference hit the airways—both on TV and the radio—the response was overwhelming, as people interested in the case, as well as the gubernatorial race, paid close attention. When asked to make a comment, Wilbur Kenyatta said Kincannon's statement was "irresponsible, defamatory, and false." He went on to say, "Under no circumstances would I or anybody in my office ever make a charge, whether serious or slight, that is fallacious. Mr. Steiger's guilt or innocence has absolutely nothing to do with any plans I may—or may not have—about running for Governor. To intimate that it does is reprehensible and offensive. I demand an apology from Mr. Kincannon."

It was obvious Sean had gotten under Kenyatta's skin. This added to the drama, which helped escalate the media's interest. This was precisely what Sean had hoped would happen. Kenyatta actually said a lot more, but this was the sound bite that played statewide and beyond, being broadcasted numerous times throughout the day and into the next.

Sean's plan was working. As the rhetoric continued to escalate, so did people's awareness about Pencil's situation, which was in his client's best interest. When the producer of *The Kelly File* learned of the events in Georgia, she planned a short segment for the evening program. Calling Captain Barbara Baird and Dr. Big Shot, who had been frequent guests since the original murder of Pretty Boy two years earlier, Ceci Drawdy booked both of them. When asked to appear or make a statement, Wilbur Kenyatta declined in favor of appearing on MSNBC.

Hoping to book Sean Kincannon, the producer called his cell numerous times. Since it went to voicemail consistently, Kelly's producer assumed the lawyer had turned it off for some reason, but she couldn't imagine why—not with all the free publicity it would generate.

But that's exactly what had happened. Sean had turned his cell phone off. Marla-Dean, Connor, and he had a longstanding engagement for the evening that couldn't be broken—at least, not according to Marla-Dean. As it turned out, her deceased husband's parents were in town, and they wanted to meet Sean and Connor, especially the baby. They wanted to see the boy that should have been their grandchild.

Their son, Grayson, was Marla-Dean's first husband. She loved him dearly, as well as his parents, who were wonderfully supportive people. Since their son died years earlier of an unexpected heart attack at the age of thirty, Marla-Dean was all they had left of him, but she had moved on. Because he was their only son, Marla-Dean kept in contact with Grayson's parents throughout the years. They were in town, and this was their only opportunity to meet Connor.

Although Marla-Dean realized it would be awkward, she agreed to meet them for an early dinner in Alpharetta. As it turned out, there couldn't have been a worse day for this, but life is frequently inconvenient.

Since Sean had abdicated the role of "Cruise Director" to Marla-Dean from day one of their marriage, he just did as he was told, even when it was problematic—like the event she had planned for that afternoon. For him, keeping his promises was more than being a good husband; it was an integral part of his recovery.

Knowing his cell phone would be ringing off the hook by media outlets desiring an interview, Sean decided the best way to make his wife happy was to turn it off. Knowing the press the way he did, he suggested she turn hers off as well, which she did begrudgingly. Because they were going to be out for the evening, Marla-Dean also gave Winky the night off, which pleased her young au pair.

The Kincannons headed north at 4:30 p.m., knowing the traffic would be a nightmare on Georgia 400. It always was in the late afternoon. Their goal was to make it home by 8 p.m., so that Connor could be put to bed at his normal time.

As they passed I-285, traveling slowly outside of the perimeter, Marla-Dean gasped, just like she always did when she forgot something. Turning to her husband, she said, "I forgot the camera, Sean. I wanted to shoot some video of Connor with Grayson's parents. Now, what will I do?"

"I guess you'll just have to use your iPhone. It's equipped for that," he replied.

"Damn it. I suppose that will have to do. Winky and I had the camera all set to take some really high quality video." Turning to him, she asked, "I don't suppose we have time to turn around, do we?"

Without commenting, Sean simply snorted his response, which let her know that wasn't an option.

CHAPTER TWENTY-ONE
"I Will Bring You Down"

After picking up the house, folding laundry, feeding Asta, and vacuuming, Winky was ready to call it a day. Having the evening off, she planned to eat chicken Parmesan at Pasta Vino, a restaurant just a couple of blocks from the house. Since it was still early, she decided to drop by Barnes & Noble first to see if Hal Lindsey's new book on prophecy had arrived.

Winky was very concerned about the survival of Israel, and Lindsey's treatise provided a unique perspective about what the Persians, Assyrians, and Egyptians were planning, all based on biblical prophecy. Reading it would give Winky the upper hand in discussions with Sean and his ignoramus sponsor, which was something she greatly desired.

Arriving at 5:45 p.m., she was delighted to see the book was in stock. Sitting down, she became intrigued by what she read—oblivious to what was happening around her. As she began Chapter 2, which traced Syria's checkered past, going back as far as to the time of Solomon, she was interrupted by a woman's voice.

"Hello, do you remember me? I was the woman you gave the ring to not long ago."

Surprised to have been approached, Winky was thrilled to see the woman. Winky still had not come to terms with parting with her favorite piece of costume jewelry. As she said hello to the smiling woman, Winky started to think of a gracious way to ask for its return.

Smiling, the woman asked, "May I sit down for a minute?"

"Certainly," Winky replied. "It's so nice to see you again. My name is Winky Weller, by the way."

"And I am Gabriela Sabata, Winky. It's so nice to put a name with the face of someone as loving and generous as you," Gabriela replied graciously.

Winky was surprised by the woman's genuine warmth. She decided to chat for a while, before asking for her ring. As they talked, Winky noticed that Gabriela was well mannered and well spoken. In her early fifties, Winky could tell Gabriela must have been very beautiful in her youth. Even now, she had a regal elegance, despite the deep stress lines that suggested either hardship or sadness.

Returning Winky's look, the woman reached for the young lady's hand and said, "The day you gave me your beautiful ring was one of the worst days of my life. I felt so hopeless, but then you walked up. With love in your eyes and generosity in your heart, you said you had a gift for me from God. Winky, I was so surprised I couldn't say a thing. You probably didn't think I could speak English well enough to understand what you said, but I do. I understand English very well."

As her eye misted, Gabriela continued, "For me, it was truly a miracle. I felt so lost and alone, but you reminded me that God still loves me. Whenever I doubt that, I just touch the ring you gave me and rub it. Then, I feel strong again."

Holding up her hand with a grin, Gabriela showed Winky the ring she had proudly worn since that evening. Flabbergasted, Winky abandoned her intention to ask Gabriela for its return, knowing Joyce Meyers had been right. God had used her sacrificial gift for a higher purpose. Mortified by her selfishness and lack of faith, Winky scolded herself for being so petty, while simultaneously smiling at Gabriela.

Unaware of Winky's thoughts, Gabriela continued. "I am a good, God-fearing woman who has seen incredible evil for years. My husband is a drug dealer, and he has done many terrible things. The night you approached me, I was at the end of my rope and didn't know what to do. But you helped me make a decision—a decision to fight against my husband's evil—not just that day but from that day forward."

As she was getting deeper into her story, four teens from Westminster High sat next to them. Laughing and carrying on, exactly the way normal teens do in a store, they talked loudly, when being quiet was required. Gabriela became reluctant to continue.

Sighing, she said, "I would really like to talk further, but what I have to say isn't suitable for these young people, and they are being too loud for you to hear me whispering."

Without giving it a second thought, Winky suggested, "I live just around the corner. We could talk there. I can make a pot of coffee and a sandwich if you like?"

Knowing how badly she wanted to talk to her godly benefactress, Gabriela smiled, nodded her head, and indicated she would enjoy that. "My car is right outside, Winky. Should I follow you?" Gabriela asked.

"I've got a better idea. Let's go in my car, and I'll bring you back later. Would that be alright with you?"

"Certainly, that would be fine."

Putting Hal Lindsey's book back on the shelf to be purchased later, Winky left the history of the Assyrian Kingdom for another day. That evening the Lord was about to use her in a special way, and she knew it.

Ten minutes later, Gabriela Sabata was sitting at the Kincannon kitchen table, pouring out her heart and her life to an American woman in her late-twenties, and it was all because Winky had displayed genuine compassion and caring by giving away her ring.

Having made tea, which Gabriela preferred, Winky served a ham and Swiss sandwich with potato chips. Gabriela ate her tasty supper eagerly, while her hostess just nibbled. When they were finished, Winky suggested they go into the office to continue their discussion, which appealed to Gabriela.

As they sat in Sean's office, Gabriela told Winky about being the witness to her husband's criminal activities for years. At one point, Gabriela spoke for nearly an hour without interruption. As Winky was listening, she continued to feel ashamed for having been so petty, for having wanted her ring back so badly. It was worth so little, and yet it had already accomplished so much.

When Gabriela was finally finished, she sighed, relieved to have unburdened her soul. Looking at Winky, she added, "I've been trying to help one of my husband's men break free from his life of crime. I was supposed to meet him at the bookstore at 5 p.m., but he never showed up. I'm worried sick about him."

"I'm sure he will get in touch with you, Gabriela. Maybe he forgot," she suggested.

Looking at Winky incredulously, Gabriela said, "When I have $100,000 for him? I don't think so."

"Oh," Winky replied, startled. She added, "He would never forget about a meeting like that, would he?"

"Hardly," Gabriela replied, laughing. Becoming serious again, she said, "I'm afraid something has happened to him. My husband's men have been searching for him for days."

Winky interjected, "I'm concerned about your safety, Gabriela. From what you've told me, you could be in danger."

"I really don't think so, but I don't care anymore." Concluding, she added, "I've sent my boys off to school. Keeping them out of my husband's business is my only reason to live."

Before I take you back to your car," Winky said, "I want to try and call my boss one more time." Dialing Sean and then Marla-Dean for the tenth time each, she sighed, realizing they still had their cell phones turned off.

As Gabriela and Winky walked out of the house to get into the car, Gabriela turned and gave her new friend a big hug, holding her tight for a long moment. Brushing back a tear, she told Winky how special she was.

When they drove back to Barnes & Noble, Winky turned into the entrance adjacent to Publix. Intending to drop Gabriela off at her car, the woman told Winky to stop and let her out.

"I've got a long drive home," Gabriela said, "but I don't have any half & half for my husband's coffee in the morning. I'll just run in and get some. Thank you so much for welcoming me into your home and for providing me with so much love and acceptance."

"You're welcome, Gabriela," Winky replied. "I wish it was my house, but it's not. I actually live in the apartment above the garage, but it was more comfortable for us to talk in the main house."

With that, as Gabriela got out of the car to head into Publix to buy cream and a few other items, Winky handed her a note with her name and address on it.

By the time Gabriela finalized her purchase and walked to her car, Winky had already returned home.

When Gabriela raised her hand out to click the door open, Ricardo Castillo said, "Ola, Gabriela."

Frozen with fear, Gabriela didn't say a word.

Knowing how this would play out, Castillo simply opened the door to the panel truck that was parked next to Gabriela's Mercedes, gestured for her to get in, and said, "Entra, Gabriela."

Handing the keys of her Mercedes to Castillo, as well as her sack of groceries, she entered the panel truck without protesting. Assisting her, Castillo held out his hand for her bag, which she gave to him as well.

Signaling for one of the men to drive Gabriela's car, they left the parking lot at Barnes & Noble without incident, headed out of the city.

Realizing there were no loose ends with Tweedle-Dum, Castillo thought they might survive the consequences of Amiglio's sexual indiscretion with the gringo woman. The gay bandito had not yet given a statement to the authorities and, unless they were mistaken, neither had Amiglio's wife, Gabriela.

When Daniel returned home from the salon, he was shocked to discover Ernesto absent. Suspecting foul play, he checked the doors, windows, and anything else he could think of that might suggest his lover had been kidnapped. But nothing was amiss. Everything was as it should be, except for Ernesto being absent.

Becoming extremely apprehensive, he raced to the safe. Suspecting he had been played, he thought the $10,000 would be gone, as well as everything else in the safe, which contained many valuables. When he opened it, he sighed with relief. Everything was still there—just as it had been—including Tweedle-Dum's money, which was the $10,000, minus three $100 bills.

Wondering if Ernesto had become tired of being cooped up, he thought he might have gone for a walk. So, Daniel drove around the neighborhood, Piedmont Park, and the shopping center several times, hoping to spot him, but he never did.

At 7 p.m., Lance arrived. When he told him what had happened, Daniel was close to hysteria. Lance knew Tweedle-Dum's return was highly unlikely. Lance didn't want to seem callous by congratulating Daniel for having made $9,700, but it was the truth. As behind as Lance had been financially, he wished some Latin lover would pop into his life for a few days, have wild sex, hand over a huge wad of cash, and leave with no strings attached, but Daniel was the kind of guy who had that kind of luck—not Ring Man.

Returning home by 8 p.m. was wishful thinking, and Sean knew it.

When they rolled in at 9:15 p.m., which was way past Connor's bedtime, the infant was particularly fussy. Giving him her breast, Marla-Dean settled him down quickly.

Still wide awake, but delighted to be home, Sean turned on the TV and watched several news segments on *The Kelly File*. When the one concerning his case aired, he paid particular attention.

Once it was over, however, he became tired quickly. Making a security check, just as he did every night, he made sure the house was locked and the alarm was armed. Looking out the back, noticing Winky's lights were still on, he made a mental note to have a second burglar system installed for her garage apartment. As valuable as Winky was, he didn't want anything to happen to her.

Getting ready for bed, he noticed Marla-Dean was already asleep. How she beat him to bed every night amazed him, but she always did. Saying goodnight, he turned out the light. In reply, Marla-Dean simply grunted, which she did often but would never acknowledge. She snored a little too, which she steadfastly denied.

When the panel truck and Mercedes arrived at the abandoned warehouse, Gabriela was given a chair and treated respectfully by Amiglio's men. Although none had been rough with her, nobody was willing to make eye contact with her either. Neither had they spoken to her during the trip, which let her know her worst fears were about to become a reality.

Mustering as much dignity as she could under the circumstances, she sat straight up in the chair, held her head high, and smiled confidently, rubbing her ring to give her fortitude, knowing God was with her every step of the way.

A minute later, her husband approached with a hard expression on his face—one she had seen and come to loathe. He didn't possess it in the beginning, when they were young and carefree, but it had become his trademark in recent years. Having lost interest in her more than a decade earlier, it wasn't a look he used with her. Being indifferent, he treated her more like the family maid than anything else—but not now. He was enraged, and it was obvious.

Walking straight up to her, glowering over her in an intimidating way, he asked, "Gabriela, mi esposa, porque?"

Returning his look defiantly, she replied, "Amiglio, since I suspect this will be the last conversation we will ever have, I prefer to have it in English, if you please. After all, this is the United States of America."

Stunned, he stepped back in amazement. They had always spoken in Spanish—never English. For years, she refused to learn the language of the gringos, complaining that it was too difficult; but here she was, speaking to him in English, like it was her native tongue.

"Does it surprise you that I can speak English, Amiglio?"

"Si? Yes it does," he answered honestly.

"There are a lot of things about me that would surprise you, but you haven't bothered to notice for years. I've been invisible. I've been here to raise your two sons, cook your meals, clean your house, and tend to you when you were sick. I haven't been a real person to you for years, but I am a real person, Amiglio. I am your wife."

Dumbfounded, Amiglio still couldn't believe she could speak English. Even more astounding, she was being bold and assertive, which was completely out of character. She had always been a dishrag—never like this. He wondered how she learned English so well.

As if she had been reading his mind, Gabriela said, "When I suspected you intended to bring our two sons into your criminal enterprise, I learned to speak English. I wanted to know what was going on. You never suspected a thing, did you? Of course, you didn't. It's because you never paid any attention to me. You've been too busy smuggling drugs and bedding whores to pay attention to your wife."

Amiglio said nothing. He just listened—something he had not done for years.

"You think you're so smart, don't you? But, you're not. Since you didn't think I could understand what you were saying, I have been like 'a fly on the wall' for years." Shaking her head contemptuously, she continued. "You have turned into an evil man. You're going to hell for what you have done, but you will not take our sons with you."

Concerned by what she was saying, several of Amiglio's men looked at one another nervously. Being focused on Gabriela, Amiglio didn't notice how apprehensive they had become.

Gabriela announced proudly, "I've been siphoning off money from you for years—not for me—but to provide for our sons who will never become an evil, whore-mongering criminal like you."

By this time, Amiglio had had enough of her critical tongue and was about to silence her, until she said something that stopped him.

"That's why I have $100,000 in my purse. It's all your money, Amiglio. It was to help Ernesto escape this life of crime, but he won't be needing it, will he?"

Refusing to answer her question, which he considered rhetorical, Amiglio pointed to Gabriela's bag. Understanding his boss's non-verbal command, Ricardo reached inside and grabbed a large package. Putting her bag in the van earlier, he wondered why it had been so bulky. Now, he knew.

Tearing the package open, it was filled with crisp, neatly packaged $100 bills. Ricardo also noticed a piece of paper with a name, address, email, and phone number. It was for a woman named Winky Weller.

Unaware of the additional discovery, Gabriela continued. "Mi esposo, do you remember seeing *Star Wars*, when we were young?"

"Yes," he replied, wanting to end the charade but captivated by what she was saying.

"Do you remember when Obi-Wan Kenobi was fighting Darth Vader?" she asked.

"Yes, of course, I do," Amiglio replied.

"Just before Obi Wan allowed Vader to kill him, Obi Wan said that by dying he would become stronger than ever. That is what is going to happen today, Amiglio. When you kill me, which I suspect will be very soon, I will become stronger than ever, and I will bring you down. You think that killing me will save you, but it won't. It will destroy you instead."

When she finished, she just sat there and looked defiantly at her husband of three decades.

Having had enough, Amiglio gestured for the man holding the syringe to inject it into Gabriela's arm. Knowing that resistance would be futile, she allowed it to happen without protestation, other than to rub her ring, which was God's present, assuring her of His eternal love. Then, she looked at her husband for the last time with cold contempt in her eyes.

Everything Gabriela had said and done had been a surprise to Amiglio. Her words stung deeply, troubling him more than any conversation he had ever had with her. Maintaining his supremely confident façade, he barked one order after the other. On the inside, however, he was not nearly as resolute and self-assured as he appeared.

Gabriela's words had created something in him he hated and didn't know how to handle—doubt.

His men pretended not to notice the difference in his demeanor, but they did. Besides, each of them had known Gabriela for a long time and, being genuinely fond of her, they didn't like being involved in her death. Murdering a defenseless woman just didn't seem right— not to any of them.

Amiglio was genuinely shaken. Feeling apprehensive, he knew he had to get back on top of his game quickly. For a drug lord, there was nothing worse than being hesitant and irresolute. It could be fatal, foreshadowing the kiss of death.

CHAPTER TWENTY-TWO
Up the Stairs Like a Navy SEAL

Paying a hefty surcharge for expediting Luke's DNA test, Landria had the results confirming the lineage of her toddler in record time. Having no idea Landria switched the hair samples Luke was completely fooled.

When Landria brought the findings to his attention, she was wearing black leather boots, black nylons with a seam up the back, a black garter belt, a black leather halter-top, and nothing to impede a full view of her snake tattoo. Her outfit captivated Luke's attention more completely than the DNA report, which was Landria's intent.

She wasn't certain her hoax would stand up to careful scrutiny by a trained physician, but she was certain she could divert his attention, which she accomplished quickly and easily. She enjoyed fooling men like this, especially ones as smart as Luke. Because bright guys always felt confident, they were much easier to deceive than simpletons who were far more wary.

When her scheme proved to be successful, which she knew it would, it heightened the intensity of her orgasm. The DNA results, coupled with her leather ensemble, aroused and mislead him to the point where it allowed her to achieve greater sexual satisfaction than him. This was rare for her but she loved every moment of it.

She enjoyed fooling Luke. It was easy, but part of Luke's vulnerability was his need to belong. Being adopted, his desire to feel attached and secure was substantial, often clouding his judgment. It was a weakness Landria routinely exploited to her advantage.

Satisfied by having seen the DNA report, Luke would never question Ellen's parentage, which Landria knew would become an issue in the future. Carefully misfiling the document so that Luke would never get a second look at it, she smiled. Having accomplished so much so quickly, she slept well that night.

◦◦◦

When he went to the ER the following evening, Luke was just as nervous about seeing Melissa as she was about seeing him, but for a much different reason. Although he didn't love Landria—at least not yet—he planned to stick with her. After all, she was the mother of his child, and the two needed him. Like Dwayne, Luke thought he was being given a second chance in life, and he intended to make the best of it.

He had moved on from Melissa. At the same time, he didn't want Melissa to move on from him—at least not any time soon. He wanted to enjoy himself and watch her suffer, while he pursued a new romance. He would never allow her to realize how he felt, of course. He didn't want Landria to know either. There was no telling what she might do if she found out.

Essentially, Luke wanted his cake and for Melissa to watch him eat it. He knew he was being shallow and unfair, even a little vindictive, but this is exactly how he felt. Melissa had dismissed him summarily, and he wanted her to pay a huge emotional price for doing so.

From Melissa's perspective, she didn't have an ounce of jealousy— just the opposite. She had dodged a bullet, and she knew it. Luke's relationship with Landria involved deep pathology, destined to create problems for years. Those who live with "borderlines" always pay a heavy price for doing so. She hated this for him, but she was also relieved to no longer be a participant in his drama, especially a sexual participant.

Luke had no idea how much she knew about Landria, and Melissa didn't consider it her job to enlighten him. He wouldn't believe her anyway. He was already too enmeshed with Landria to see her for who she really was. Understanding would come to him in time, but he was far too busy believing her lies to even consider entertaining the truth.

That Luke believed Jo Ellen was his child was particularly troubling. Plus, it was bizarre. Melissa was the child's grandmother. Until a short time earlier, she had also been the lover of the man who now believed he was the child's father, but wasn't. The real father was her son. The first time she thought about it, she was mortified, but now it seemed comical. People always told her she needed to lighten up. Maybe she was beginning to do just that.

The first evening they worked together after ending their intimate relationship, Melissa's mood was anything but light. She and Luke had done a good job of avoiding each other, but there was definite tension between them. The whole unit was on pins and needles because of their personal circumstances.

Being in charge, it was Melissa's responsibility to correct the situation, so she set out to do just that. Shortly after midnight, she noticed Luke had gone to the cafeteria for a break. Heading that way a short time later, she walked straight up to him, held out her hand, smiled, and said, "Luke, let's be friends."

Looking at her, his heart melted. He missed her smile, her smell, her personality, and everything about her, but he wouldn't give her the satisfaction of knowing it. Showing "good form," however, he returned her smile. Then, like a gentleman, he stood, took her hand, pulled her to him for a brief fraternal hug, and said, "That's a great idea, Melissa. Let's."

On the inside, he was hurting. Being a man, however, he knew how to suck it up for the sake of others.

With this, the tension was broken, and things returned to normal in the ER, which was necessary if they planned to continue working together, which both intended to do.

Melissa knew a confrontation over Jo Ellen was coming, but there was much that needed to be done before that could occur. Until then, Landria would seem to be the winner in this Chess game, with Melissa appearing to be the gracious loser.

Landria had pulled a fast one on Joseph and Luke, but Melissa knew the snake-tattooed tramp's day of reckoning was looming. What day that would be, she didn't know, but she knew it would happen. Regardless of how devious and clever a "borderline" may be, they always self-destruct. The question wasn't *if* they would, it was *when*.

On Peachtree Battle Avenue, everybody was sound asleep in the Kincannon household. About 2:15 a.m., while Sean was sleeping soundly, Asta put her front paws on the bed and nuzzled his hand. Turning away from the dog, he returned to sleep. Not content to leave him alone, Asta pulled at the top sheet and comforter, which really annoyed Sean. Giving his bedding a good yank, he moved away from the side of the bed. He thought Asta would get the message and leave him alone, but the dog was persistent. Finally, Asta jumped on the bed and licked Sean's face, which surprised him. She had been trained to keep off of the bed.

Finally awake, Sean sat up and looked at Asta who jumped off of the bed and went straight to the large ceiling-to-floor window that showcased the backyard. Pushing the sheer aside, Asta looked out. Definitely agitated, the dog uttered a very low, guttural growl, but didn't bark.

Instantly alert, sensing danger, Sean stealthily tiptoed to the window, and slowly pulled the sheer aside a quarter of an inch. Although the moon was not yet full, it was bright enough for him to view the backyard and garage clearly.

He saw two men crawling up the stairs adjacent to the garage. They were headed for Winky's apartment. Instantly, Sean hastened to his closet and retrieved the shotgun he had just purchased for the lake house. Loading the weapon in the dark, which wasn't difficult, he pumped it, chambering a shell. The sound was unmistakable, awakening Marla-Dean, who sat up straight in bed. She was obviously alarmed but, seeing Sean, she intuitively knew to remain silent.

In a firm but quiet voice, Sean said, "Call 911 and get the police here fast. Two men are breaking into Winky's apartment."

Following instructions, Marla-Dean grabbed her cell, went into the hall, and dialed emergency services.

Opening the shutter doors, which triggered the alarm and the flood lights, Sean stood in the darkness of the bedroom and discharged the shotgun, pumping the gun to chamber another round immediately.

The assailants, who had nearly reached the top of the stairs, froze for a split second, arrested by the lights and the noise from the alarm. When they heard gunfire, they leaped over the railing. Landing hard, they got up quickly and headed for the back fence. Scurrying over it quickly, they disappeared into the darkness of the woods. As they were running, Sean stepped outside and fired several more shots but, at that range, his efforts were more symbolic than anything else.

The intruders were gone, and he doubted they would return. Returning to the house, Sean turned off the alarm system, which stopped the incessant blaring noise. Within seconds, the security dispatcher called to check on the Kincannon's safety. Taking the call, Marla-Dean said the police had already been notified and were on their way.

While he was shooting, Sean was concerned Asta would run after the intruders into the woods and get hurt. She might even have been wounded by buckshot but, for whatever reason, she didn't chase after them. As soon as Sean knew the criminals were out of sight, he headed straight for Connor's room—even before checking on Winky—which is what any dad worth his salt would do. When he reached his son's bedroom door, Asta was vigilantly standing guard. Amazed the dog was smart enough to do this, Sean's love and respect for Asta soared.

Walking into Connor's room, Sean saw that his son was sound asleep. He hadn't even stirred. Bending down to kiss him quickly, Sean knew how important it was to always protect him. Sean also loved the loyalty of Asta, who was committed to guarding her charge.

Having no time to linger, Sean raced out of the house, telling Marla-Dean to lock the door behind him, which she did. Nevertheless, she kept close watch.

As Sean approached the stairs with his shotgun poised—just in case—he kept a watchful eye. Walking up the stairs like a Navy SEAL, he swung his shotgun from side to side with the agility of a twenty-year-old. By the time he reached the landing to Winky's door, the sound of police sirens could be heard, and they were becoming louder by the second.

In his most insistent and authoritative voice, Sean said, "Winky, it's Sean. Don't be afraid. I'm coming in. Taking the keys he had grabbed and stuffed in his robe pocket, he put the safety on his shotgun, lowered his weapon, took a lingering look at his surroundings to ensure everything was as it should be, put the key in the lock, turned the handle, and entered Winky's room.

Squinting his eyes to adjust to the darkness, he couldn't see her. The large room over the garage looked empty, but he remembered seeing lights on when he returned home earlier, so he was certain she was there. Switching the lights on, he still didn't see her. That's when he became genuinely alarmed.

He called out once again loudly and authoritatively, "Winky?"

Then, he heard a feeble voice answer, "Sean, is that you?"

Relieved, he replied, "Yes, where are you?"

"I'm in the closet," she said.

Walking over quickly, he opened the door, and there she was, cowering in the darkness. She was clutching her Bible and her laptop computer. Although Sean thought this was an odd combination, he was so relieved to see her he forgot about it.

Lifting her to her feet, he held her in his arms firmly, and she began to cry. She was terrified and for good reason. Too distraught to speak, crying was all she could do, and she did quite a bit of it. Sensing her need, Sean held her like her dad would have.

A few minutes later, they heard people talking in the backyard. Realizing the police had arrived, before walking outside, Sean yelled, "This is Sean Kincannon, and this is my house. I'm walking out with Winky Weller, our au pair. I have a shotgun. The safety is on, and I'm holding it down."

"Okay, Mr. Kincannon, come on out," Sean heard one of the policemen reply. Sean said this because he didn't want to be mistaken for a perpetrator and get himself shot. He knew what being shot felt like, and it was an experience he didn't want replicated. Wearing a robe and slippers made such a mistake highly unlikely, but he wanted to be certain.

In the minutes that followed, everything was a blur. Numerous patrol cars arrived. Since it was the middle of the night, however, no detectives came. The officers wrote a report and took Sean's statement. Since Winky was so upset, Sean was the one who dealt with the police.

Replacing Sean as Winky's comforter, Marla-Dean held her au pair for a long time. Finally, being a doctor, she pulled out her medical bag, which she rarely used, and gave Winky a 10 mg. Valium tablet to help settle her down. It also made Winky very sleepy. Leading Winky to one of the guest bedrooms on the second floor, Marla-Dean comforted her until she fell asleep soon thereafter.

For most people, calling the police would have been enough, but not for Sean. In the back of his mind, he wondered if this intrusion had anything to do with the case involving William Steiger. Sean couldn't see how, especially since the assailants went after Winky and not after him but, if he erred, it would be on the side of caution. Calling their security agency, he asked for a patrol car, with two armed off-duty officers, to sit outside his house for the remainder of the evening. It was expensive, but he did it anyway. They were affluent, and this was something he considered to be essential.

∽

At the Waffle House on Howell Mill Rd., Amiglio sat with Ricardo Castillo, awaiting the return of the two amigos that had been sent to take care of Winky Weller. Sitting at a booth as far away as possible from other patrons of the busy restaurant, the banditos enjoyed a measure of privacy. When the two men tasked with Winky's assassination walked in, Amiglio could tell immediately things had not gone well. Both looked disheveled, defeated and downcast, while one had a slight cut on his arm.

Infuriated, but unwilling to display it publicly, Amiglio gave the two men a look that would have made Pencil wet himself. Other than that, the only thing Amiglio said was, "We'll talk later."

Paying the bill, the four left. Amiglio wanted Winky dead. Thanks to Gabriela, the young woman knew far too much about him, as well as about his illegal operation. On the other hand, Winky couldn't prove a thing. Maybe her near-death experience would do the trick and scare her into silence. He thought it might but, in the back of his mind, doubt returned with a vengeance, rocking his world.

Troubled, he wondered: *Could Gabriela have been right? Is she going to be like Obi-Wan Kenobi? Now that she is dead, will she become stronger than ever? Could she bring me down, just like she promised?*

CHAPTER TWENTY-THREE

"Nothing but Trash and Trouble"

At 6:30 a.m., Lance's cell phone rang. Not an early riser, it didn't awaken him, so he was surprised to hear it ringing. Looking at the screen, he saw "Daniel."

Answering immediately, Lance said, "Daniel, what's up?"

Not wasting time with pleasantries, Daniel came straight to the point. "Tweedle-Dum didn't return last night after you left. He's gone, and I'm afraid something terrible has happened to him." Pausing for a second to steady himself, Daniel added, "I don't think I'll ever see him again. He was so troubled but, on the inside, he was a really good person." Once Daniel said this, he burst into tears.

Lance did his best to console his friend, but his mind was racing, thinking of what might have happened. He was certain Tweedle-Dum had been discovered by those pursuing him—those intent on his elimination. Never having met the man, the Mexican's fate didn't trouble Lance as much as wondering how the man's whereabouts had been discovered. Had it been by chance, or had the gang been tipped off? In his heart he knew the answer, which bothered him deeply. It meant there had to be a leak coming from law enforcement.

Disconnecting, Lance promised to do everything he could to discover what had happened to Tweedle-Dum, and when he had any information, to contact Daniel and let him know. Less than a minute later, Lance dialed Renfro, updating him about the gay bandito's missing status. That Tweedle-Dum hadn't returned didn't surprise the detective either.

Anxious, Lance said, "Michael, we need to sit down and talk right away—but not at your office. Can you meet me at the West Paces Starbuck's in about an hour? Say . . . 7:45?"

"I don't know, Lance. I've got a pretty full day."

"I see," Lance replied frostily. "I'll bet your schedule would clear up quickly if you were dead."

When Lance said this, complete silence ensued for a very long moment, as Renfro reevaluated the seriousness of the situation. "Do you really think that's a possibility, Lance?"

"Hell yes, I do," he practically screamed into the phone.

Lance's response rattled the detective, who finally grasped that the two might be in real danger. Michael replied, "All right. I'll see you there, but I can't stay long."

Luke returned home from his nightshift at the hospital earlier than usual. Because Ellen would remain asleep until at least 9:30 a.m., Landria asked if she could run to the YMCA for a quick workout, while Ellen was still asleep? Being a good dad, Luke consented graciously, as he headed to the shower and then to bed.

Grateful, Landria kissed him on the cheek, just like they were married, and headed for the Y, taking a brief detour to get a cappuccino at Starbucks first. Although there were two locations closer, she went several miles out of her way to purchase her beverage at the West Paces Starbucks.

Having discovered that Patricia worked there as a barista, Landria hoped to spot Luke's ex and let her have a good look at who Luke was now bedding. Her workout clothes were skintight, which enhanced her figure and, best of all, with a bare midriff, her outfit revealed the snake tattoo. She had no real purpose for harassing Patricia, but hurting a rival was Landria's favorite sporting event. She did it often— just because she could.

As she walked in, she spotted Patricia immediately but pretended she didn't. Although they had never met, she knew who the woman was from her photos posted on Facebook. Going to the counter, Landria nonchalantly ordered a cappuccino. Wandering around the store, looking at items for sale while waiting for her beverage to be brewed, Landria knew the instant it dawned on Patricia who she was. For Landria, this moment was priceless. Borderlines relished moments like these.

Having no idea she was being taunted, Patricia recognized how beautiful her customer was long before it dawned on her who she was. Mortified, Patricia felt trapped, but she maintained her composure— just like any sophisticated Kappa would. She had been trained for moments like these. Refusing to be less than ladylike, she smiled, handed Landria her drink, while never making eye contact with the woman again.

Having stung Patricia thrilled Landria. It added inspiration and motivation to her workout. Once she had her drink, Landria smiled politely and headed for the door. As she passed a table where two men were sitting, the straight guy eyed her lasciviously. Intuitively knowing he was a policeman, she smiled coquettishly, while thinking, *Only in your dreams, cop, . . . only in your dreams*. With that, she headed to the YMCA.

✑

Sitting at the Starbuck's table, Lance watched the little adventure between the snake-tattooed woman and Detective Renfro comically.

When the woman passed out of sight, Michael's attention returned to his conversation with Lance.

"Talk about a man being ruled by his erections; oh my God," Lance commented, touching a sensitive nerve in Michael.

"What?" the detective winced defensively, as if he was completely innocent.

Nailing him, Lance reproached, "Our lives may be in danger, Michael. So, you might want to pay attention. Besides, that woman is nothing but trash and trouble." When it came to discerning the intentions of women like Landria, it's nearly impossible to fool a savvy gay man like Lance.

Knowing he had been caught and feeling the sting, Michael smiled. "You're right, Lance. I know you're right. But did you see her tattoo?"

"Of course, I did." Thoughtfully, Lance added, "I don't know who that woman is, but I'll bet her entire wardrobe has been chosen to accentuate that tattoo." Getting a little testy, he asked, "Can we get back to the case now?"

"Sure," Michael replied, properly chastised.

"Okay then, since neither you nor I have told anyone about Tweedle-Dum, the leak must have come from someone at the meeting you had with the brass." Seeking reassurance that his theory was correct, Lance asked, "Isn't that how you see it?"

"Yes," Michael added, "but I doubt it was the FBI agent or Captain Baird. Neither has a vested interest in the case. That means we can rule the two of them out. Don't you agree?"

"Yes, I do," Lance replied, delighted they had come to the same conclusion. "That means it has to be either the Atlanta Police lieutenant or one of the two guys who is working for Wilbur Kenyatta."

"Right."

"Any idea which one of the three it might be, Michael?"

"No," Michael answered, "but, if I had to venture a guess, I would pick one of Kenyatta's guys. They have too much to gain, as well as too much to lose, for it to be anyone else. If I'm correct, and I'm pretty sure that I am, this means we have to keep everything we're doing confidential, completely away from them. Agreed?"

"Agreed," Lance replied.

Now deep into their conversation, Michael's cell rang. The call was from his office. Answering immediately, Renfro listened for a long moment, as the blood drained from his face. Paying careful attention as he listened, he finally thanked the caller and disconnected.

Returning his attention to Lance, he said, "There was an attempted break-in at Sean Kincannon's house last night."

"Steiger's attorney?" Lance asked, keenly aware of how significant this might be.

"Yes," Renfro replied. "Apparently, somebody tried to take him out, or at least take out his au pair."

"Whatever happened, I believe it has something to do with this, don't you?" Lance asked, but his question was more like a rhetorical assertion. Pulling out his laptop, Detective Renfro started punching keys. Wondering what he was doing, Lance asked.

"I'm looking up Kincannon's phone number. Since he's the attorney for Steiger, it will be in the case file. Retrieving the number, Renfro called and left a voice message, introducing himself and telling the counselor he needed to speak with him as soon as possible. When he finished, he closed his computer, set his cell on the table and continued his conversation with Lance.

Less than three minutes later, Renfro's cell rang again, exasperating Lance, who had been speaking nonstop. He asked, "Why didn't you put that damn thing on vibrate?"

Looking at the caller ID, Michael recognized the number. Answering immediately, he said, "Mr. Kincannon, thanks for returning my call so promptly." As he was speaking, he gave Lance a look, letting his companion know he knew exactly what he was doing.

⁓

Ten minutes later, Sean was in his car headed for Starbucks. The detective had asked if they could come to his house but, since Winky was still asleep and Marla-Dean was busy tending to Connor, Sean offered to meet Renfro at Starbucks instead. Arriving, Sean ordered a grande cappuccino, asking that it be foamier than the last time. Galled at already having been stung so early in the morning by Landria, Patricia smiled and promised to make Sean's drink precisely the way he liked. She wanted to spit in his cup but, with so many people present, this wasn't an option.

Barely paying attention to Patricia, who had become increasingly invisible as each month passed, Sean looked around until he spotted the cop. When he did, Michael signaled for him to join them. After meeting Renfro, as well as his CSI tech, Sean grabbed his cappuccino, which had been brewed to perfection. Smiling at Patricia, after taking his first sip, he walked back to their table, pulled up a chair, and sat down.

Getting straight to business, Renfro asked numerous questions about the intruders. Were they armed? Could he tell if they were Mexican or not? Were they in their twenties or older? Had Sean ever seen them before? The questions were endless, but both men paid keen attention to each answer Sean provided.

Finally, Renfro said, "I'll need to talk to Winky Weller right away. Do you think she's awake?"

Looking at his watch, Sean noticed it was just past 9 a.m. Answering, he said, "I suspect she is. Do you want to follow me back to my house?"

"Yes, that would be perfect. You lead the way, and I'll be right behind you," Renfro said. Not willing to miss out on anything as exciting as this, Lance called his office and told his boss he wouldn't be in until later. The woman didn't like it, but she knew better than to demand conformity from her best tech.

In the unit, Lance was often referred to as "The Queen Bee." Had his boss known about his other nickname, Ring Man, she would have preferred it. Realizing this, Lance was very careful to keep that juicy tidbit of information to himself.

Ending the call, he followed the other two. Like a mini caravan, the three cars left Starbucks two minutes later, headed for Sean's Peachtree Battle home.

∽

When they arrived, Marla-Dean was doing her best to remedy a crisis. She had been shooting a video of Connor taking a bath. She wanted to send it to Grayson's mother, just as she had promised at dinner the evening before. Her former mother-in-law adored Connor. The infant seemed to thrive on attention, cooing every time the woman looked his way, which was often.

While filming, with Winky still sleeping, thanks to the Valium, the au pair was unable to assist Marla-Dean. Trying to bathe Connor with one hand and film him with the other, the infant slipped in his bath and came close to going underwater. Putting the camera down instantly to rectify the situation, Marla-Dean inadvertently knocked it into the bathwater. She got everything under control quickly but was certain the camera was ruined, as well as the existing footage in its memory.

When Sean walked in the front door, she told him what had happened, but he was far more concerned about other matters to pay much attention. A moment later, as the other two men entered, Sean introduced Detective Michael Renfro and CSI tech Lance Rector to his wife.

Recognizing Marla-Dean instantly as one of the physicians on duty the night he gave Dr. Easton the nickname Big Shot, Lance was embarrassed.

Returning his look, Marla-Dean recognized him just as quickly. Instead of calling attention to the awkward incident, which would have humiliated the CSI tech, Marla-Dean held out her hand instead. "Welcome to our home, Mr. Rector—you too, Detective Renfro."

Truly grateful to have been spared the humiliation, Lance smiled at his hostess gratefully. Despite the seriousness of what was happening, Lance thought Marla-Dean was the kind of woman Michael needed— not some snake-tattooed tramp like the one he was flirting with at Starbucks.

Missing the mini adventure that had just occurred, which was not unusual, Sean asked if Winky was awake. Saying that she wasn't, Sean asked Marla-Dean to awaken her. The police detective needed to speak with her about the previous evening's events. With Connor busy in his playpen, Marla-Dean went upstairs to do as her husband had requested.

Leading the two men to his office, Sean waited for Winky to make an appearance. While they were waiting, Lance took the lead, which wasn't his place to do, but he did it anyway. Looking directly at Sean, he said, "Michael and I have been talking, and we think your break-in is somehow connected to the Steiger case." Looking at Sean, he added, "Have you considered this, Sean?"

"Yes, I have."

"Well, instead of talking around the subject—never actually saying what's on our minds—I'm going to be honest and tell you exactly what we think." Again looking at Sean, he asked, "Would that be all right with you?"

Again, Sean replied that it would.

Taking a quick look at Detective Renfro, who simply nodded his approval, Lance began. He told Sean about his friend, while not identifying him by name. Then, he told Sean about Tweedle-Dum, which fascinated the lawyer.

After talking non-stop for several minutes, Lance paused and said, "Can I tell you something off the record?"

"Certainly," Sean agreed.

Again, Lance looked at Detective Renfro who nodded his assent.

"Sean, we think this is a bullshit case. The evidence just doesn't support the allegation that Steiger had anything to do with his wife's murder." Becoming animated and somewhat indignant, Lance added, "We think Wilbur Kenyatta is pushing for a conviction to become governor. He wants it so badly, he'll do anything, including railroading Steiger for murder. There I've said it, and I'm glad I did. It's what we've all been thinking."

In response, Sean switched his glance to Renfro, who nodded once again, acknowledging his agreement with the CSI tech's conclusion.

Lance added, "By the way, I saw your press conference on the news yesterday, and I agree with every word you said."

"Thanks, Lance," Sean replied. "I really appreciate your candor."

Although Sean was just beginning, Lance stopped him. "There's more, Sean, and I want to finish, if that's all right with you?" A little surprised, Sean simply sat back and kept quiet, content to yield the floor to Lance.

Continuing, Lance said, "Last night, Tweedle-Dum went missing. Michael and I don't think he's coming back." Looking directly into Sean's eyes, Lance announced, "We think he's dead."

Once again, Sean started to speak but was stopped by Lance. "If this is true, and we're pretty sure it is, this means there is an inside leak, and we think it's coming from Kenyatta's people. Sean, they will do anything to win, including murder. That's the real reason I came with Detective Renfro. This part of the investigation certainly isn't in my job description, but staying alive is. Knowing as much as we do, we suspect our lives might also be in jeopardy. The people who got Tweedle-Dum may consider us to be loose ends."

As he thought of it, Lance also needed to put Daniel in that column. He was also a loose end. With dramatic flair, Lance asserted, "If anything happens to us, we don't want Kenyatta to get away with it." Now done, Lance sat back, allowing Sean and Michael to have a turn speaking.

Looking at Detective Renfro, Sean asked, "Have you come to the same conclusions, detective?"

"Off the record, yes," Michael verified.

Sean was about to continue when there was a soft knock on the door. Turning his head, Sean said, "Come in."

It was Winky Weller, looking nervous but resolute. She had a cup of coffee in her hand and a smile on her face, ready to answer the detective's questions.

After introductions and a brief potty break, the four sat down to discuss the events concerning the attempted break-in at Winky's apartment. After having answered numerous questions from Detective Renfro, trying to think if there was anything he might have missed, he asked if she had any idea why someone would want to harm her?

Replying promptly, Winky said, "Yes, I do," which surprised Sean. Elaborating, Winky began to describe her story about giving away her ring, which bored the two straight men but fascinated Lance. Befuddled about the relevance of her tale, Michael was about to interrupt. Before he could though, Winky reached the part of her story where the woman introduced herself as Gabriela Sabata, the wife of Amiglio Sabata. When Winky said this, she had the complete attention of all three, as they looked at one another in stunned disbelief.

Continuing, Winky said, "Gabriela told me all kinds of things about her life. She talked about murder, drug smuggling, and lots more, going into vivid detail about many things. She also told me her husband was responsible for the murder of the wife of Sean's client."

Interrupting, Detective Renfro looked at Sean and Lance. Reasoning out loud, he said, "When they got Tweedle-Dum, he would have told them about Gabriela helping him, probably through torture. That's why they came after Winky. It means they must have found out about Gabriela, too."

"This means we'll never hear from Gabriela again," Lance interjected.

When she heard this, Winky started to cry, which made Lance wish he had kept his mouth shut.

Continuing with his analysis, despite Winky's whimpering, Renfro said, "that means they were after Winky because of some evidence she may have that would incriminate Amiglio." Looking at Winky, Michael asked, "Did she give you anything?"

"No," Winky replied, stifling her tears.

"Then, what could it be?" the detective wondered out loud.

Interrupting Michael's reverie, Winky said, "Maybe they were after the video I made of everything she said?"

Shocked, all three men just looked at Winky in astonishment. Sean broke the silence by asking, "So, you took a video of everything she told you?"

"Yes."

"How did you record it?" he asked.

"With the camera you and Marla-Dean forgot when you left last night. It's all in the camera's memory," she answered matter-of-factly.

Thinking they had hard evidence exonerating Steiger, Michael and Lance gave each other a hi-five. Sean was dejected though, and shook his head in despair.

When Lance asked what was troubling him, Sean replied, "The camera containing Gabriela's statement just fell into my son's bathwater. It's ruined. We don't have anything—not a damn thing."

CHAPTER TWENTY-FOUR
The Truth Would Finally Be Known

"Sean," Marla-Dean said, knocking insistently, while opening the door at the same time, intent on interrupting the meeting, regardless of the seriousness of what was being discussed. Surprised by her intrusion, Winky, Lance, Michael, and Sean turned their heads in unison, like choreographed dancers would, to see what was happening.

"You have to watch this," Marla-Dean said, as she used her universal remote to click on the large TV above the sofa in the office. Explaining her breach of etiquette without apologizing, she said, "I was watching the local news. Just before the commercial break, the anchorman said, 'Stay tuned for an analysis of the hard-hitting ad just released by the Kenyatta for Governor Campaign.'"

Marla-Dean continued, "From what I've gathered, apparently Kenyatta's ad makes tacit reference to your press conference, Sean."

Getting up from the couch and walking over to the side of Sean's desk, Michael and Lance stood with Marla-Dean, while Winky just switched positions in her chair. Sean remained seated behind his desk. During one of the numerous commercials, Winky got up and quietly excused herself.

As the anchorman returned, he said the Kenyatta campaign had just released the following ad statewide. It was playing in all six major markets, with a huge buy in the metropolitan Atlanta market, which accounted for more than half of the state's voting population.

As the ad began, Wilbur Kenyatta was sitting behind a desk with the American and Georgian flags prominently and majestically draped in the background. The commercial was set up to look like Kenyatta was already the Governor, in an apparent effort to make him appear like the natural choice. The gubernatorial aspirant began by saying he had served the people of Georgia in one capacity or another for more than a quarter of a century, and nobody had ever called his ethics into question—not until yesterday. With a look of righteous indignation, he said that to insinuate he would even consider doing anything morally reprehensible for political gain, and not out of genuine heart-felt service, was a lie and an affront to him as well as to the good citizens of Georgia. With the camera zooming in to get a close up of his face, Kenyatta added, "What offends me most is the apparent racial motivation behind these charges. For most of us, the days of racism have passed but, apparently, not for all."

After playing the ad in its entirety, the anchor deferred to the station's political commentator who made a direct reference to Sean's news conference the day before, indicating that Kincannon's defense of Steiger was playing the race card and Wilbur Kenyatta was calling him out on it. The commentator concluded that Kenyatta was just the kind of hard hitting, take-no-prisoners kind of guy Georgia needed to "get this state moving in the right direction again." When the commentator finished his editorial, the segment concluded and was followed by a commercial, so Marla-Dean switched off the TV.

Infuriated by what she had just seen, with flared nostrils, she looked at her husband and said, "Racially motivated! There's not one speck of truth to that. They are making you look like you're nothing better than a Klansman. I'm so furious, I can't even see straight."

"I agree, Marla-Dean," Lance replied. "That's the way Kenyatta plays. He's never fair, but there is one good thing about it."

Piquing the interest of everybody in the room, Lance explained, "By making you the enemy, at least you are safe—physically safe, that is. He needs you alive to be the bad guy—just like he needs Steiger to be a cold-blooded killer."

When Marla-Dean heard this, the blood drained from her face. Looking at her husband, she was mystified, but Sean wasn't. He understood Lance's reasoning, which had a sobering effect on him.

Both furious and frustrated, Detective Renfro added, "It's too bad we don't have that video. If it hadn't been destroyed, we would have a powerful rebuttal, but now we don't." Shaking his head, he added, "We don't have squat!"

Confused by what the detective had just said, Marla-Dean looked to Sean for an explanation, which he was about to provide, when Winky reentered the room.

Carrying the case for her laptop over her shoulder, she took charge of the meeting. "I can't believe you guys think I'm a brainless nitwit." She added, "Knowing how important Gabriela's statement was, the first thing I did was email it to my computer, where I downloaded it for safekeeping. I have backup."

Thinking like the policeman he was, Renfro asked, "So, what you're telling me is we still have a copy of what Gabriela Sabata told you? In her own words?"

"Yes, that's exactly what I'm telling you, detective," Winky replied.

Lance interjected, "Am I the only one who is curious about what Gabriela has to say? For God's sake let's see it."

Not having to be told twice, Winky opened her MacBook Pro, clicked on the video, turned up the volume, and hit the sideways triangle, starting the clip. As it began, the setting was the room they were in, with Winky sitting in Sean's chair and Gabriela sitting across from her. Before Gabriela began her long soliloquy, Winky rose, picked up the daily paper, and held it in front of the camera for whoever might be watching. It showed the front page of *The Atlanta Journal*. Covering all of her bases, she used the newspaper to establish the date of Gabriela's message.

When Detective Renfro realized what she had done, he looked at her differently. He was impressed, as was everybody in the room.

In the video, as Winky took her seat, she nodded for Gabriela Sabata to begin, which she did. Gabriela explained how her husband had become involved in a life of crime, and how he became consumed with the riches it provided. As Amiglio's corruption escalated, he became increasingly evil, which included sexual sadism. Abandoning the marital bed for perversion and brutality, Gabriela became a non-person in their home, doing little more than cooking, cleaning, and raising their two boys.

For Gabriela, it was an unacceptable life. Determined that her children would not end up like their father, she did everything she could to keep them from following him into his business, finally sending them off to college to protect them from his criminal influence.

As the people in Sean's office watched the video of Gabriela telling her story, they became engrossed in it. Her statement was a riveting indictment of Amiglio's operation, as well as of his escalating sexual perversion.

After twenty minutes, Gabriela reached the critical point. She said, "Amiglio started having sex with Anne Steiger. They were lovers for quite a while. Since there had been so many before her, I had become used to it. Following a predictable and well-established pattern, Amiglio started getting very rough with her. Instead of scaring her off, his brutality seemed to excite her. She liked it rough." Being sensitive to the young woman she was addressing across from her, Gabriela added, "Winky, you are very young and probably cannot understand a woman like Anne Steiger. I cannot either, but they do exist."

Gabriela continued, "Finally, Amiglio had had enough of her, but she wouldn't let go of him. So, he got rougher with her—much rougher. But she still wouldn't let go. She kept coming back for more. That was her mistake. Finally, one night, she followed him to our house on the lake. I had come down much earlier in my own car. Because I was tired, I went to bed early, and was already sound asleep. I was awakened by hearing noise out on the deck. It didn't sound like two people who were just having sex. If that had been the case, I would not have gone out there. That's not something I would want to see." When Gabriela said this, she looked at Winky, who nodded in an understanding way, knowing she wouldn't want to witness it either.

Then, Gabriela said, "It sounded more like Amiglio was beating her up. Anyway, I went out on the deck to do something to stop him. Finally, I yelled. '*Parate Amiglio! La vas a matar.*' I always spoke Spanish to Amiglio, Winky. I don't want him to know I can speak English, but that's another story for another time. Anyway, what I yelled means, 'Stop it, Amiglio. You'll kill her.' But he didn't stop. Instead, he told me, '*Cayate mujer si intiendes lo que es bueno para ti.*' That is a very vulgar way of telling me to shut up and mind my own business."

With a look of wounded indignation, Gabriela added, "Winky, I am his wife. He was doing this on the deck of our house, and this is not my business?" At this point in the video, Gabriela shook her head contemptuously at her husband, disgusted by his behavior.

Marla-Dean said, "Winky, pause the video for a second, please." Looking at her husband incredulously, she said, "Sean, do you think this is what you heard that night at our house on Lake Oconee?"

"Yes, I believe it is," he replied with equal astonishment. For a long moment, the couple just looked at each other, astounded by the coincidence, while also being grateful for having an answer to the origin of the mysterious voices Sean heard that evening.

Detective Renfro asked Winky to start the video again, which the young woman did.

Gabriela continued, "But Amiglio didn't stop. Because he didn't, he killed her, and there was nothing I could do to stop him. It all happened so fast. That poor woman didn't deserve to die like that—choked to death while having sex—but Amiglio didn't want her body to be found at our house on the lake. So, he called two of his men—Tweedle-Dee and Tweedle-Dum—to take her to her ex-husband's apartment and make it look like that poor man had done it. Since her ex-husband was an alcoholic and passed out every night, which Anne Steiger had told Amiglio, they thought it would be easy to make it look like he had murdered her, and Amiglio was right. That's what has happened."

At this point, Gabriela started to cry. Finally, pulling herself together, she continued. "Seeing the look on that woman's face, with her dead eyes, has haunted me ever since. I knew I couldn't take anymore. When I saw you at Barnes & Noble that day, I was at the end of my rope. I knew I had to get out. I looked at a couple of condos on Peachtree, but I realized Amiglio would never let me go—not alive anyway. Nobody ever leaves Amiglio. That's why I looked so sad sitting there all by myself."

The video continued for a few more minutes, describing Winky's kindness, but everybody had heard the essentials. Looking at her husband, Marla-Dean was the first to speak.

"I still can't believe it, Sean. The sounds you heard that night were from Amiglio Sabata strangling Anne Steiger to death across the bay."

"That's what it must have been, Marla-Dean. Some of the words Gabriela said I remember distinctly." Looking at Detective Renfro and CSI-tech Rector, Sean explained in detail what had happened that night, including how words from that far away can be carried by the wind, although they seemed to come from right outside of Sean and Marla-Dean's bedroom.

Lance asked, "What time did you hear those voices, Sean?"

"Just before midnight," he replied.

"That's within the timeframe we've established for Anne's death," Lance replied, as his mind raced, considering the evidence based on this new theory.

Renfro added, "It also explains why the blood settled on her side and not on her back, which is the way the crime scene was staged. Anne Morrow-Steiger must have been on her side in the trunk of a car or on the bed of a van for several hours before she was placed on her back. Now, for the first time, the discrepancy in her blood lividity makes sense."

Thinking of something else, Lance added, "It's also why the bruising on her neck couldn't have been inflicted by Steiger. I'll bet Amiglio's hands are much bigger."

At this point, Winky asked, "But why did he have to kill Anne? What would make somebody want to do that?" Nobody was willing to go into detail about this, so Marla-Dean offered to provide Winky with a thorough explanation of death by sexual asphyxiation at a later time, which seemed to pacify her au pair.

Looking at the young woman, Sean asked, "So, that's why you were holding your laptop and your Bible to your chest when I found you in the closet last night?"

"Yes, Sean, that's why," she said. When she said this, everybody gave her a puzzled look. Recognizing how bewildered they were, Winky decided to provide them with a complete explanation. When she did, addressing Sean, she said, "After I dropped off Gabriela, I tried calling you several times, but you and Marla-Dean still had your cell phones turned off. So, I prayed and asked the Lord what to do."

"And?" Lance asked.

"I knew how important my video was, Lance. I also knew I needed to make sure somebody in authority could have access to it. As I drove home, after dropping Gabriela off, I became nervous something might happen to me, which it nearly did. So, I not only uploaded the video to my computer, I also attached it to my blog."

Not being very computer savvy, Detective Renfro asked, "I'm not sure I'm following you, Winky. Take your time, but tell me exactly what that means. Explain it in a way that someone like me can understand. Can you do that?"

"Of course," Winky said. "I have a blog on Wordpress.com. It's called *Winky's Words of Wisdom*."

When she said this, Lance chortled, which made Winky blush.

Turning to him, Detective Renfro stared knives at his CSI tech, which made Lance stop immediately.

Continuing, Winky said, "Anyway, I uploaded the video to YouTube, and marked it private. That means nobody can access it, but I also posted it to a blog entry I created about the murder that's linked to my Yahoo email contacts, Facebook, Twitter, Pinterest, and Linked-In accounts. I thought that if anything was about to happen to me, I would let the world know exactly who was responsible."

She added, "I had it ready to send when I heard Sean call, so I aborted it, but it's still saved as a draft to be posted on *Winky's Words of Wisdom*." When she said this, she looked at Lance to see if he was going to laugh at her again, but he put his hands up in surrender, smiling as he did. She could tell he was sorry, so she returned his smile, accepting his non-verbal apology, non-verbally.

Thoroughly impressed by the young woman's resourcefulness, Detective Renfro knew he would be asked many questions about the video at trial. Hoping to appear intelligent when this happened, he asked, "Winky, can you show me exactly what you did? I will need to know precisely how all of this works. Show me, step-by-step, please."

"Sure, it's quite simple," she said, and she meant it. Nobody in the room was following her, except for Lance, who—like Renfro—was genuinely impressed with the attractive young woman. Looking at her, he thought she would be a perfect girlfriend for Michael, but the CSI tech wisely kept this to himself.

While Lance was entertaining these thoughts, Michael leaned over Winky's shoulders as she opened her Blog—winkyswordsofwisdom. wordpress.com. When she did, she brought up her dashboard, clicked on her posts, and opened her saved drafts. Opening the draft with its attachment of Gabriela's video, she said, "There it is, Detective."

"So, when you were in the closet, all you needed to do was click on that 'Publish' button, and the video would have gone out to several people, right?"

Answering, Winky said, "It would have been broadcasted to my

3,000 email contacts, my 3,700 Facebook friends, the 125,000 people following me on Twitter, my 4,500 Linked-In contacts, my 100,000 followers on Pinterest, as well as all the search engines connected to Word Press."

Standing straight up, Michael looked at her flabbergasted. "That's a lot of people, Winky."

"That's just the tip of the iceberg, Detective Renfro. The potential audience could be millions, especially when it concerns an actual murder case that's all over the news."

"Unbelievable," was all the awed detective could say in response, as he chuckled under his breath, clearly amazed.

Knowing exactly what Winky had done and how, Lance was equally impressed. Getting up from his seat, he said, "Move over, Michael. I want to see for myself what she's done. May I, Winky?"

Moving her shoulder aside, as Michael stepped back, Winky gave Lance access to her screen and keyboard. Having a MacBook Pro himself, in less than two seconds, he moved the curser to "Publish," hit the button, and sent the video out to all the places *Winky's Words of Wisdom* would reach.

Speechless, everyone in the room looked at Lance with incredulity. All they could do was stare, nervous about the consequences, but delighted the truth would finally be known.

Returning to his seat, Lance simply said, "Oops!"

CHAPTER TWENTY-FIVE
"Which Street Would Bear His Name?"

That afternoon, as Luke got up from sleeping after his night shift, Landria greeted him with a good morning kiss and a cup of coffee.

Groggy, Luke reached for it and said, "I feel like I've been shot out of a cannon."

"I know, darling. You work so hard, and you're so good at what you do," she said, comforting him, rubbing his back, as she spoke.

Smiling, he didn't reply, choosing instead to grin at her lasciviously.

Returning his smile with a wry grin, she added, "That too, but I was referring to your medical skills."

Enjoying the moment, both laughed, as Ellen came in and gave Luke a big hug, which he just loved. Having another child was something he never anticipated, and Ellen seemed to respond to him quite well. He felt like a truly blessed man. His heart still ached for Melissa, but that would pass in time. He was sure of it.

While he was sipping his coffee, Landria said, "The movers have everything set up at the Lullwater house, so it's ready for occupancy right away. I think Ellen and I will move over there tomorrow, and you can follow whenever you feel ready, if you still want to, that is?"

She knew the answer, of course. If she had any doubt about his desires, she wouldn't have asked, but tantalizing him intensified his interest.

Luke, fearful of losing her, replied immediately. "I'm ready. Now that we're back together, I don't want to be apart again—not for anything. Do you?"

"Of course not, darling," she said. "I just needed to hear it from you. That's all. Maybe we'll just stay here with you until the weekend. Then, we can all move together. How would that be?"

"That would be perfect. I'm off this weekend," he added. As he walked over to the coffee pot to pour himself a second cup, she sidled up behind him, and gave him a hug that was more like a grope, which she knew would arouse him. Every man she had ever known loved the way she did this.

As afternoon turned to dinnertime, the airways remained filled with Wilbur Kenyatta's ad, which victimized the gubernatorial aspirant, while castigating the state's few remaining racists—most notably, Sean Kincannon. Kenyatta's consultant, Swag Wheeler, was beside himself with glee, overjoyed by his surgical strike, eviscerating Steiger's lawyer. Although hastily put together, Swag's ad was the most effective one he had ever crafted, gratifying him immensely—Kenyatta too.

By playing the race card against Kincannon, political support for Kenyatta was increasing by the hour. The campaign had already experienced its best fundraising day ever—with the evening yet to come.

When Kincannon held his news conference, he had scored against Kenyatta, wounding the candidate, but Swag's counterpunch had landed solidly, sending Kincannon and Steiger to the mat. Kenyatta's consultant doubted they would ever recover. Smiling, Swag planned to villainize Steiger and his lawyer all the way to the election, making him the Willie Horton of Georgia.

Adding to the political momentum, the news programs that editorialized the situation universally supporting Kenyatta. Although this turn of events had not been anticipated, the political consultant was so pleased with things that, if it had been possible, he would have hugged Sean Kincannon. When Swag went to bed that evening, the prospects for the future couldn't have looked better.

∽

By late afternoon, just a few hours after Lance had his "Oops," the blog entry on *Winky's Words of Wisdom* had not received many hits. Because the clip hadn't generated a stir, Sean, Marla-Dean, and Michael were concerned, but this didn't trouble Lance or Winky—not in the least. They knew traffic would come. Winky asserted confidently that the post was like the tree in Psalm 1, bearing "fruit in its season"—not before. Everybody hoped she was correct but, with the exception of Lance, the others remained skeptical.

∽

As Melissa was settling down to watch the local evening news, her cell phone rang. The caller ID read, "Joseph," so she answered it instantly, smiling cheerfully as she did.

"Hi, Mom." Coming right to the point, Joseph said, "There's something I need to tell you. Do you have a minute?"

"Of course, I do," she replied.

"I've made a decision," he said. "I'm leaving Belmont University at the end of this semester."

"Son, are you sure you want to do that?" Melissa countered.

Interrupting her, he said, "Hear me out, okay?"

"Of course, I'm sorry, son. Go ahead," she said, already thinking about what she would say in rebuttal.

"I'm not quitting college. I'm just going to transfer and change my major."

This was different, Melissa realized. "I see," she said. "What are your new plans?"

"I'm pretty sure I can get into Emory, especially as an upper-classman, and it's a lot closer to Jo Ellen," he said. "They don't have a great music department like Belmont, but I've been thinking about changing my major to business anyway."

"Hmmm, that's a lot to think about, Joseph," she replied.

"I'm not thinking about it, Mom. I've already sent in my application. This is what I'm going to do." Taking a long breath, he added, "With Molly going to Stanford, Dad gone, and you and Jo Ellen in Atlanta, there's no reason for me to be here any longer. I'm going to rent a condo in Decatur, near the campus," he added.

"When are you planning to do this?"

"Right away," he said. Becoming firm, he added, "There's one thing I can promise you, Mom. There is no way in hell I'm going to allow Landria get away with stealing Jo Ellen from me. She may get away with stealing Dad's furniture and his artwork, but not my daughter."

Normally, Melissa would have reprimanded Joseph for using profanity, but not this time. Replying in kind, she said, "Damn right. I'm with you all the way, son."

"I knew I could count on you. I'm coming home, Mom."

Disconnecting a minute later, Melissa thought about everything Joseph had said, especially the part about not allowing Landria get away with keeping Jo Ellen from her real father and her real grandmother. That part made her mad too, but the part that made her cry was when Joseph said, "I'm coming home, Mom." It was a sentence she would replay in her mind a thousand times. Being an answer to prayer, she enjoyed it each time she did.

⚬⁓⚬

By 8 p.m., several people had watched Gabriela's video about being an eyewitness to the murder of Anne Morrow-Steiger. Since *Winky's Words of Wisdom* was oriented toward a Christian audience, church people were the first to take notice.

One of them, a regular at Haynes Bridge Baptist Church, understood its importance instantly. Calling her good friend, Captain Barbara Baird, the woman said, "Barbara, have you ever read anything on the blog site, *Winky's Words of Wisdom*?"

Not following the woman and taken by surprise, Barbara answered, "Winky's what?"

"*Winky's Words of Wisdom*, Barbara. The blog is quite good and very practical. It's written from the perspective of a single au pair," the woman added.

"No, Estalena, I can't say that I have," Barbara answered, wondering why this old busybody had called her in the first place. Mildly irritated, Barbara wondered what she really wanted.

Sensing Barbara's impatience with her, Estalena said, "Well, you need to check out her latest entry."

"Why is that, Estalena?" Barbara answered bluntly, close to cutting the woman off.

"Because there's a video clip from a woman name Gabriela, saying she saw her husband, a drug dealer named Amiglio Sabata, strangle the wife of that Steiger guy. You know who he is, don't you? The one they call Pencil; he's in jail accused of killing his ex," the Haynes Bridge Baptist busybody replied, knowing she had struck a nerve—the true purpose for her call. Barbara had been unaware of the video. Estalena, a master at discerning nuances—like all busybodies, was certain of it.

Stunned, Barbra's mouth became dry, and she couldn't sit still. She stood and walked around nervously as she listened, while attempting to appear calm. Finally, she thanked Estalena for the information and hung up abruptly.

Racing to her computer, she Googled *Winky's Words of Wisdom*, which opened to the smiling face of a young woman holding a Bible.

In a vertical column, running alongside the photo were numerous entries. With trembling hands, Barbara clicked the first. It opened to a brief statement and a video of the two women sitting in a room, which reminded her of one of the rooms at Marla-Dean's house.

Paying rapt attention, Barbara started the video and watched the entire clip. She was nervous Amiglio's wife would mention her husband's association with a female police officer. To her relief, there was no mention of Captain Barbara Baird—not even a casual intimation. Panicked that she would have to "make a run for it," Barbara felt somewhat safe, once the video finished.

Not yet satisfied, she watched the entire interview a second time— just to make certain. While watching, she paid closer attention to the furnishings in the office, which she concluded were Sean's. In the bookcase behind the desk, there was a picture of Vince Dooley and another of Bear Bryant. Only a few people in the world would have a picture of both, and Sean was one of them.

After being shot nearly two years earlier, Sean said he was "out of the game." Apparently, he was back in it, and he might prove to be a threat once again. She would have to keep an eye on him—that's for sure.

Going to her kitchen, she poured herself a large glass of Chablis, went back to her computer, and watched the clip for a third time, becoming thoroughly knowledgeable about everything Gabriela divulged. She needed time to think, and the wine would calm her nerves, while she pondered her predicament.

The negative ad continued to run, and the Kenyatta campaign was bringing in far more money than it was spending—a rarity for any political campaign, especially one so early in the election cycle. The ad was scheduled to run for two more days. By that time, Kenyatta's name recognition and approval rating would be sky high. At least,

Swag thought this is what would happen.

On the 10 p.m. news in Valdosta, however, there was a report of an alternate theory that had been posted on *Winky's Words of Wisdom*, which the news anchor read skeptically. Not having seen the clip, the anchor just reported, allowing the audience to decide.

In the subsequent ten minutes, there were more than one hundred hits on Winky's website, fifteen shares on Facebook, and thirteen re-tweets. Some people were beginning to watch the clip, and they were sharing it with their friends.

At the Kincannon home, after the adventures of the past twenty-four hours, everybody was exhausted and went to bed early. The Internet, however, never sleeps nor does it slumber. By the time Sean and Marla-Dean were awakened by Connor early the next morning, Gabriela's statement had circulated throughout the state and beyond. More than 1,000 people had viewed it, and this was just the beginning.

By 8 a.m., the number doubled, doubling again in the next hour. The interest in *Winky's Words of Wisdom* became so intense Word Press featured it, and Yahoo put *Winky's Words* in their national "Trending Now" column. That's when the video went viral. By mid-afternoon, several million had viewed Gabriela's clip.

Someone finally alerted the Kenyatta campaign. Viewing it, a hasty meeting of Kenyatta's leadership team was called. Making a quick call to the telemarketing center, Swag was informed donations had nearly dried up.

A pragmatist, this was the precise moment that Swag knew Kenyatta's political prospects had evaporated. He was dead in the water. Predictably, Kenyatta was not ready to give up. He wanted to denounce *Winky's Words of Wisdom*, but his consultant brought him back to reality, by saying, "Wilbur, my contract runs through November of next year. You have to pay me regardless of what happens. You know that, right?"

Hearing this, the candidate winced, finally grasping that he was not destined to be the first African-American governor in the Deep South.

Within a few hours, his candidacy was in free-fall, the likes of which few have ever witnessed. Meanwhile, the hits on *Winky's Words of Wisdom* made it the number one blog entry on Word Press for the day, then for the week, and finally for the entire year, eventually eclipsing a former winner from *American Idol*.

When the press and TV shows began calling for a statement, despondent, Kenyatta was unwilling to make a capitulatory comment. Bitterly resentful, as a former Georgia Bulldog, he hunkered down for two more days before finally ending his campaign unceremoniously.

Respect for him plummeted as well. His name became a joke—like O. J. Simpson's. Eventually, Wilbur Kenyatta, stripped of his dignity, was forced to resign his position as the district attorney a month later and move out of state, eventually taking a job as the City Manager in Dunedin, Florida, where few knew him and those who did were so old they quickly forgot.

Winky received a call in the afternoon from the producer of *The Kelly File*, asking her to be a guest. Winky went to the Fox studio where two other guests from Atlanta were also scheduled—Captain Barbara Baird, who was asked to discuss what should be the next steps in the investigation; and Dr. Big Shot, who was asked to explain what happens when a woman is asphyxiated while having sexual intercourse. Dr. Big Shot's interview was something Winky didn't want to miss.

Not having been in front of the television camera before, even locally, Winky was nervous, but she asked the Lord to use her for His glory. After that, she left it in His hands, and did her best to be herself, paying less attention to what she was wearing or how she looked than she had ever done in her life, which helped keep her priorities straight.

Megyn Kelly devoted the second segment of her show to what was happening in Atlanta. When she asked Winky how she managed to get the video clip to go viral, Winky said, "Well, the ingredients were already there, Megyn. Mr. Steiger was in jail and still is, falsely accused of killing his ex-wife. The real killer is still on the loose, and to my knowledge, the police haven't even been looking for him. Because I had the video, two men tried to break into my apartment, but my boss, who just happens to be the lawyer for the accused, chased them off with a shotgun. And the defendant saved my boss's life by shooting the man he's accused of killing," Winky rambled nervously. "When something dramatic like all of this happens, and you know how to use Yahoo, You Tube, Facebook, Twitter, Pinterest, and Linked-In, it's easy to get a blog entry to go viral."

Having said all of this, right off the cuff, Megyn was very impressed with the young woman's social media savvy. Focusing on the case, Megyn said, "You've brought up some great points, Winky. We put in a call to the prosecutor's office, but they refused to respond. You've caused Wilbur Kenyatta and his staff a lot of trouble."

"That's because they are accusing an innocent man, and they know it," Winky added. "I'm sure the prisoner did kill Pretty Boy Sabarisi, but he shouldn't be put in jail for that. He's a hero. Instead of trying him for murder, they should name a street after him."

Concurring, Megyn said, "I tend to agree with you. I'm not sure whether or not Mr. Steiger is able to watch this from jail, but if he is, he owes you a big debt of gratitude."

Winky just smiled and replied, "I did what I did and have said what I've said because it's the truth, and it's the right thing to do. I have no other agenda."

"I wish we had more solid citizens like you, Winky," Megyn added. "Before I let you go, let me ask; have you heard anything from Gabriela Sabata?"

With a concerned expression, Winky commented, "No, I haven't, and it worries me sick. It really does. I hope the police are looking for her but, since all of this has happened so quickly, I'm not sure they are."

"That's why we are having Captain Barbara Baird for our next guest, Winky," Megyn added. "Rest assured I'm going to ask her about the whereabouts of Gabriela Sabata."

"Thank you for caring about Gabriela and about Mr. Steiger, Megyn," Winky said.

"Before you leave, I have to ask one more thing. If I don't, I'll get a thousand emails. Are you single?"

Blushing, Winky said, "Yes, but I'm only interested in a Christian man. I don't do missionary dating."

"There you have it, guys. She's single, and the whole world knows how to reach her. What's the name of your blog again?"

"It's *Winky's Words of Wisdom*—winkyswordsofwisdom.wordpress. com," she said, spelling it out, smiling as she did.

Megyn Kelly's segments with Captain Barbara Baird and Dr. Big Shot were equally interesting. For whatever reason, Dr. Easton refused to wait in the Green Room with Captain Baird, which was specifically for guests. He chose to stand in the hallway instead.

Captain Baird was a particularly good guest, talking about how important it was to be tough on criminals but to never forget—despite the enormity of the evidence—that a man should always be considered innocent until proven guilty.

Megyn Kelly's final Atlanta guest was Dr. Big Shot, who gave a detailed description of death by sexual asphyxiation. When she heard it, Winky wished she hadn't. As she left the studio, she couldn't get the perverseness of it out of her mind, but it gave her a better understanding of why Gabriela had come to the end of her rope. Under similar circumstances, Winky knew she would have reacted the same way. Concerned about Gabriela's safety, this was all Winky thought about for the rest of the evening, so she prayed for her friend's safety repeatedly.

In the heart of the city, at the Garnett Street Pre-Trial Detention Center, William Steiger, now known to everybody as Pencil, was allowed to watch Winky Weller, Captain Barbara Baird, and Dr. Big Shot that evening on Megyn Kelly's show. Earlier in the day, Sean had come by and spoken with the jail officials—one of whom had watched the video clip on *Winky's Words of Wisdom*.

Because the prisoner had been important to the district attorney, Pencil had been treated well. When the guards realized he was probably innocent of his ex-wife's murder, he was treated even better, based on this alone. None of his jailers would reproach Pencil for shooting Pretty Boy Sabarisi, who had killed one of their favorite judges and had narrowly missed killing Sean Kincannon, who was a prosecutor at the time.

So, when *The Kelly File* aired, Pencil was allowed to watch it. In fact, several guards watched it with him—all hooting when Winky affirmed America's Hero like she did. As he was returned to his cell—now completely sober—he wondered which street would bear his name? He didn't think it would be Peachtree Rd., but one never knew. Regardless, he was looking forward to seeing the sign bearing his name. Now, his daughters would be proud of him. He wished Anne could have been around to see it too.

Drifting off to sleep, he realized Megyn had been working tirelessly behind the scenes on his behalf, but he didn't know it. He felt guilty for having doubted her, but he decided to keep his misgivings to himself. Looking forward to freedom, he slept well.

CHAPTER TWENTY-SIX
Like Obi-Wan Kenobi

For a gangster—any gangster—life is similar to a chess match. There is no place on the board of life that is safe. Someone is always trying to take your spot. Your job, if you want to live, is to stay two or three moves ahead of your opponents, knowing your survival depends on it.

Your position is even more tentative and precarious, if you are a drug lord. Being the King and the Queen rolled into one, a drug lord must have eyes in the back of his head. Everybody is his adversary, or his potentially adversary. Being wary becomes an all-consuming way of life, and there's never a break from it. If you are the kingpin, you never have just one opponent either. You have to play several concurrent matches. You always have numerous opponents working simultaneously against you—the local police, the Feds, rival gangs, and even those from within your organization. Each opponent is either ready to bring you down or to replace you.

To take anything for granted—even for a day—could prove to be your undoing. There is no such thing as taking it easy; there is no such thing as retiring to a life of leisure; and, there is no such thing as a drug lord who dies naturally of old age. By becoming involved in organized crime, regardless of the ethnicity of the gang, having a shortened lifespan is part of the job description. It comes with the territory. If it wasn't such an easy road to wealth and power, recruitment would be difficult, but every gangster convinces himself that he will beat the odds, cheat death, and enjoy a long and prosperous life.

Amiglio Sabata understood this, having beaten the odds for many years. He achieved his position by never trusting his associates, by being ruthless and intimidating, and by being smart. His current situation had come close to undoing him but, by eliminating his loose ends, he believed he had once again dodged a bullet.

His wife, Gabriela, said she would become more powerful after her death—like Obi-Wan Kenobi—but what did she know? She was just a stupid woman. But he had to give her credit; she had come close. That she had spoken English to him was a shock, but she wouldn't be speaking English ever again, or Spanish, for that matter.

He wouldn't miss her—not really—but he had become accustomed to having her around. If she hadn't startled him on the deck that night, interfering with his pleasure, he might have paid better attention to what he was doing, and not killed that stupid whore. It was Gabriela's fault. If she hadn't interfered, Anne would still be alive. Now that Anne was gone, he had to admit he did miss her too—not as a person but as a sex partner. That she loved being hurt really turned him on.

Now that it was over and in the past, he realized he had a problem. He needed an outlet. Powerful men like him often do, but he couldn't just kill women because he enjoyed it—not in America. He had to learn to control his impulses. If he continued meeting his needs the way he had been doing, his behavior would eventually destroy him.

Strangling Anne, while having sex with her, had given him a real rush though. Just thinking about it again was stirring. This didn't make him a monster. He just needed to do a better job of controlling himself. That's all—no big deal.

Now that his wife Gabriela was gone—God rest her soul—Amiglio started to think about what he was going to tell his two sons. He may not have loved her, but his sons certainly did. He had to make sure they never learned the truth about what happened to her. He wasn't certain how he would accomplish this, but an idea would come to him. It always did.

⚬⚭⚬

The afternoon *Winky's Words of Wisdom* went viral, Amiglio and his men were among the last to learn about it. They understood guns, knives, syringes, and cash, but not the Internet, email, or paying bills online. Their world was tangible. They might steal a laptop, but few would bother to own one.

Nevertheless, when one of the gang members was eating lunch, he happened to catch the local news on the TV behind the bar. Recognizing Gabriela when her photo came on the screen, he paid keen attention to what she divulged about his boss. Finishing quickly, he returned to the house and told Ricardo and the others what he had seen. Each was concerned, obviously.

Shortly thereafter, Amiglio called one of them to perform an errand. The man did as he had been told, but Amiglio sensed a slight hesitation coming from him—something he had never seen before. Intuitively, the Master Chessman knew something was amiss. The king was in danger.

Nonchalantly but quickly, he headed to his bedroom to pack a small bag—just in case. Turning on the TV to provide background noise, he saw a special news report with Jaye Watson, featuring Gabriela. In her own words, spoken in English, Gabriella told everybody listening that Amiglio Sabata was a drug lord, a murderer, and a sexual deviant.

Stunned, he watched in horrified fascination, as his entire world collapsed around him. When the news report concluded, Amiglio sat on the bed, knowing his time had run out. Gabriela had done what she had promised. From the grave, she had become more powerful than ever, destroying him, as she said she would.

But he didn't have time to think about that—not now. Putting a Glock in his waistband, he finished packing a small satchel and left, taking the back exit from his Gwinnett County estate. Knowing his car might be watched, he drove Gabriela's instead. Luckily, it still contained the $100,000 from her handbag—the one Ricardo had placed in the trunk. At the time, taking care of the funds she had pilfered wasn't that important. Now, it was all he had, and he would certainly need every penny of it.

The police and his own men would come after him. He had become a liability to them—a person who could take the gang down, sending everyone to prison. Because of this, they would want to eliminate him. He was certain of it.

Driving off, he wondered if the chess match might be over. Although still free, he was cornered, having only one move left before being checkmated, which he intended to play. For Amiglio, it might be the difference between life and death.

When Barbara Baird returned home from her appearance on *The Kelly File*, she knew she had done a good job, but she hadn't anticipated receiving the call she did. On the other line was the consultant who had been running Wilbur Kenyatta's gubernatorial bid. Swag Wheeler indicated that Kenyatta was finished, even though the gubernatorial aspirant had not yet accepted this reality. Consequently, the consultant, a modern day Sophist, was already looking for another viable candidate.

Flattering Barbara, which she loved, Swag stated, "I liked what you had to say tonight. So did everybody else, Captain Baird—some very powerful people, I might add."

"Thank you. Call me Barbara, Swag," she replied, savoring the compliment.

"Then, Barbara it is. Here's the reason I called. I think you should consider making a run for the governor's office. Jump right in, especially while this story is so hot. If you do, we can boost your name recognition quickly. After this debacle, Georgians will be ready for a law and order candidate whose willing to abide by the law of the land."

Continuing, he added, "Who would be better to serve as governor than a decorated police officer? A sharp, articulate, beautiful one, I might add. What do you think, Barbara? Any interest?"

"I don't know," she replied. "I've never considered it."

"Well consider it now," Swag insisted. "Let's talk again in a couple of days, after you've had a chance to think about it. I'm serious about this. With me running the show, I think we could win." With this he disconnected, after promising to call her again soon.

Pouring herself a glass of wine, she smiled, thinking about all the power a governor wields. It was a thought she liked.

The morning after *Winky's Words of Wisdom* created such a sensation, while sitting at her desk, the au pair opened her laptop and saw 133 messages waiting for her on her blog. Some were from the media, inquiring about a potential interview, but most were from men seeking a relationship. Looking at several, she was amazed by what she read. They all seemed to be so self-serving. None of them interested her, and several seemed downright weird.

On Facebook, there were hundreds of "Friend Requests," nearly all coming from bizarre looking, lonely men—some old enough to be her grandfather. Unwilling to deal with this, she closed her computer and took Connor and Asta for a long walk. She loved being with the two of them, but it made her want to have a home of her own and be a mom. This thought saddened her. If all that was available out there were guys like the ones who had just contacted her, she knew she would be single for a long time.

When she returned an hour later, Detective Renfro was waiting to see her. Not having called beforehand, she hadn't expected him. Putting Connor in his crib for a nap and Asta in the backyard, she sat down with the detective in the sunroom, ready to answer his questions.

After going over everything again, he closed his notepad and said; "I really liked what you said in your interview last night. You were straightforward and classy. I like that in a woman, Winky."

Not sure what he was intimating, she simply replied, "Thank you, detective."

"I don't meet many women like you." Correcting himself, he said, "Actually, I don't meet any women like you."

Not knowing how to respond, although curious, she just sat in silence.

Finally coming to the point, he said, "This case will be over soon. When it is, I would like to take you to dinner—not as part of the investigation, but as a date. I don't know whether or not that would interest you, but it definitely would interest me."

The Words of Wisdom woman was speechless. She hadn't expected this, nor had she given it any thought. Not having considered it, she didn't know how she felt about dating a detective.

Concluding, Detective Renfro said, "I can't ask you until this is over. It would be unethical but, when the time comes, I'm definitely going to ask. I'm bringing it up now, because there will be many guys knocking at your door, and I don't want one of them to snatch you up before I get a chance to take you out."

By putting his ethical commitment above his personal desires, Winky was impressed. For her, character mattered; it mattered a lot. This made her look at Detective Michael Renfro from a different perspective. From that precise moment, she knew she would be interested in dating him—quite interested.

Looking at him, she answered, "When the season is right for both of us, ask. When you do, I will be honored to have dinner with you."

Hearing her positive response delighted him. It was an electrifying moment for both, as they looked at each other. Finally, taking the lead, Michael smiled and Winky followed suit.

Leaving a few minutes later, Michael, feeling very confident, strutted to his car. While driving to his office, his cell rang. Seeing it was Lance, he just opened the phone but said nothing.

On the other end, Lance asked impatiently, "Well?"

Michael didn't say a word, but he did smile from ear-to-ear.

As Amiglio headed out of town, he needed to formulate a plan that would work. He only had one chance, and he knew it. His survival depended on it. Knowing law enforcement would be looking for him— as well as his own men—he went in the opposite direction from the one they would anticipate. Instead of heading out of the country or to a Spanish speaking area of the city, he headed for the North Georgia Mountains, hoping to find safety in rural America.

By remaining out of sight throughout the fall and winter, he thought he could emerge in the spring, sporting a well groomed, manicured beard. If he were twenty pounds lighter, that would help as well. He thought it might work. Like all drug lords, he had an alternative identity, but with his picture being all over the TV, he was too well known. To be seen in public again, things needed to settle down a bit. When they did, he would relocate to Marbella, Spain, the city of his ancestors.

Once he arrived in España the following spring, he could live out his years in peace, but to do so, he needed more than the $100,000 in the trunk. He had millions stashed away, but he would never be able to retrieve his funds. It would be suicide for him to even try. This is why his plan needed to work.

Opening his disposable phone, he sent a coded text—"Go Red Sox"—and waited for the response.

Within a minute, his disposable cell rang. Picking it up, he said, "I can give you 3.5 for 1.5, if you have the cash."

"I do," the person on the other end replied.

"Wal-Mart parking lot, Blairsville, noon tomorrow."

"Got it."

With that, the call ended. Securing a room for the night, Amiglio made a detailed map to guide Barbara Baird to the place he had the $3.5 million hidden. With the $1.5 million he would receive from her in exchange, he could make a new start. Relieved, he looked forward to meeting her the following day. Gabriela had come close to fulfilling her prediction but, in the end, he had outsmarted her. He always did.

After disconnecting, Barbara thought long and hard about Amiglio's situation. She had known him for many years, but she had no personal loyalty to the man. Such a concept never entered the equation for people like Amiglio or her. She could make $2 million in one day, but Amiglio had become a liability and a potential threat. He could bring her down, and nothing was worth that—nothing.

Finally, having made her decision, using another throwaway phone, she dialed a number.

On the other end, a man's voice answered, "Si."

"Tweedle-Dee, I think it's time you became the boss. How would you like that?"

CHAPTER TWENTY-SEVEN
"They'll Be Proud of Their Dad"

Early Saturday morning, Joseph got up, showered, dressed, and began his long drive to Atlanta. Headed southward, his mind raced faster than his pickup truck. Upon arrival, he planned to sign the paperwork, securing his condo for the following two years. It's where he intended to live, while finishing his undergraduate degree at Emory.

Although nothing prevented Molly from accompanying him on his brief trip, she chose not to. Watching him begin his move back to Atlanta was too painful, even though she planned to leave for California soon thereafter. Somehow, it felt like he was leaving her, which wasn't the case, but it was how she felt, nevertheless.

Both had tried to be so mature about their desire to pursue differing educational goals, which necessitated being apart, but it hadn't worked. Thinking they could handle the situation easily, they were learning one of life's valuable lessons. When there is a disruption in a romantic relationship one cherishes, the emotional part of humans always trumps the rational side—not sometimes, but always. They tried to be like Spock, but they couldn't. Being out of sync with each other was painful. It also made them quarrelsome, which was rarely a part of their relationship, other than fighting about Landria, of course. Each was grieving the loss of the other before it became a reality, making their last days together difficult rather than joyous and memorable.

When he left, although it was only for a few days, she cried; it's just human nature that she did. She loved Joseph and didn't want to be without him, so she became increasingly miserable in his absence. Having caught up with her studies, with him gone for the weekend, she decided to see what life would be like as a single woman. So, she went clubbing in downtown Nashville with several of her girlfriends.

For Joseph, the situation was even worse—much worse. Having just lost his dad, while also having his daughter ripped out of his life by his father's widow, Joseph's grief was tripled. With Molly's departure looming, his young heart was overwhelmed by sorrow, and it showed. He hadn't eaten well for days. Losing weight as a result, he was thinning appreciably. Always trim and muscular, he would need to punch an extra hole in his belt soon, just to keep his pants up.

His weight loss didn't detract from his good looks though. If anything, his wiry handsomeness, coupled with his chiseled muscles, made him even more appealing. Working out twice a day just to relieve all the stress in his life, he started to resemble a sprinter, rather than a rugby player.

Leaving Nashville quite early, he arrived in Atlanta by 10 a.m. He stopped to pick up his mom and the pair headed for his new condo, which he had located online. It was adjacent to the university. Having been accepted at Emory as a transfer student, which only required a couple of days, he planned to start classes in January.

This meant there would be no break in his studies—something that pleased his mother. If anything, Emory was more expensive than Belmont University, but Joseph assured her he had all the funds necessary, thanks to what his dad left him in his Will.

When they inspected the condo, both liked it. Having been painted and re-carpeted, it was bright and cheery. With an east view, it would let in the morning sun and not be oppressively hot, like the units facing the west, which received the full heat of the sun in the late afternoon.

Since most of the furnishings in his Nashville apartment belonged to Molly, Joseph was essentially starting from scratch. Melissa planned to buy him a bedroom suite that afternoon at IKEA, but he needed numerous other household items as well. At 11:30 a.m., Joseph and Melissa arrived at the Target store located on Druid Hills Road—narrowly missing Landria, Luke, and Ellen, who had left that same store five minutes earlier. This is how close they would be living to each other in a city of 6.5 million. Although none of the players in this yet to be told part of the drama were aware of it, they were neighbors.

Amiglio arrived at the Blairsville Wal-Mart Shopping Center early. Carefully surveying his surroundings, the gangster scouted the location for telltale signs of treachery. He didn't expect to find any, but he had not survived for as long as he had without being cautious. Everything looked fine to him. Sighing with relief, he drove to the Waffle House nearby and had an All-American breakfast, which was tasty and filling.

Returning at 11:58 for his noon meeting, the parking lot was filled with shoppers, which is precisely what he expected and desired. Knowing there would be security cameras watching the parking lot, hiding in plain sight was his safest recourse. He knew this, but more importantly, so did Barbara Baird. After all, she was a cop. Even if she wanted to, she wouldn't endanger herself by doing something foolish. Amiglio counted on this.

As he cruised the large parking lot, he spotted Barbara's Jaguar backed up to the large tree-lined hill on the south side of the store. Looking around, he didn't notice anything that looked suspicious. Proceeding, he backed his car—Gabriela's Mercedes—into the empty parking spot on the left of Barbara's Jag.

Less than a minute later, he spotted Barbara. She was wearing a sweatshirt, sunglasses, and an Atlanta Braves hat with her hair tucked inside. Normally well dressed, she looked like a typical Wal-Mart shopper, which seemed like a smart idea to him. Seeing her look frumpy made him smile.

Spotting him immediately, she signaled for Amiglio to come help her, which he did. To anyone looking, they appeared like a normal couple—the wife doing all of the work, while the lazy husband sat in the car listening to the radio.

As he walked up, he looked in her buggy and noticed it was filled with normal household items. There was nothing that alarmed him— nothing that looked out of place.

Turning to him, she said, "Help me get these in the trunk, Amiglio. But first, you'll have to take out the large satchel that has your money in it. It's all there. Then, put this stuff in the trunk, please," she said, pointing to the items she had just purchased.

"Of course, Barbara," he said deferentially. "Here is the location of the $3.5 million. This is a good deal for you," he added, trying to be the person in charge, which he clearly was not.

"It's a better deal for you, Amiglio," she replied. "I'm taking a huge risk being seen with you."

"But the security tapes will soon be erased, and nobody will be the wiser," he replied, reassuringly.

"That's what I'm counting on," she said pleasantly, as they reached the trunk of her Jag. Popping the lock, the trunk opened, and Amiglio saw a large sailor's bag at the far end of the trunk, tucked away snugly. Taking a quick look around, everything continued to look normal. All he saw was a Ryder truck moving slowly, obviously looking for a space large enough to park.

Reaching down, he noticed the bag was heavier than he anticipated, but $1.5 million in cash would weigh a lot. When he reached in to give it a good yank, Barbara tasered him from behind. With his weight moving forward and her hands guiding his fall—aided by a vigorous push—he fell naturally and easily into the trunk. Lifting his left leg and pushing it in, she closed the lid quickly and easily.

The truck that had been passing was driven by one of Amiglio's men, who now worked for Ricardo Castillo—Tweedle-Dee. The tall moving truck obscured the security camera's view of the Jaguar at precisely the right moment, as planned by Barbara. The entire operation, which had been choreographed to perfection, required less than ten seconds from start to finish.

With a simple nod of her head, the man-riding shotgun got out of the truck and walked to the Jag. Catching the keys she tossed, he got in, started the engine, put the car in gear, and drove off. Using the spare set of keys for Gabriela's Mercedes, brought from Amiglio's house by Ricardo, Barbara put on her driving gloves, got in the Mercedes, and followed the truck out of the parking lot.

Nobody noticed a thing, including the security guard monitoring the cameras, who was busy munching on a slice of pepperoni pizza at the time. It was as if nothing had happened.

An hour later, Amiglio awakened, groggy and confused, just like Tweedle-Dum had several days earlier. Finally gaining his bearings, Amiglio tried to move his hands, but he couldn't. Neither could he move his legs. Both had been bound tightly.

"Amiglio, are you awake?"

"Si."

"That's good, boss. I'm glad to hear it. I don't want to spend all day up here, but the mountains are very beautiful, don't you think?" Ricardo asked.

Looking at the remote mountain setting that dwarfed the small valley they were in, Amiglio knew they were as alone as anyone could be. Responding, he said, "Yes, Ricardo, it is beautiful." With his mind now racing a mile a minute, Amiglio added, "I think we can work out a deal, my friend."

"Maybe we can, boss," Ricardo replied. "First, let me ask you this: did you know Ernesto—Tweedle-Dum—was my first cousin?"

Immediately aware of how precarious his situation was, Amiglio replied, "No, Ricardo, I didn't know that."

"You really need to pay better attention to the people who work for you, boss," Ricardo added.

"You're right. I plan to do that, Ricardo," Amiglio stated with conviction.

Laughing at the absurdity of Amiglio's response, Ricardo added, "Ernesto's mother, my aunt, practically raised me. It was very difficult for me to torture my cousin. Did you know that, boss?"

"I didn't, but now I do. That will never happen again," Amiglio asserted, which again seemed comical to Ricardo, as well as to the others.

"Last night, I had a dream, boss. In my dream, Ernesto came to me and said, 'Avenge me, cousin. Don't let that fat shit get away with what he has done.'" Looking at Amiglio with cold, hard eyes, Ricardo said, "I told Ernesto I would avenge him. If I didn't, I would never be able to face my aunt again. Now, your time is up. You are about to suffer—just like my cousin did."

Terrified, but without options, Amiglio begged for his life, just like Ernesto had, producing the same, predictable measure of compassion from his tormentors—none.

Bright and early Monday morning, Sean sat at a table in the Garnett Street Pre-Trial Detention Center waiting for his client, William Steiger. Two minutes later, the prisoner arrived. When he did, Sean was smiling broadly.

Knowing something was up, Pencil simply said, "What?"

"You're getting out of here today, that's what."

"I am?"

"Yes, you are," Sean reiterated. "Based on the video statement by Gabriela Sabata and the discrepancies in the forensic evidence, the state attorney general's office started asking questions. So, Kenyatta's office relented and dropped the charge against you for killing your ex-wife. Currently, they are hunting for Amiglio Sabata but, so far, they haven't come up with a thing. He seems to have vanished into thin air."

"I hope they get him," Pencil replied, wishing he could be the person who found him.

"But that's not all. They have dropped the other charge as well," Sean added.

"They have?"

"Yes, they have."

Looking at Sean with appreciation in his eyes, Pencil said, "Oh, thank you, Jesus. Looking at Sean, Pencil added, "Thank you too, Sean. Without you, they would have locked me up for the rest of my life."

With equal gratitude, Sean replied, "Without you, I wouldn't be alive to help you get out of jail, Pencil."

With that, both smiled. Not yet finished with his surprises, Sean reached into a large sack and retrieved his old UGA football helmet. Having been told about the importance of Pencil's Georgia helmet in understanding Megyn Kelly's cryptic messages, Sean told Pencil he had a helmet too.

Being very clandestine, Sean said, "Here's what's going down. Tonight, you and I are going to be guests on Megyn Kelly's show. She's doing this to honor you for being the hero that you are, but you must not divulge anything about the secret messages she has been giving you for years. Do you understand?"

Sitting straight up in his chair and becoming deadly serious, Pencil replied, "Of course I do. You can count on me, Sean. So can Megyn. I won't let on about the President or the Illuminati. I promise."

Looking pleased, Sean said, "We knew we could depend on you." Telling Pencil he would be picked up and taken to the studio, the attorney added, "I think you should call your daughters and tell them to watch. When they see Megyn's segment, they'll be proud of their dad."

When Pencil heard this, being completely vindicated, he cried. He couldn't help it, but he didn't wet his pants.

At noon on Tuesday, pursuing an anonymous tip, the Georgia State Patrol located the body of Amiglio Sabata in a remote valley close to the North Carolina border, within a mile of where Barbara Baird's husband's body had been found years earlier.

Obviously tortured, Sabata's corpse had been slathered with honey and peanut butter, attracting the area's wildlife. Consequently, the cadaver was disfigured. The crime scene was gruesome, but there were no clues left to determine who had murdered the victim. This didn't surprise any of the law enforcement officials. Gangland executions rarely result in arrests or convictions. Looking at the mutilated man, with his face half eaten away, it was difficult to recognize him, but his wallet contained his Georgia Driver's License, which helped establish the identification.

As they placed Amiglio in a body bag, zipping it up, they could not have known his wife had been right. From the grave, Gabriela Sabata had become more powerful than she ever had been in life, checkmating her husband, destroying him in the process, just like Obi-Wan Kenobi had done to the Dark Side in *Star Wars*.

Kenyatta's former consultant, Swag, picked up the phone on the first ring. Recognizing the number, he answered, "Barbara, how nice to hear from you. Have you given my proposal any thought?"

"Yes, I have," she replied cheerfully, as a new adventure in her life was about to begin. "I've decided to throw my hat into the ring."

"That's great news," he said. "We'll need to get started right away, especially with name recognition and fund raising."

"I know that," she said. "I've already talked to some of my friends who have encouraged me to run. They want to help by seeding my candidacy."

Surprised but delighted, he asked, "I sure like the sound of that. It's music to my ears." After a moment, he asked, "How much are we talking about?"

"I have $3.5 million at my disposal, ready to be used whenever it's needed," she replied matter-of-factly, knowing it would surprise Swag.

After a moment of silence to assimilate what he had just heard, Swag announced, "Then, I believe I am talking to Georgia's next governor—its first female chief executive."

Loving the sound of it—Governor Barbara Baird—she didn't say a word, but she was sporting a wicked, wry grin.

CHAPTER TWENTY-EIGHT
"Spanish Moon"

In Georgia—as often as not—the weather remains mild until Christmas. This was one of those years. It was a beautiful early December weekend, and Georgia was scheduled to play Alabama in the SEC Championship game in Atlanta. The Dawgs were 11-1, and the Crimson Tide had the same record, having lost to Vandy earlier in the season. Despite this, the Tide was a heavy favorite. The winner was slated to get a birth in the National Championship Series. The final game was scheduled to be played at the Sugar Bowl in New Orleans.

Tickets for the SEC Championship game were outrageously expensive, but Sean didn't care. He wanted to go. Unfortunately, he couldn't find a ticket. Doing the next best thing, Marla-Dean arranged a hasty trip to their lake house, inviting a few friends to accompany them. While there, they would watch the game, have a cookout, sit on the deck, and spend the night.

Everybody invited accepted the invitation. So, early that Saturday morning, several cars headed for Lake Oconee in Greene County for the last weekend excursion before winter. Since they traveled in a caravan, everybody arrived at the same time.

Sean was in charge of bringing things in—like always. Winky, accompanied by her new beau, Michael Renfro, was in charge of looking after Connor and Asta, while Marla-Dean, queen of the roost, was in charge of showing the place to their guests, as well as getting everybody situated. Since Winky had her own room, Marla-Dean assigned a room to Joseph, Melissa, and Michael, making it a full house.

The first thing Sean did was turn on the large flat-screen TV—just to make sure it was working. Firing up the grill after that, he began to prepare the food like he was a master chef at Joni P's. An event like this was just the kind of thing he loved, and it showed.

When she finished getting her guests settled, Marla-Dean made everybody an Arnold Palmer, which was particularly delicious because she made the lemonade from scratch, using Luzianne tea as well. It was as refreshing as it was tasty.

While getting the coals hot, Michael walked out on the deck to keep Sean company. Pointing across the bay, Sean said, "Although I didn't know it at the time, when we bought this place, Amiglio Sabata owned that house over there."

"So, that's the house," Michael said knowingly. "When we were looking for Sabata, it's one of the first places we checked out—not me, but some of the other guys. It looks pretty far away."

"Not that far," Sean replied knowingly, as he remembered hearing the voices that seemed so close the evening Anne Morrow-Steiger lost her life.

Reminiscing about the case, Michael said, "We never did find the body of Tweedle-Dum or Gabriela Sabata. You know that, right?"

"You probably never will," Sean replied, remembering how another witness went missing several years earlier—the first time he tried to convict Sabata of drug running and racketeering.

"Sean, I'll never forget how stupid I looked the day I told the bigwigs we had a witness named Tweedle-Dum. They laughed their ass's off at me, especially that woman cop whose running for governor."

Turning his head toward Michael, riveted by his last statement, Sean asked, "Barbara Baird was at that meeting?"

"Yeah, she was," Michael replied, curious by Sean's change in temperament. "Why? Does that surprise you?"

"Yes, it does," he admitted, flipping the steaks that had been marinated in teriyaki sauce. "You never mentioned this before."

"I didn't think it was important. Is it?" he asked like a cop and not like a dinner guest.

"It is," Sean answered matter-of-factly. "But that's a conversation for another day, Michael, and for another setting—not for here and not for now. I'm sure I won't need to remind you about it."

"Damn right, you won't," Michael replied, as his mind raced, wondering what the significance might be.

After a few moments, smiling, Sean said, "This is the happiest I've ever seen Winky. You understand why, don't you?"

Forgetting about Barbara Baird, Michael smiled. "Me too. So many people are following *Winky's Words of Wisdom*. Simon & Schuster wants to publish her book. Did you know that?"

"I did know that, Michael. I've helped her negotiate the contract. It's with their Christian label, Howard Books. Winky has a bright future. You probably should hang around."

Being perfectly serious, without a hint of levity, Michael replied, "I intend to, Sean. I intend to."

✐

Melissa was thrilled Marla-Dean had asked her to come, as was her son. Having just moved into his condo near Emory a short time earlier, Joseph remained melancholy, which troubled his mother.

The day Molly left for Stanford, Joseph kept a stiff upper lip, but he cried numerous times afterward. He didn't talk about it, but his mom could tell he missed her terribly.

Getting away from Atlanta was just what Joseph needed, according to Melissa. He seemed to be enjoying himself with Sean and Michael. When he was called to the table, worried about his weight loss, Melissa thought Joseph ate more than he had in quite a while. When Sean saw how little he ate, having seen him devour huge quantities of food in the past, the chef wondered if he hadn't grilled the steak to the young man's liking. Regardless, everybody dined upon the cornucopia provided by their hosts until they were full, and then some.

After dinner, each person helped with the cleanup, including Asta, who ate the scraps that fell on the floor, pouncing on them before any do-gooder could retrieve them and throw them into the trash.

The women hoped the SEC Championship would be entertaining enough to keep the men occupied while they sat and talked on the deck, but that wasn't in the cards. The Dawgs fumbled the opening kickoff, and the Tide scored three plays later. From that disastrous start, things went downhill for Georgia, with Alabama winning in a rout, 42-10.

As the game was winding down, the front door bell chimed. Not expecting anyone, Sean looked at Marla-Dean who shrugged her shoulders. Going to the door to see who was there, Sean opened it. Molly was standing there, looking nervous.

"Hi, Molly. Come on in," he said, moving aside to provide her entrance. "I thought you were in Palo Alto?"

"I was, Sean." Looking at him anxiously, she asked, "Is Joseph here?"

"Yes. Come on in. Are you hungry?" he asked.

Not having eaten a bite all day, she answered honestly, "I'm starved."

"Hmmm, it will seem funny serving you a steak, instead of the other way around, but let me see what I can 'rustle up,'" he said, leading her into the great room, where Joseph was sitting on the couch.

Seeing her, Joseph couldn't have been more surprised. Motioning for him to follow her to the deck, he obeyed instantly. When the two walked out, Melissa and Marla-Dean started to say something but intuitively knew to wait. As Joseph and Molly strolled toward the deck railing, the two women found a reason that necessitated them returning inside immediately.

Standing in front of him, Molly, having rehearsed what she intended to say a hundred times, wanted to speak, but she couldn't. She cried instead. After a minute, she braced herself and said, "I can't do this, Joseph, not without you. I hate Stanford. I don't belong out there with all those freaks. I belong here with you—that is, if you still want me?"

"Are you kidding," he said. "I've been miserable without you, Molly. Of course, I still want you, but what about law school?"

"There's been a cancellation at Emory, and I've taken that person's spot."

With a knowing smile and a mischievous grin, Joseph said, "So, you knew I would want you back, huh?"

"Of course, I did," she said playfully, as they were about to embrace.

While she was finishing her sentence, Sean walked out with a raw steak to cook. Not nearly as sensitive as the women, he just barged in, reasoning that Molly said she was starved. Poor man, he couldn't help himself. Sober or not, he was still Irish and a lawyer to boot. Being obtuse was part of his nature.

Looking at Sean, as he strode past, Molly added humorously, "Besides, when I graduate, I'm going to be Sean's associate. By that time, even a pathetic shyster like him will need some help."

When she said this, Joseph roared with laughter, as did Sean, although he wasn't quite sure why. As he put her steak on the gas grill, asking her how she wanted it, Joseph interrupted, saying, "I'm still hungry, Sean. I'll have another steak with Molly, if that's okay?"

"No problem, Joseph," Sean replied, as he headed back to the kitchen to get another rib eye.

Unable to wait any longer, Molly kissed Joseph tenderly. Breaking away quickly, fearful his mom might be watching, Molly looked into his eyes and said, "We're still pretty young, but you know this is for keeps, right?"

"I wouldn't have it any other way, Molly." He wanted to kiss her again but squeezing her hand instead, knowing that everybody was watching them.

✐

When things began to quiet down toward evening, Joseph, Molly, and Asta went for a long walk. Before they did, Sean turned off the electric fence so Asta wouldn't get shocked, coming and going. There was another football game following Georgia's humiliation at the hands of the Tide that the men intended to watch.

The lake was calm with a gentle easterly breeze blowing, which cooled the evening. Being so pleasant, Melissa and Marla-Dean walked onto the deck to smell the sweet air. Pointing to the lights across the bay, Melissa said their twinkle reminded her of Christmas lights.

Since the house had just been sold to an older couple retiring from Newton, Massachusetts, it was the first time Marla-Dean had seen lights flickering since the place had been confiscated. While they were talking, Melissa turned. Distinctly hearing a voice, without seeing anyone, she inquired, "Whose there?"

When she did, Marla-Dean just smiled, shaking her head.

Bewildered, Melissa asked what was so funny? Turning her head again, she continued to look for the person who had just spoken.

"There's nobody there, Melissa. The noise is coming from the couple that lives across the bay. They must be out on the deck."

"No way," Melissa replied, as she looked at the lights twinkling in the distance. With a full moon, the house was beautifully silhouetted on the lake with a forest of trees in the cascading hills, accenting the lake house magnificently.

"I know it sounds weird, but it's true," Marla-Dean said. "The breeze carries the sound, and the words are often intelligible. When it happens, which isn't often, I call it a Spanish Moon. Some other time, I'll tell you why."

At the end of the evening, Joseph offered to give up his bed to Molly, but Michael insisted he should be the one to sleep on the couch. Being a cop, he was accustomed to it, he assured everyone. When her beau made this offer, Winky looked at him and liked what she saw. Being enamored with him, she had even convinced him to watch Joseph Prince with her a couple of times a week on the religious channel.

The following morning, Melissa, Joseph, and Molly headed back early. For whatever reason, Asta stood at the front door, asking to be let out, which Sean was not about to allow. When Winky opened the door for Connor's stroller, however, Asta seized the opportunity and squeezed between the wheels, gaining her freedom.

Sean and Michael chased after her, but she was gone in a second. Not expecting to see Asta for several hours, Sean was surprised when she reappeared a few seconds later, pointing to the woods, and growling but not barking.

Instantly, Sean knew something was amiss. Scurrying back to the house, he retrieved the shotgun he had brought. Looking at Michael, he asked, "Where's your weapon?"

"Right here," Michael replied, pointing to the small of his back. His gun was hidden under his sweater. "I always carry it with me," he added.

"Good. Keep it handy," Sean said, as both men followed Asta into the woods.

Since most of the leaves had already fallen, it wasn't difficult keeping up with her. A little past the bend in the bay, she stopped, sniffed the ground, and growled again. Puzzled, Sean and Michael couldn't figure out what Asta was doing. Then, the dog went to another spot and did the same thing. In all, she went to five spots—all close to one another.

Finally, recognition dawned on Sean's face. Looking at Michael, he said, "Oh my God, do you know what I think this is?"

"No," Michael replied, clearly bewildered.

"It's a graveyard."

When Sean said this, Michael's deportment changed instantly. Looking from one spot to the other, he said, "I think you're right." Reaching for his phone, he dialed the Greene county Police, introduced himself, and asked for immediate assistance.

Within an hour, the place was swarming with police, including the best cadaver-sniffing dog in the Southeast, which was unnecessary since Asta had already discovered the graves. One hour later, the press arrived, and another round of national attention accompanied it, lasting throughout the Christmas season and well into the next year.

Ultimately, five bodies were retrieved—all murdered.

As they returned to Atlanta that afternoon, nobody talked. Except for the persistent inquiries by the media, the following day was quiet at the Kincannon house. On Tuesday morning, however, Sean received a call. After listening for a few minutes, he hung up. Patting Asta, he told her what a great dog she was—worthy of belonging to Nick and Nora Charles.

Then, he turned to Marla-Dean and Winky. "They found Gabriela, Tweedle-Dum, and three others, including my missing witness from a few years back. He still had his driver's license in his pants pocket."

Looking directly at Winky, Sean added, "When they found Gabriela, she was wearing your ring."

CONCLUSION
There Is Still More to Tell

Well, that was quite a tale, wasn't it? Sean and Marla-Dean certainly do live eventful lives, don't they?

Do you remember my question at the beginning? About the saying, "Crime Never Pays?" After what you've just heard, there doesn't seem to be a clear answer, does there? Several people died gruesomely. For them, crime certainly didn't pay. But for others, like Landria and Barbara Baird, it seemed to have worked quite well—at least, so far.

Of course, I know the outcome and you don't, which has to be a little irritating. I'm sorry about that. I wish I had time to tell you what happens next. I really do, but you'll just have to wait. You don't want to miss it, though. Of that, I can assure you.

Right now, I just want to sit down and watch a ballgame. So, I guess you'll have to come back another time, and I'll update you. Until then, remember to keep your eyes open because you never know what's coming your way.

98869846R00157

Made in the USA
Columbia, SC
02 July 2018